PAIGE TYLER

If You
DARE

ELLORA'S CAVE
ROMANTICA PUBLISHING

EROTICE EXPOSURE

Liz Bellamy agrees to pose for a provocative calendar to help raise money for the animal shelter where she volunteers. Although it's for a good cause, she's a little shy about posing half naked.

When Liz arrives at the photography studio, she discovers hot photographer Kent Draper. She almost chickens out, but ends up having not only one heck of a sexy photo shoot, but discovering that being half naked in front of a hunky photographer and his camera is one hell of a turn-on. And when a girl gets that aroused, a little shyness isn't going to keep her from getting what she wants.

JUST RIGHT

The sexy tale of Goldie and the three werebears.

When Goldie Lockwood gets lost hiking and comes upon an isolated cabin, little does she know it belongs to three hot and hunky werebear brothers. The guys aren't thrilled to discover Goldie ate their food and slept in their beds. Not wanting to go to jail, she suggests the men punish her for her naughty misdeeds—with an arousing round of spanking.

Goldie *loves* getting spanked and decides that after having her bottom warmed, she needs a little sex to make the night complete. The only question is whether she's going to sleep with one of the brothers—or all of them.

MR. RIGHT-NOW

Kate Gentry is always the bridesmaid, never the bride. When her best friend asks her to be maid of honor, it just reminds her of how crappy her luck is when it comes to finding her own Mr. Right. Her friends point out she's trying too hard to find Mr. Right instead of having fun with Mr. Right-Now. They convince her to put her search for the perfect man on hold and have some meaningless sex with a hot guy.

Kate takes their advice and propositions the gorgeous best man, Dawson McKenna. When he eagerly agrees, she finds herself doing things she never dreamed of doing—spanking, bondage and some amazing anal sex!

Despite knowing Dawson isn't supposed to be Mr. Right, Kate finds herself falling for him big-time anyway. But since she was the one who made the rules, how can she now tell him she wants more than just a weekend fling?

GOOD COP, BAD GIRL

When a hunky guy shows up at Julie Hanson's apartment to tell her the police received a complaint about the noise from her birthday party, she assumes he's a male stripper her girlfriends hired. Upon discovering the gorgeous Kirk Chandler really is a police officer, she's completely mortified, especially since she teased him about giving her a birthday spanking.

Kirk appears at her door for a second time later that night, bearing gifts and asking if she got her birthday spanking. Julie not only gets her bottom nicely warmed, but is treated to a night of pleasure that qualifies as the best birthday present any girl could ask for.

An Ellora's Cave Romantica Publication

www.ellorascave.com

If You Dare

ISBN 9781419961601
ALL RIGHTS RESERVED.
Erotic Exposure Copyright © 2009 Paige Tyler
Just Right Copyright © 2009 Paige Tyler
Mr. Right-Now Copyright © 2010 Paige Tyler
Good Cop, Bad Girl Copyright © 2010 Paige Tyler
Edited by Raelene Gorlinsky.
Cover art by Syneca.

This book printed in the U.S.A. by Jasmine-Jade Enterprises, LLC.

Trade paperback publication August 2010

IF YOU DARE
Paige Tyler

ഇ

EROTIC EXPOSURE

JUST RIGHT

MR. RIGHT-NOW

GOOD COP, BAD GIRL

EROTIC EXPOSURE

ଌ

Chapter One

ഔ

"You know, if this weren't for such a good cause, there's no way I'd be doing this," Liz Bellamy said to her precious chocolate lab Godiva.

She was half hoping the dog would talk her out of it, regardless of the cause, but her pet just gazed up at her as if to say, "Don't look at me, this was your idea." In fact, from the canine grin on Godiva's face, she'd almost think the animal was amused by the whole thing.

"Of course, you'd find this funny," Liz muttered. "No one is asking you to take your clothes off."

Godiva gave her a pointed look that said, "That's right. And don't you even think of touching my collar!"

Well, maybe saying taking off her clothes was an exaggeration. She might do a little arty exposing of the shoulders, maybe even show a little leg. Nothing more than that.

"Right, Godiva? We draw the line at shoulders and legs."

It really was for a good cause, though. The no-kill animal shelter where she'd gotten Godiva two years ago was putting together a sexy naked-for-a-cause type of calendar to raise money. Liz and the other women who volunteered there had agreed to be the pin-ups. There was an animal rescue organization in Portland that had done the same thing last year and it had been a big hit, pulling in thousands of dollars to help support their shelter. When the woman who owned the one where Liz volunteered asked if she would do it, she hadn't been able to say no.

Now that she was standing in front of the door to the photography studio in downtown Seattle, though, she was beginning to think she should have just donated some money instead. It wasn't that she was a prude or overly shy or anything like that. It was just that she had never done anything as bold and daring as posing half naked for a pin-up calendar.

But she had said she would do it, so there was no backing out now. She'd never be able to face the other girls at the shelter if she did. They had all done their photo shoots already and hadn't been able to stop talking about how much fun it had been.

So, tugging Godiva closer on the leash, Liz opened the door and went inside. A little bell attached to the top of the door jingled, announcing their arrival. She looked around the studio, expecting to find the photographer waiting for her, but the woman was nowhere in sight. The other girls who'd done the photo shoot already had described her as down-home as apple pie and easy to work with. That made Liz feel better. Posing for a nice older lady wouldn't make her feel so self-conscious.

After a few moments went by and no one came out from the back room of the studio, Liz decided the woman must not have heard the bell. Maybe she was busy setting up stuff for the photo shoot.

Telling Godiva to sit, Liz stepped forward to ring the bell on the front counter. It was louder than she'd thought it would be and she winced as it echoed around the room. She gave Godiva an apologetic look.

"Sorry about that. I'm a little nervous."

Godiva just gave her a look that Liz translated to mean, "Whatever," before lying down to lick her paws. She probably wanted her nails to look nice for the photo shoot, Liz thought, wishing she could be as relaxed as her dog.

Knowing she was only going to make herself more nervous if she kept thinking about posing for the pictures, Liz let her gaze wander around the room. In addition to the leather couch and two matching chairs, there were a coffee table and several potted plants that gave the room a warm, cozy feel. But it was the mounted photos on the walls that caught her attention. Everything from kids and animals to weddings and family portraits to wildlife and landscapes, they were a mix of color and black and white photos that were both beautiful and artistic. She could see why the owners of the shelter had chosen this photography studio to take the pictures for the calendar. If they came out even half as elegant as the photos on the wall, the result was going to be a work of art.

"Can I help you?"

Liz was so mesmerized by the photographs she didn't hear anyone come into the room and she jumped at the sound of the man's voice. Hand to her throat, she whirled around to see the most gorgeous guy she'd ever laid eyes on standing before her. Tall and muscular with dark hair and a chiseled jaw, he had the kind of soulful brown eyes a girl could get lost in if she wasn't careful.

The grin he flashed her was almost enough to make her melt right there on the spot. "Sorry," he said. "I didn't mean to startle you."

"You didn't." She felt her face color as she realized how lame that sounded, especially when it was obvious he had. "Well, maybe you did startle me a little bit. I was just looking at the photographs and didn't hear you come out."

Duh. She reached up to tuck her long dark hair behind her ear as she tried to hide her embarrassment. Before she could say something else more intelligent, however, Godiva got to her feet and padded over to greet the man, her tail wagging wildly. Liz instinctively opened her mouth to scold her, albeit gently, but the man had already dropped to one knee to give the dog an affectionate pet.

"Godiva," Liz admonished, then gave the man a sheepish look. "Sorry about that. It's her first time at a photography studio so she's a little excited."

The man chuckled. "It's okay. She's just being friendly. Aren't you, girl?"

Liz couldn't help but smile as he rubbed Godiva behind the ears. Not only was the guy totally hot, but he liked animals, too. She wondered if he had a girlfriend. If not, maybe he was in the market for one.

He gave Godiva another rub, then got to his feet. "You must be Liz Bellamy, right?"

She nodded, wondering how he knew her name. Her confusion must have been obvious because he explained. "I'm Kent Draper, one of the photographers here. Maxine mentioned you'd be coming by for a photo shoot with your dog, so I just put two and two together. "

"Oh." Liz looked past him to the door leading to the back of the studio. "Is Maxine here?"

"Actually, she had to take off early. Her daughter went into labor a couple of hours ago, so she and her husband headed down to Olympia."

"Oh."

Liz didn't know whether to be relieved about having to put off the photo shoot or not. She'd spent most of the day psyching herself up for it and now she was going to have to do it all over again.

"Maxine asked me to take the pictures instead, if that works for you," he said.

Liz blinked in surprise. She hadn't expected that. "She did?"

He shoved his hands in the back pockets of his jeans. "Yeah. Unless you'd rather come back. I understand if you'd be more comfortable having her take the pictures."

Liz chewed on her lower lip. While part of her wanted to come back when Maxine was there, the other part wanted to get the whole thing over with. But could she pose in front of a guy? She wasn't so sure of that. Then again, the short robe she'd brought to wear wasn't all that revealing. It wasn't like she'd be stripping naked for him.

On the other hand, she couldn't deny the excited little hum that was starting to course through her body at the thought of a hot guy like him taking pictures of her scantily clad body. She did a mental double take. Where the heck had that come from? A minute ago, she was terrified at the thought of Maxine even seeing her shoulders. Now she was getting all hot and bothered over the idea of Kent seeing the same thing? Well, he was the hunkiest guy she'd ever seen.

"No," she said in answer to his question. "We're both already here, so we might as well go ahead and do it." Yikes, had she just said that out loud? Color suffused her face as she realized that must have sounded as if she wanted to jump his bones right there. "The photo shoot, I mean."

He grinned. "I figured."

Her color deepened even more and she reached up to tuck her hair behind her ear again. Even Godiva was looking at her as if she was an idiot.

"So, which animal shelter are you doing the calendar for again?" Kent asked.

Liz smiled, relieved he'd changed the subject. "People for Pets. Over on 12th Ave."

"No kidding? I got my dog there."

"You have a dog? What kind?"

"He's a border collie." Kent gestured to the photograph on the wall behind the front counter. "That's a picture of him."

Her smile widened as she gazed at the photo. The black and white dog looked playful, yet alert and watchful at the same time.

"What's his name?" she asked, turning her attention back to Kent.

"Bob."

Her brow furrowed. "Bob? That's not a dog's name."

15

Kent regarded the photograph for a moment, then shrugged. "I don't know. He looks like a Bob to me."

Liz turned to study the picture of the cute dog again. No, she didn't see it.

"The bathroom's in the back if you want to get changed," Kent suggested. "Second door on the right."

Liz turned back around to look at him. She'd been so interested in talking about his dog, she almost forgot the real reason she was there. "Okay, thanks." She gave the leash in her hand a gentle tug. "Come on, Godiva."

"She can stay out here with me while you change, if you want," Kent offered.

She glanced down at Godiva, then back at him. "Sure. If you don't mind."

Handing Kent the dog's leash, Liz told Godiva she'd just be a few minutes, then made her way to the back of the studio. As she walked past the lights, umbrellas and various other photography equipment, she was amazed by how professional it all was. It made her feel like a real model. *Right.* Like real models were ever this nervous before a photo shoot.

Shaking her head, Liz went into the bathroom and closed the door. She slipped off her jeans and tank top. Since the pictures in the calendar were supposed to be on the sexy side, she and the other women posing for it had come up with the idea of wearing lingerie for the photos. The cami-top and bikini panties some of her friends had worn seemed a little too revealing for her, though, so she'd decided on her favorite short, silk jacquard robe instead. Gazing at her reflection in the full-length mirror as she tied the belt around her slim waist, she was glad she'd chosen the garment. Not only did the pretty powder blue robe accentuate her slender curves, but it showed off her long legs, too. She had put on make-up right before coming over to the studio, so all she had to do was touch up her lip gloss, run her fingers through her long, dark hair, and she was ready.

She took a deep breath, gave her reflection one last look in the mirror, then opened the door.

When Liz walked into the studio, she found Godiva lying at Kent's feet with her head on her paws while he studied the camera he had in his hands. At her approach, both of them lifted their heads to look at her. Godiva immediately got to her feet and walked over to greet Liz. Kent, on the other hand, stood there, the camera in his hands seemingly forgotten as he took in her slender, robed figure and long, bare legs. Liz felt her cheeks blush at the obvious appreciation in his dark eyes and she shyly bent to give Godiva a pat on the head.

Kent cleared his throat. "We can get started whenever you're ready."

Liz straightened to give him a sheepish look. "I've never done any modeling before, so I'm not really sure how I should pose."

He grinned. "No problem. Why don't you and Godiva go on the dais and stand in front of the backdrop and we'll start with some warm-up shots? I've got the camera hooked up to that monitor, so you can check yourself out on it as I take photos."

She nodded. That was a fancy setup. "Okay. Come on, Godiva."

Tail wagging, Godiva eagerly followed Liz up onto the raised platform and obediently sat down.

"That's good," Kent said. "Smile for me."

Liz did as he instructed, tilting her head slightly and giving him what she hoped was a natural smile.

"Great." Kent lifted his camera and snapped a few pictures. "Okay, same smile, but this time, put your hands on your hips."

She complied, resting her hands loosely on the curve of her hips and bending one knee a little. Remembering what he'd said about checking herself out in the monitor, she darted a quick glance in that direction and saw that she and Godiva looked pretty darn good. That monitor thing was rather cool. It would leave whatever picture he took up there until he snapped another one.

"Very nice." He took some more pictures, then glanced at her over the top of the camera. "Okay, let's try some with you kneeling down next to Godiva."

She dropped to one knee beside the dog and put an arm lovingly around Godiva. "Like this?"

"Perfect." He snapped more pictures, turning the camera first one way, then the other as he moved a little to the left and right.

He lowered the camera to flash her a sexy grin. "If all the women are as beautiful as you, I know I'll be picking up a calendar."

She blushed at the compliment and reached up with her free hand to self-consciously tuck her hair behind an ear.

"Hold that pose," Kent commanded.

Though she was surprised, Liz obeyed. She wouldn't have thought the almost candid pose particularly worthy of being in the calendar, but she decided to defer to Kent. He was the photographer, after all. But when she looked toward the monitor, she realized the picture did look kind of sexy.

He took what must have been twenty or thirty pictures from various angles with her in that pose before lowering the camera to give her another smile. "I knew you'd be a natural at this."

Liz laughed. "I don't know about that."

"You'll change your mind when you see how these photos come out," he assured her. "How 'bout you sit on one hip with your legs kind of tucked under you?"

She did as he asked, resting her hip up against Godiva as she tucked her legs to the side. The movement caused her robe to ride up a little higher on her thighs, but she made no move to adjust it. The pictures were supposed to be sexy and if the way Kent's gaze lingered there was any indication, then showing a little leg was definitely sexy. Who knew? It might even sell more calendars.

"Okay," he said. "Now put your arms around Godiva. Perfect."

As Kent continued to take photos, Liz glanced at Godiva out of the corner of her eye to see the dog giving the camera a huge canine grin and she had to stifle a laugh. *What a ham.*

"Lean forward a little more and show me some more of that beautiful cleavage," Kent instructed.

Cleavage? Liz blinked in surprise. She hadn't realized she was showing any cleavage, but a quick glance down showed that her robe had parted a little to not only reveal the lacy trim on her black satin bra, but the tops of her breasts as well. Blushing, she leaned forward to show the camera — and Kent — even more. She was really getting into this.

"Oh yeah, just like that," he breathed. "Hold that pose for me."

Liz wasn't sure whether it was the husky way he said the words or the provocative, sexy pose, but as Kent moved closer while he continued to snap her photo, she felt a sudden rush of heat pool between her thighs. Sheesh, she was actually getting excited.

Dropping to one knee in front of her, Kent lowered the camera and reached out with his free hand to gently brush her hair back from her face with his fingers. The contact sent a little tingle of electricity unlike anything she'd ever felt before coursing through her body and she caught her breath. Had he felt it, too? she wondered. The look in his eyes made her think so, but before she could be sure, Godiva interrupted the moment by getting to her feet and stepping off the dais to walk out of the studio. Liz watched in bewilderment as the dog disappeared through the door and into the waiting area.

Abruptly remembering the reason they were there was to do the photo shoot, Liz opened her mouth to call Godiva back, but Kent stopped her.

"It's okay," he said, dropping his hand. "We've got enough for the calendar."

Chapter Two

හ

"Oh." Liz couldn't hide her disappointment as Kent got to his feet. "I was having so much fun, I was hoping you'd need to take some more."

He regarded her in silence for a moment, then gave her a lazy grin. "Just because we have enough for the calendar, that doesn't mean I can't take a few more shots. And if you like any of them better than the others, I can just Photoshop Godiva in later."

Liz caught her lower lip between her teeth as she considered his offer. The photography studio was donating their services to the shelter, so she really shouldn't take up any more of his time. On the other hand, it wasn't every day she got to have her picture taken by such a hot guy.

"Okay," she said. "But only if you're sure you don't mind."

His mouth quirked. "Mind taking pictures of a gorgeous woman like you? It's a tough job, I admit, but someone's gotta do it."

She laughed, her cheeks coloring at the compliment. God, this guy knew exactly what to say to a girl.

Kent dropped to one knee in front of her, camera at the ready. "Okay, now that Godiva's out of the room, show me your best sultry look."

Liz wasn't exactly sure she knew how to do sultry, but she decided to give it her best shot. Putting her hands on the floor in front of her, she leaned forward to flash him a little more cleavage and gazed at him from beneath lowered lashes.

He immediately began snapping pictures. "Oh yeah, that's what I'm talking about. Work it."

She giggled at the words, unable to help herself.

He came out from behind the camera to give her a curious look. "Why'd you stop? That was perfect."

"I'm not so sure sultry is a good look for me," she told him.

"I beg to differ. And so does the camera. But if you don't believe me, do the same thing and this time check yourself out on the monitor."

Hoping she didn't look as silly as she felt, Liz struck the same pose, then glanced at the monitor after he'd snapped the picture. What she saw made her do a double take. With her full lips parted, her blue eyes half hidden underneath a thick fringe of dark lashes, and the tops of her lace-covered breasts peeking out enticingly from her silk robe, not only didn't she look silly, she looked like the very definition of sultry. That thought sent another current of excitement shooting through her pussy.

"Beautiful," Kent said. "Now let your robe slip off your shoulders a little for me."

Liz did as he asked, waited for him to take a picture, then impulsively lifted her hair up with her free hand and blew him an air kiss over her bare shoulder.

He chuckled. "That's it. Show me some more. Have fun with it."

She dropped her hand, letting her hair fall down her back as she shifted positions. Lying over on her hip, she leaned forward to give him a sexy come-hither look. As she did, the robe slid down to her elbows, completely exposing her lace-trimmed bra to the camera and the man behind it. Kent's low groan of approval was all the encouragement she needed to keep going. Rolling onto her back, she propped herself up on her elbows and lifted one bare leg high in the air.

"Hold that pose," Kent said as he snapped more pictures. "Very nice."

Forgetting all about her earlier comment to Godiva about not showing anything more than some leg and a little bit of shoulder, Liz found her hands going to the belt of her robe. But then she hesitated. Did she dare? The bra and matching panties she was wearing might be on the skimpy side, but they weren't much different than a bikini, and she did that on a regular basis. Besides, posing for some racy pictures was pretty dang fun. Like her own personal glamour shoot.

Lips curving into a naughty smile, Liz slowly untied the belt and let the robe fall away to give Kent and his expensive high-tech digital camera a good, long look at her scantily clad body. From his sharp intake of breath, she had the feeling he liked what he saw.

Rolling onto her side to face him, she braced herself on her elbow and drew her top leg up. As Kent captured the pose with his camera, she glanced over at the monitor and was pleased to see how hot she looked. While she'd always been fairly confident about her body, seeing herself like this made her feel even sexier. She'd recommend this to any girl looking to improve her self-image. Catching her lower lip between her teeth, she turned her attention back to Kent and gave him a provocative look.

"Oh yeah, that's it," he said. "Make love to the camera."

Liz hadn't thought of what she was doing as making love to the camera, but the words made her pussy quiver even more between her legs. She wondered if it was the idea of posing like a centerfold model she found arousing, or whether it was doing it in front of a guy as smokin' as Kent. As she sat up, she decided it was a little of both.

Wondering just how naughty she should get with the racy little photo shoot, Liz slowly ran her finger down her cleavage, then cupped her satin-covered breasts in her hands. Her nipples hardened beneath the material at her touch, and she had to stifle a little moan. God, how she wanted to take off her bra and just give them a squeeze. The urge was too powerful to resist and she found herself reaching around to unclasp her bra. Once her fingers found the hooks, however, she hesitated, unsure whether to continue. But then she caught the glint of anticipation in Kent's eyes and her pulse quickened with excitement. She knew right then she wasn't going to stop.

Unhooking the clasp, she slowly pushed first one strap, then the other off her shoulder. Rather than take off her bra right away, though, she crossed her arms over her breasts, then leaned forward just enough to tease Kent a little bit more before the big reveal.

Kent moved closer, his finger clicking the shutter button furiously. "Are you sure you've never done this before?"

"I'm sure." She threw one shoulder forward and gave him a pretty pout. "Why do you ask?"

"Because you know exactly how to seduce the camera."

Liz suddenly realized she had forgotten all about the camera. At some point, this had become about seducing the man behind it. She wondered if it was working. Deciding there was only one way to find out, she slowly let the bra fall away to reveal her bare breasts.

Kent lowered the camera to stare at her. "Damn," he breathed.

She gave him a coy look and crossed her arms over her chest again. "Too much for a first photo shoot?"

The corner of his mouth edged up as he went back to taking pictures. "Not at all."

"Well, in that case..."

Letting the words trail off, Liz slowly uncrossed her arms and cupped her breasts. She took each rosy red nipple between a thumb and forefinger and gave them a firm squeeze. Little tingles of pleasure zipped through her and she gasped.

"God, that's hot," Kent said.

The husky words made her pussy spasm. Wanting to see just how hot she really did look, she glanced over at the monitor and was amazed to see she not only looked sexy, but wanton as hell.

"Lean back on your hands for me and cross one knee over the other," Kent instructed.

She did as he asked, lazily swinging her top leg back and forth. "Like this?"

"Exactly like that."

Liz waited until he'd snapped a few pictures of that pose before stretching out one leg in front of her and drawing the other up. As she did, she felt moisture between her thighs and realized her panties were damp with her arousal. If she slipped her hand inside them, she knew she'd be sopping wet.

So, what's stopping you?

Throwing the camera a look that would make a Playboy model proud, she hooked her thumb in her skimpy bikini panties and slowly pushed them down over the curve of her hip. Although she couldn't see Kent's eyes behind the camera, she could tell from his sharp intake of breath that he approved of the direction the photo shoot was heading. Pretty thrilled with it herself, she continued to slowly inch her panties lower and lower until they were banded around her thighs. Then she pushed them even lower.

She wondered if Kent could tell how excited this little naughty photo session was making her. The idea that he might know was more of an aphrodisiac than she would have thought possible. Before she even realized what she was doing, she closed her eyes and slid her hand between her legs to run her fingers over the folds of her pussy. Good heavens, she was soaking wet. Her clit throbbed, begging for her touch, and this time she didn't even try to stifle the moan that escaped her lips. Unable to help herself, she began to make little circles round and round her clit.

"Do you have any idea how much of a turn-on that is?"

At the sound of Kent's voice, Liz opened her eyes to discover that he was no longer taking pictures, but was instead watching her every move, his dark eyes hot with lust. The reminder she had an audience only made the act of pleasuring herself that much hotter.

Her gaze went to the hard-on clearly visible in the front of his jeans and her lips curved into a sexy smile. The hell with playing coy any more. She wanted him. "Why don't you come over here and show me?"

Liz didn't know who was more surprised by the words, she or Kent. She normally didn't proposition men she'd just met. On the contrary, she liked to take things nice and slow. But tonight she seemed to have shrugged off her inhibitions along with her robe. Besides, she'd been attracted to the handsome photographer from the moment she met him and right now, she couldn't think of anything she wanted to do more than feel his hard body pressed up against hers.

Kent stood gazing down at her for so long, though, Liz was half afraid he wasn't going to take her up on her offer. After a moment, however, he set down the camera and stepped up on the dais. Her pulse quickened as he dropped to one knee beside her. She waited for him to say something, but instead, he slid his hand in her long hair and bent his head to kiss her.

His mouth was gentle and yet firm on hers, and she let out a breathy little sigh as their tongues met and intertwined. Eager to find out if he really was as well built as she thought, she ran her hands up the front of his chest. To her delight, he was hard and solid beneath the navy blue T-shirt, and she let her fingers glide over each muscle appreciatively. She always did have a thing for guys who worked out.

Kent dragged his mouth away to look down at her, his dark eyes hungry. "I've wanted to do that since you walked in the door."

"What took you so long?" she asked softly.

He kissed her again before answering. "The photographer's code of ethics."

Her brow furrowed. "There's a code of ethics for photographers?"

Another kiss. "Sure. You've never heard of it?"

She had a sneaking suspicion he was putting her on, but she didn't call him on it. Instead she just shook her head and pressed her mouth to his. "No."

"I'm surprised. It's very strict." He drew her lower lip into his mouth and suckled on it. "The code wasn't the only thing that kept me from kissing you, though."

She moaned as he teased her lips with featherlight kisses. "It wasn't?"

"No. I wasn't sure if there was a boyfriend in the picture or not."

"There isn't."

"Good."

"What about you? Is there a girlfriend in the picture?"

"No girlfriend. I'm a free agent."

"Good."

He captured her mouth with his in another scorcher of a kiss before she could reply and by the time he lifted his head a few moments later to trail a path of kisses along the curve of her jaw, she forgot what she'd been going to say. As he kissed his way down her neck, she tilted her head to the side, giving him an all-access pass to wherever he wanted to go. The angle put her in the perfect position to see the monitor and the last picture Kent had taken of her. In it, she was leaning back, her eyes closed, her lips parted, her hand between her legs as she pleasured herself.

"Does seeing yourself like that turn you on?"

Liz dragged her gaze away from the monitor to look up at him, a blush coloring her cheeks. "A little. Does that make me kinky?"

"Maybe. But I like kinky." He kissed her long and hard. "Don't go anywhere. I'll be right back."

Kent was on his feet before Liz could even ask where he was going and she watched curiously as he picked up the digital camera he'd been using and set it on a tripod. She frowned, wondering if he was going to take more pictures. She was about to ask him when he walked over and dropped to one knee beside her again.

"I put the camera on auto so it'll snap pictures the whole time," he explained before she could ask. "That way you can watch everything we do."

Her gaze went to the monitor and she watched in fascination as the picture changed every few moments while the camera captured them. It was like their very own private porno shoot. Her pussy spasmed at the naughty notion. When had she turned into such a bad girl?

Liz gave Kent a slow, sexy smile. "Then let's put on a show for the camera."

Pushing herself to her knees beside Kent, she slid her hands underneath his shirt and shoved it up. He reached over his head and helped pull it off the rest of the way, tossing it aside and leaving his magnificent chest bare to her hungry gaze. She stared in appreciation, taking in his six-pack abs and well-defined pecs, and wondering again why the heck he spent his time behind the camera instead of being in front of it. Damn, he was built.

She ran her hands over the smooth muscles of his chest and over his broad shoulders, sighing at the way they flexed beneath her touch. She couldn't remember the last time she had sex with a guy just because he was hot. The thought of having his hard cock inside her practically had her panting with need and she wrapped her hand around the back of his neck to pull him down for a kiss. This time, she took the lead, plunging her tongue into his mouth to seek out his.

Kent made a sound deep in his throat. Sliding one hand in her hair, he gently cupped her breast in the other. Liz moaned against his mouth as he took her nipple between his thumb and forefinger and gave it a little squeeze. She'd always had sensitive nipples, but tonight they seemed even more receptive to touch. Or maybe Kent just knew how to make love to them better than any other man she'd been with. She could have him do that all night long.

Which was why she almost protested when he took his hand away. But then she realized he had only stopped playing with her breasts so he could gently lower her to the floor.

He gazed down at her, taking in every inch of her naked body. "God, you're beautiful."

The compliment warmed Liz all the way to the tips of her toes. She would have thanked him, but Kent had already leaned forward to slowly kiss his way up the inside of her outstretched leg. She licked her lips in anticipation as he got closer and closer to her pussy. But to her surprise, he moved right past her nether regions and zeroed straight in on her breasts again, cupping them in both of his hands. She gasped as he closed his mouth over the same nipple he'd been playing with before. So, he was a breast man was he? Her lips curved into a smile. She should have known from the way his eyes had been glued to them during the photo shoot.

She glanced over at the monitor as he suckled on her nipple, unable to believe how sexy it looked. She'd stolen the occasional quick look in the bedroom mirror during sex with other men before, but this was even hotter.

Liz moaned, lifting her hand and burying her fingers in his dark hair as he swirled his tongue round and round the stiff little peak. But while what he was doing felt exquisite, it was also enough to almost drive her insane and she wasn't sure whether to be relieved or dismayed when he finally lifted his head. Before she could decide, he bent to take her other nipple in his mouth and lavish it with the same attention, driving her crazy all over again.

When he was finally done feasting on her breasts, he slowly kissed his way down her tummy to her belly button. He made lazy little circles around the indentation with his tongue before dipping it inside. She'd never had a man do that before, but at the shiver of pleasure that ran through her, she decided she just might have discovered a whole new erogenous zone.

Liz forgot all about her belly button as Kent made his way lower, however. Her breathing quickened as he got closer and closer to the juncture of her thighs. Something told her he knew exactly how to go down on a woman. And if his tongue felt even half as good on her pussy as it had on her breasts, then she was going to be in for one mind-blowing orgasm.

Cupping her ass in his hands, Kent lifted his gaze to hold hers for one long, breathtaking moment before he bent to slowly run his tongue along the slick folds of her pussy. Liz moaned, her eyes automatically going to the monitor again. Seeing picture after picture of Kent's dark head buried in her pussy made the act of oral sex even more erotic and she couldn't have taken her eyes off the screen if she tried.

Kent didn't lick her clit right away, but focused his attention on her pussy lips, teasingly running his tongue up first one side, then the other until she was so aroused she was sure she thought she would explode by the time he finally licked her clit. She was just wondering if he was ever going to take mercy on her when he put his warm mouth on the plump little nub.

Liz caught her breath.

As if to drive her even wilder, he flicked her clit with quick, featherlight caresses before finally making slow, deliberate circles around it. She arched against him, her fingers finding their way into his hair again as she began to rotate her hips.

"Oh God," she breathed. "Just like that. Don't stop."

Kent let out a groan and tightened his hold on her ass cheeks, his tongue more firm as he continued to lap at her clit. He kept it slow and steady, building her higher and higher with every passing minute. When her orgasm finally hit her, it started right at her clit, then spread throughout her whole body until she was trembling all over.

Liz tried to keep her eyes on the monitor while she was coming, but that quickly became impossible as she writhed beneath his tongue. Giving up on the visual, she closed her eyes, threw back her head, and gave in to the pleasure as Kent coaxed one breathtaking climax after another out of her until she was completely dizzy. It felt so good, she didn't ever want him to stop.

But then at some point the sensations became too intense and she tightened her grip on his hair, urging him up. Although he stopped licking her, he didn't lift his head. Instead, he pressed tender kisses to the inside of one trembling thigh, then the other, before looking up at her.

She gazed down at him from beneath half-lowered lashes. She had been with guys who were good at licking pussy, but that had to be the best oral sex she'd ever had in her life. This guy was an artist with his tongue. While her clit might be satisfied, however, her pussy was still aching with a need that almost bordered on desperation. And only one thing was going to satisfy that yearning.

"I need to have you inside me," she begged.

Kent didn't reply, but simply got to his feet and tugged open his belt, then unbuttoned his jeans. She felt her pulse quicken as she waited for him to undress. With an upper body as gorgeous as his, the rest of him had to be just as mouthwatering, she was sure. When he finally shoved down his jeans to reveal long, well-muscled legs, she was thrilled to discover she was right. But as fascinated as she was with his well-toned legs, it was the sizeable bulge in the front of his boxer briefs that held her attention, and she caught her breath when his hard cock finally came into view. He was bigger than any guy she'd ever been with, and as she watched him roll on the condom he'd grabbed from the pocket of his jeans, she could only imagine how glorious he was going to feel inside her. Her pussy throbbed in anticipation. She was going to find out soon enough.

It occurred to Liz then she should probably compliment his body like he had complimented hers, but by the time she opened her mouth, Kent had already joined her on the floor again. He obviously didn't want to waste any time. That was fine with her. There would be time for compliments later.

Bracing his arms on either side of her head, he settled himself between her thighs, then bent his head and covered her mouth with his. She wrapped her arms around his neck, a moan escaping her lips as she felt the head of his cock press against the opening of her pussy. She expected him to slide in right away, but instead, he teasingly slid up and down along the slick outer lips. She moaned against his mouth again, impatient to have him inside her.

Kent must have interpreted what she wanted, because he positioned the head of his shaft against the entrance to her pussy and slowly eased himself inside.

Liz gasped as he entered her. His cock filled her so perfectly and so completely, it was as though he was made for her.

Above her, Kent groaned hoarsely. "God, you're so tight."

She wrapped her legs around him, pulling him in even deeper. "That's a good thing, right?"

He made a sound that was somewhere between a chuckle and another groan. "That's a very good thing."

"Then fuck me," she ordered softly.

She blushed at her own brazenness. She didn't normally talk dirty in bed, but posing for nude photos had brought out her inner bad girl. Kent didn't seem to mind, though. In fact, from the grin tugging at the corner of his mouth as he began to move his hips, she suspected he probably liked it.

He thrust slowly, sliding out until just the head of his cock was in her pussy, then burying himself all the way inside her again until he was touching her very core. She tightened her legs around him even more, pulling him in as deep as he would go, gasping as his shaft stretched her pussy wide. He dropped his head and buried his face in her neck, kissing the sensitive skin there as he pumped in and out of her.

Liz was so close to coming, she wouldn't have minded if Kent had picked up the pace right then. She tried to urge him to go faster by yanking him in with her bare heels, but he refused to comply. Instead, he continued his slow, steady rhythm, keeping her balanced on the edge of orgasm.

She wondered if he knew what he was doing to her, but from the look in his eyes, she could tell he enjoyed driving her crazy.

Then, just when she thought she would go insane from the pleasure, he pulled out and sat back on his heels.

"I want you to ride me," he said hoarsely, taking her hand and urging her up.

As Kent rolled onto his back, Liz obediently straddled his hips and carefully sank down on his cock. She caught her breath as he filled her pussy once again, savoring the feel of him inside her. He must have wanted to change position because he'd been just as close to coming as she was.

Leaning forward, she placed her hands on his chest and slowly began to ride up and down on him. The motion drove his shaft deep inside her each time and she moaned with pleasure. She had planned on going nice and slow, teasing him as he had done to her, but he gripped her ass in both hands, making her move faster. God, it was such a turn-on when a guy took charge like that during sex.

Abruptly remembering the camera, she glanced over at the monitor and stared in amazement at how incredibly hot she and Kent looked together. The camera had captured them just as she was about to take him deep again, with his cock poised to plunge into her pussy and his strong hands clutching her ass cheeks.

She turned back to Kent to see a grin tugging at his mouth. "Hot, huh?"

Her lips curved into a smile. "Very hot."

Bending forward, she slid her hands in his hair and kissed him. He groaned against her mouth and tightened his hold on her ass, moving her up and down on him as he pumped his hips. The rhythmic motion sent his shaft deeper and deeper with every thrust. With him taking care of the pace, all she had to do was give herself over to the pleasure and enjoy the ride.

"Harder," she demanded against his mouth. "Fuck me harder!"

Kent obeyed, thrusting into her so forcefully she probably would have bounced right off him if he hadn't been holding onto her. Her pussy spasmed around his cock, signaling her impending orgasm, and she dragged her mouth away from his.

"Oh yeah, just like that," she urged. "Don't stop. Please don't stop!"

"I won't," he promised, his deep voice husky in her ear as he pumped into her. "Come for me, baby. Come for me."

The words were all it took to send Liz over the edge. Clutching his shoulders, she let out a scream of ecstasy loud enough for the entire city of Seattle to hear. Kent made some noise of his own, groaning deep in his throat as he reached his own climax.

When her orgasm finally subsided, Liz slid off him and collapsed against his chest, panting for breath. "That was amazing."

He slid his arm up to her waist, holding her close. "Yeah, it was."

They lay there quietly for a moment, Kent's heart beating in time with hers as their breathing slowed to normal. In the background, Liz could hear the camera still clicking away. She smiled at the thought of the x-rated photo shoot they'd just put on, but then frowned as she wondered if it was something Kent made a habit of doing. While she wasn't sure she wanted to know the answer to that, she couldn't contain her curiosity.

She lifted her head from his shoulder to regard him thoughtfully. "So, do you sleep with all the women you take pictures of?"

"You're the first."

What else had she expected him to say? Even so, the words pleased her and she smiled. "Good answer."

He reached up to gently brush her hair back from her face. "I'm just being honest. I've never wanted to do something like that with any other woman I've photographed."

There was a sincerity in his dark eyes that made Liz believe him and as she snuggled against him again, she couldn't help but feel a little giddy. It made what they'd just shared even more special.

As she lay with her head on his chest, basking in the warmth of that thought, Liz looked down and realized Kent had taken off the condom. When the heck had he done that? As she was trying to figure that out, she also noticed his cock was beginning to stiffen again. Smiling, she ran her finger along his length from the base of his shaft to the tip.

"Looks like someone's ready for round two."

He chuckled. "Always."

She leaned up to kiss him on the mouth. "Mmm, I like that in a man."

Pushing herself onto her knees, Liz trailed kisses along his jaw line and down his neck. Then she moved lower, exploring the chiseled contours of his chest and abs with her lips and tongue until she came to his cock. She was going to make him as hard as he'd ever been in his life. Wrapping her hand around the base of it, she swirled her tongue over the head to lick the glistening bead of pre-cum on the tip. He was sweet and musky, and she let out a little moan of appreciation as his taste filled her mouth.

She lifted her other hand and cupped his balls in her palm. Despite having come a little while ago, they were heavy with arousal and she gently massaged them as she ran her tongue up and down the length of his shaft. Remembering how he'd teased her when he was going down on her, she decided a little turnabout was fair play. So, rather than take him in her mouth right away, she closed her lips around the head and suckled gently.

Kent inhaled sharply in what she was sure was anticipation, but she only continued to swirl her tongue round and round the tip until he let out a groan of frustration. Deciding she'd tortured him enough, she closed her lips over his cock and took him completely in her mouth.

Above her, Kent groaned again, this time in obvious approval, and Liz almost smiled as she slowly moved her mouth up and down on his length.

"Damn, you're good at that," he said, his voice raspy with need.

This time, Liz did smile as she traced a path up his shaft with her tongue. When she got to the top, she swirled her tongue over the head before taking him deep in her mouth again. Then she took him even deeper and swallowed.

Kent sucked in a breath and slid a hand in her hair, urging her head up. "If you keep that up, I'm going to come in that pretty mouth of yours. And while that wouldn't be a bad thing, right now I need to be inside you again."

While the idea of making him come in her mouth made Liz shiver with anticipation, she decided she wanted him in her pussy just as much as he wanted to be there.

He pulled her close and kissed her long and hard on the mouth. "Get on your hands and knees facing the camera."

Liz did as he asked, her pussy quivering. She absolutely loved it when a guy took her from behind. And she had no doubt it was going to look spectacular for the camera.

As Kent dug in the pocket of his jeans for another condom, she glanced at the monitor and saw that the camera had captured their kiss. Damn, they looked hot together.

Behind her, Kent grasped her hips and Liz caught her breath as she felt him tease the opening of her pussy with the head of his cock. The urge to have him inside her was impossible to resist. When he began to enter her, she tried to push back against him, but he held her in place and slid into her pussy inch by glorious inch. Once he was finally in as deep as he could go, he held himself there, filling her completely.

Kent felt so perfect inside her Liz thought she might actually come from the sheer pleasure of their joining.

But then he did something that took her pleasure to another whole level. He sat back on his heels, urging her to sit back on him. The position shoved his cock even deeper and she gasped as she leaned back against his chest.

"Does that feel good?" he asked, his mouth brushing her ear as he reached around to cup her breasts.

"Mmm-hmmm," she breathed, resting her head on his shoulder.

He pressed his lips to the curve of her neck. "How about this?"

"God, yes!"

He gave her nipples a little squeeze, making her jump. "That's it. Ride my cock."

Liz put a hand on each of his muscular thighs and slowly began to move up and down on him.

"Just like that," he murmured in her ear. "Nice and slow."

She obeyed, undulating her hips slowly. He felt so good inside her that it was difficult to keep up her leisurely pace, though, and she was glad when he distracted her by whispering in her ear again.

"Check out the monitor."

At the mention of it, she turned her attention to the screen. The camera had caught them with Kent cupping her breasts and her leaning back against him, her lips parted, her eyes half closed, and a look of pure, unadulterated lust on her face.

"You're very photogenic," he said softly.

She smiled at him over her shoulder as she came down on his cock again. "So are you."

Kent groaned in reply, murmuring something she couldn't quite catch as he grasped her hips and urged her forward onto her hands and knees again. Tightening his grip, he began to thrust in and out with a fierceness that left her breathless.

Liz tossed her head back to gaze at the monitor. The position looked even more primal on the screen and she was mesmerized by the image. Behind her, Kent's shoulders and chest rippled and flexed on camera, the lighting he'd set up for the photo shoot accentuating his gorgeously chiseled muscles as he pumped in and out of her.

"Harder!" she demanded, bracing her hands on the soft material covering the dais and pushing back against him.

He complied, shoving his cock so deep with every thrust she was sure she was going pass out from how wonderful it felt. When her orgasm washed over her a moment later, though, she didn't lose consciousness like she thought she would. Instead, she threw back her head and cried out over and over as the riptide of pleasure carried her away.

Liz was so wrapped up in her own climax she was barely aware of Kent coming with her until he buried himself in her pussy with one smooth motion and a very loud groan of satisfaction.

It was a long time before Liz could catch her breath and when she finally did, it was to gasp as Kent slid out. She wasn't sure how it was possible, but that orgasm had been even better than the others.

Kent took her hand and gave it a little tug, pulling her against his chest as he lay back on the floor. Liz snuggled close and let out a sigh.

"That was off-the-charts good," she said softly.

He ran his fingers up and down the arm she'd thrown across his broad chest. "I'm glad you liked it. I think so, too, by the way."

Liz smiled. Who would have thought she'd end up making love to her photographer? And to think she had almost chickened out about coming here tonight and getting her picture taken for the benefit calendar.

The thought made her remember Godiva still waiting for her in the front room and she stifled a groan. While she would have preferred to stay right where she was all night, she really needed to go check on her precious pooch.

She reluctantly pushed herself up on an elbow. "I should get dressed and go see what Godiva's up to. She might be trying to eat one of the plants out there."

Kent's brow furrowed. "Damn, she's so quiet, I forgot she was even here."

Liz laughed. "Me, too."

"Well, while you check on her, I'll transfer the photos from the camera so we can take a look at them. Sound good?"

Her pulse skipped a beat at the thought of looking at all those naughty pictures with him and she smiled. "Sounds great."

He slid his hand in her hair and pulled her down for a long, slow kiss before helping her to her feet. As they got dressed, she couldn't help glancing over her shoulder to catch one more glimpse of Kent's naked body. Dear God, he was gorgeous.

Stifling a moan, she tied the belt of her robe around her waist, then ran her hand through her disheveled hair and hurried into the front room to see how Godiva was doing. The dog was on the floor by the couch, fast asleep with her head on her paws, but at the sound of Liz coming in, she lifted her head to give her a drowsy look.

"Okay, girl," Liz said, crouching down to give the dog an affectionate rub on the head. "You can come back in the studio now."

Godiva wagged her tail, but made no move to get up. Instead, she just put her head back on her paws and went back to sleep.

Liz laughed. "Or you can just stay here and sleep while I get changed, lazybones."

Shaking her head, Liz got to her feet and walked back into the studio. Kent was already dressed and had taken the camera off the tripod and over to the computer.

He glanced over at her. "Godiva okay?"

"She's fine. She's just being lazy."

He chuckled. "I'll have the photos up in a minute."

"Great. Let me go change and I'll be right back."

Hurrying into the bathroom, she shrugged out of her robe and shoved it in her shoulder bag, then quickly put on her jeans and tank top. She glanced in the mirror and smiled. Damn if she didn't look like she'd just been thoroughly and completely boffed. It was a good look for her. Throwing her bag on her shoulder, she went back into the studio, feeling the sexiest she'd ever felt in her life.

"The photos of you and Godiva came out great," Kent said as she walked over to him.

Eager to see them for herself, Liz sidled up next to him. As she studied them, she couldn't help but smile. Kent was right. They really did look good.

"Any idea which one you want to use for the calendar?" he asked.

She chewed on her lip thoughtfully for a moment, then pointed to the one where she was kneeling next to Godiva with her arms around the dog and her cleavage on display. "This one."

"Nice choice. That's my favorite, too." He grinned. "At least among the photos of you and Godiva."

She jerked her head up. "You looked at the others."

His grin broadened. "I glanced at them."

"Let me see, too."

He laughed and reached for the mouse. A moment later, a new set of pictures popped up on the screen. God, there were an awful lot of them. The computer displayed them in the order they were taken and Liz slowly let her gaze wander from one photo to the next, amazed at how sexy she looked as she went from fully clothed to completely naked.

"So, what do you think?" Kent asked.

She smiled. "I think you're an excellent photographer."

He chuckled. "It's all you, babe. I just took the pictures."

She blushed. "Can I see the rest?"

He leaned over to click the mouse again and the photos of her and Kent making love came up on the screen. They were even more breathtaking than the others and all she could do was stare in awe. Though extremely erotic, thanks to the seductive shadows the lighting created, they were both sexy and tasteful at the same time. Like true works of art.

"Do you like them?" Kent asked softly.

She turned to look at him. "I love them. They're beautiful."

"Just like you," he said, kissing her gently on the mouth. When he lifted his head a moment later, he reached down to click the mouse a few times, then pulled the memory card out of the card reader and held it out to her. "As much as I'd love to keep the photos, I don't want you worrying about them ending up all over the internet, so you'd better take them with you."

Liz's brow furrowed in confusion as she took the memory card. She'd been so caught up in the moment she hadn't even thought of asking him for the pictures. "What about the pictures for the calendar?"

"I saved them to the hard drive, but just the ones of you and Godiva."

"Oh." She regarded the memory card for a moment, then gave him a teasing look. "Aren't you worried I might post your pics on the internet?"

"Not really." He gave her a wink. "I'm a pretty good judge of character and I don't think you're that type of person."

She laughed. "You're right. I'll guard them with my life."

Liz took her time slipping the memory card into her purse as she wondered how to bring up the subject of getting together with Kent again. Not just for sex, either. While she definitely wouldn't mind a repeat performance of tonight, she'd like to go on a more conventional date just to see if she was right about the connection she felt between them.

Kent reached out to brush her hair back from her face. "You know, I take Bob to the dog park over on Fourth Avenue every Saturday afternoon. I was wondering if you and Godiva would like to go with us this week. After the dogs run us ragged, we could go out to dinner, then maybe take in a movie or something."

She smiled. Not only was he sinfully handsome and great in bed, but he could apparently read minds, too. "I'd love to."

"Great." He took a step closer. "By the way, that memory card can hold a lot more photos."

Her pulse quickened. "Really?"

"A lot more."

Liz looked up at him from beneath lowered lashes and gave him a sexy smile. "So, are you going to bring your camera on our date then?"

Kent slid his hand in her hair and tilted her head back. "Count on it," he promised, his mouth closing over hers.

JUST RIGHT

Trademarks Acknowledgement

The author acknowledges the trademarked status and trademark owners of the following wordmarks mentioned in this work of fiction:

Cosmo: Hearst Communications, Inc.

Playgirl: Playgirl Key Club, Inc.

Chapter One

ഗ

She was not lost. She hiked these trails all the time, so there was no way she could be lost. But if she wasn't lost, then why didn't she recognize anything around her? Because she was momentarily disoriented, Goldie Lockwood told herself. She would see something she recognized soon enough. There'd be a trail marker or a big rock formation she'd recognize just around the next bend. She was sure of it.

Two hours and about a hundred bends later, however, she was still wandering around the Tualatin Mountains outside of Portland with no clue where she was. She had only planned on taking a short hour-long hike to clear her head after a crappy day at work, so she hadn't brought any food or water, or even a map with her. And to make matters worse, she couldn't get a signal on her stupid cell phone. So much for more bars in more places.

Thoroughly frustrated, Goldie stopped in the middle of the nearly overgrown trail and put her hands on her slender hips. Dammit, why hadn't she just gone out with the girls for a drink after work? If she had, maybe she'd be cozying up to a hot guy right now instead of being stranded in the wilderness. But no, she had wanted to go hiking. So, she'd changed into the shorts, T-shirt, and comfy pair of hiking boots she always kept in her car, then driven up to the mountains and hit the trails.

It wasn't really as impulsive or as reckless as it sounded. She loved the outdoors and hiking always relaxed her, especially after a long day at work. But today had been different. Today, Bob Ashton, the cute guy at work she'd been trying to get to notice her for months, had gone out to lunch with one of the girls from accounting. And not just any girl, either, but the office slut, Marissa Conway. To top it all off, they hadn't gotten back until after two. Combine that with Bob's tousled hair and the silly-ass grin on Marissa's face and Goldie hadn't needed a neon sign to figure out the little tramp had spent her lunch hour snacking on him instead of some uber-healthy salad. It was infuriating! Everyone in the office knew Goldie was interested in Bob, but that hadn't stopped Marissa from going after him.

That was the reason Goldie was lost. If she had been concentrating on where she was going instead of alternately wondering where she had gone wrong with Bob and what he could possibly see in Marissa, she wouldn't be in her current predicament.

She could be in really big trouble, too. She had broken the number-one rule when it came to hiking by not telling anyone where she was going. Considering it was Friday, it was likely no one would even notice she was missing until Monday morning when she didn't show up for work. Even then, someone would have to find her car at the trailhead to figure out she was out here. It could take a search party days to find her. That was a long time to be lost in the woods without any food or water.

She fought the surge of panic gripping her. *Stop being such a drama queen and start navigating your way out of here.*

Goldie took a deep breath to calm herself down, then looked around, trying to decide which way to go. After this long, though, all the Douglas fir and big-leaf maples looked the same and it was difficult to pick a direction. She was so disoriented she couldn't even figure out which way led down the mountain. She frowned at the stream of late afternoon sunlight coming through the canopy of trees. It would be dark soon, which would make finding her way back to civilization even harder, especially since she didn't have a flashlight. All kinds of wild animals came out at night, too, didn't they? She really didn't want to be some grizzly bear's midnight snack.

Behind her, a twig snapped and she jumped. Okay, time to get moving. If she were lucky, maybe she'd come across another hiker and they'd be able to point her in the right direction.

Until then, though, she was going to have to find her own way out. Wildwood Trail was one of the biggest ones in the area, so it should be the easiest to find. Using the sun as a guide, she turned around and headed east, figuring she had to be somewhere west of the trail. Hopefully, she'd just stumble on it.

That plan didn't quite work out, however. The farther she walked, the more lost she ended up. The trail she was currently on was so overgrown it looked like it hadn't been used in a couple seasons. Tears stung her eyes and she blinked them back as she glanced down at her watch. Crap, she'd been wandering around the woods for almost four hours. Not only was she frustrated and scared, but she was hungry and thirsty, too.

She turned around in a circle, desperately looking for some sort of landmark she recognized, when something caught her eye through the trees. She leaned down to try to get a better look, but couldn't quite make out what it was. She only knew it was big and looked like it was man-made. Maybe it was a camping shelter. They usually had maps and information in them.

Hoping that's what it was, she ventured off the path and started toward it cross-country, pushing aside branches and stepping over downed trees in her hurry to get there. She squinted in the dim light, trying again to make out what it was, only to gasp as she stepped out into a small clearing. Holy crap, it wasn't a shelter, it was a cabin!

Even as she rushed over to it, Goldie couldn't help but wonder who the heck would have a cabin out in the middle of nowhere. Every scary movie she'd ever seen involving a cabin in the woods popped into her head at the same time and she came to an abrupt halt halfway to the steps leading up to the front door. The cabin could belong to an axe-wielding psychopath. Or even the Big Bad Wolf, for all she knew. Maybe she should turn around and go back.

To what, wandering around the woods some more until it got dark?

"I don't think so," she muttered.

Besides, the place looked like it was deserted. Even axe-wielding psychopaths wouldn't want to live this far out in the middle of nowhere.

Telling herself there was only one way to find out if it was deserted, she ran to the cabin and knocked on the door, then waited. When no one answered, she knocked again, louder this time.

"Hello!" she called. "Is anyone home?"

Still no answer.

Brow furrowing, Goldie put her nose to the glass on the door, cupped her face with her hands, and peeked inside. She was half afraid she would find it empty, but instead there was a small kitchen with a stove, a fridge, and a table to one side, as well as a pair of overstuffed chairs and a matching couch over by the fireplace on the other.

She sighed with relief. Someone definitely lived there. Unfortunately, that same someone didn't appear to be home. And considering the place was in the middle of the woods, it could be a hunting cabin, which meant the owner probably wouldn't be making an appearance anytime soon.

Goldie's stomach growled and her gaze went to the fridge again. She looked longingly at it, imagining all the tasty food inside. Knowing it was a long shot, she grasped the doorknob and turned anyway. It was locked.

She chewed on her lower lip, wondering if she should break in. Since it was not only wrong, but illegal as well, probably not. But she was so hungry. And it would be getting dark soon. She turned to look back the way she had come and realized the sun had already gone down. Crap, it would be pitch black in thirty minutes. There was no way she was staying out in these woods in the dark.

Besides, if there was a fridge in the cabin, it meant the place had to have power of some kind, maybe solar panels on the roof or something. If there was power, there might be a phone she could use. Surely, the owner of the cabin wouldn't be angry once she explained her situation. Especially if she reimbursed him for the food she ate, as well as the window she'd have to break to get inside, of course.

Goldie stepped back from the door and looked around for a rock. Since she was in a forest, there were quite a few lying around and she hurried over to pick up one. Looking over her shoulder to make sure no other hikers had suddenly stumbled upon the same cabin she had, she tightened her grip on the rock and walked back up the steps to the door. Taking a deep breath, she drew her arm back and smashed the pane of glass closest to the lock. It was louder than she'd thought it would be and she cringed as the sound echoed through the forest. Tossing the rock on the ground, she reached through the opening and unlocked the deadbolt, then pushed open the door.

* * * * *

Gregory Bauer hated loggers, especially loggers who made their living illegally. The forest was protected and there wasn't supposed to be logging of any type going on, especially in the old-growth areas. Of course, those same old-growth trees were what attracted the loggers. Those old trees were worth a lot of money and some less-than-scrupulous dirtbags didn't mind risking a minor state park fine in order to get to cut them down. As Oregon State Troopers, he supposed he and his brothers could always use their badges to scare off the jerks, but they'd discovered a much more effective way to do it. A way that guaranteed the loggers wouldn't ever want to come back to this particular forest again.

He darted a quick look to his right, then his left as he ran, catching sight of the two grizzly bears through the trees on either side as they kept pace with him. His brothers Orson and Barrett were close. Good.

Gregory leaped over a long-dead Douglas fir in his path, his enormous paws barely touching the ground as he continued to close the distance between himself and the unsuspecting loggers with an unnatural speed only a werebear possessed. The sounds of chainsaws urged him on and he ran even faster.

He sometimes wondered if the assholes even knew the destruction they caused. Logging in an old-growth forest didn't just affect the ancient trees they killed, but the animals that lived there as well, some of which were in danger of becoming threatened thanks to their greed. Then again, maybe they knew exactly what they were doing and they just didn't care.

Gregory growled deep in his throat at the thought. Well, after the scare he and his brothers gave them, these particular loggers would think twice before coming back to cut down any more trees in this forest.

As he neared the area where the men were working, Gregory automatically slowed his step. On either side of him, his brothers did the same. While charging out from the trees might be more satisfying, the subtle approach tended to work better. The sight of three huge grizzly bears slowly and deliberately approaching was usually enough to frighten off most loggers.

As always, Gregory took the lead, slowly emerging from the trees ahead of his brothers. He kept his head low as he walked, something he knew not only emphasized the breadth of his shoulders, but made him look even more menacing to his prey. On either side of him, Orson and Barrett had stepped out from the woods and were doing the same.

Fortunately, the loggers hadn't gotten into any of the big old-growth trees yet. But they had taken down a few small firs and spruces to make it easier to get at the ones they were after. They hadn't even bothered to do more than chop up the smaller trees. They weren't interested in them, even if it meant the trees would just sit there and rot, or worse, serve as underbrush fuel for the wildfires that frequently swept through the forest. The big trees could usually handle these fires, but not if there was a huge pile of limbs and logs piled up near them. The damn jerks didn't even care.

The loggers didn't notice Gregory and his brothers at first, probably because the men were too intent on what they were doing. As Gregory drew nearer, however, one of the men must have caught a glimpse of him because he did a double take before his eyes went wide. Heavyset with a thick, red beard, he wore a plaid shirt and a knit cap.

Gregory opened his mouth just enough to show his teeth. *That's right, asshole. You're in deep shit.*

The man stared at Gregory in stunned silence for a moment, then frantically thumped the skinny logger beside him on the arm to get his attention. When his coworker glared at him an annoyance, the man pointed at Gregory with a trembling hand.

The skinny man took one look at Gregory and immediately began to backpedal. "Bear!" he shouted to the other loggers, loud enough to be heard over the chainsaws. "Three of them!"

At the words, the rest of the men stopped what they were doing to turn wide eyes on Gregory and his brothers. The stench of fear filled the air and Gregory's nostrils flared at the odor. He shook his head from side to side, baring his teeth in aggression, then following it up with a fierce growl for good measure. Orson and Barrett did their own variation, both of them sounding just as ferocious.

Their combined display of open hostility sent a good portion of the loggers running for their trucks, with Orson hot on their tails. He wouldn't hurt them, but he would claw up their vehicles a bit and make sure they had something to remind them of their stupidity.

Some of the men weren't as easily scared off, though. Instead, they stood their ground, chainsaws and axes at the ready. Gregory didn't know if they were brave or just stupid. *Okay, time for phase two.*

Gregory growled again and stood up on his powerful, hind legs. At twelve feet, he was taller than most normal grizzlies. Letting out a massive roar, he threw his front paws over his head, making sure the men got a good look at his long, sharp claws as they came clearly into view. Beside him, he caught a glimpse of Barrett raking his own claws down the nearest tree trunk. Nothing like a close-up view of a set of razor-sharp, three-inch claws and a demonstration of what they could do something as tough as a tree trunk to make a person decide discretion really was the better part of valor.

A chainsaw and two more axes hit the ground as three more of the men hightailed it to their trucks with Barrett providing an escort.

That left two more men, one with an axe and the other with a chainsaw held firmly in front of him. These two looked more resolved and Gregory knew they weren't going to fall for a simple display of strength. They would need a more direct approach. *All right, enough screwing around.*

Gregory dropped his forelegs to the ground with a thump that shook the nearby trees. Without hesitating, he launched himself at the axe-wielding logger. The fool actually tried to take a swing at him with the axe, but like most humans, he didn't realize how fast a bear, especially a werebear, could be.

Gregory let the blade pass by him harmlessly, then stiff-armed the man's shoulder with a closed paw. He could have ripped the guy's head off, but while that might have been satisfying, it wasn't what he was after. Nonetheless, the guy did go sailing through the air in a most gratifying manner. When he finally hit the ground, he lay there in a heap, moaning in pain.

Deciding the man wouldn't be going anywhere for a while, Gregory turned back to find the guy with the chainsaw approaching him, the chain churning at full speed. Gregory was fairly confident he could have avoided the deadly implement like he had the axe, but he didn't want to take a chance.

Instead he reached down to the forest floor and grasped one of the sections of smaller trees trunk the loggers had already cut down. He couldn't really grab it, of course. Even as a werebear, his paws weren't dexterous enough to do that. But he could clasp either end of the five-foot long log as if it were a great big medicine ball. Then, as the logger's eyes widened, he executed a perfect chest pass, like he would if he was playing basketball with his brothers.

The log probably weighed about two hundred pounds and it hit the dumbass right in the chest. Fortunately for the man, the chainsaw went flying in a safe direction as the man fell backward. Although the fall must have hurt like hell, the guy immediately scrambled to his feet and started backing away from Gregory, his eyes registering equal parts pain and bewilderment. Gregory could just imagine the guy trying to convince his friend a grizzly bear had just hit him with a log. *"I swear I'm telling you dudes the truth! The damn bear picked up a log and threw it at me like it weighed nothing!"*

When Gregory let out one more mighty roar, the logger finally decided to call it quits. Swearing under his breath, he grabbed his coworker up off the ground and gave the man a shove toward the lone, remaining pickup truck already slowly moving down the access road.

Gregory bounded after the men, his big paws kicking up dirt behind him as he ran. He was actually a little surprised the other loggers hadn't simply left these last two. Gregory expected the truck to stop so the two men could get in the cab, but instead the driver kept going, making the two men jump in the back. Orson caught up with the truck just in time to swipe the rear side panel with his claws before the vehicle picked up speed.

Gregory gave his brother a loud woof. The equivalent of saying, "You show 'em," in werebear. Orson woofed in reply, then followed Gregory over to where Barrett was surveying the damage the loggers had done. Fortunately, the three of them had gotten there before the men had been able to cut down more than a few trees. It still pissed him off, though.

Barrett made a gruff sound and jerked his head toward the wood line, his way of asking if Gregory and Orson were ready to head back to where they'd left their truck and change into their human forms. Gregory was all for that idea. While he loved shapeshifting into his bear form, he had already spent the better part of the day roaming the woods with his brothers before they had heard the loggers. That had been on top of a double shift they had already worked at the station. He was tired, hungry, and more than ready to go back to their cabin and relax for a while.

Chapter Two

ℰᴑ

Goldie felt another little twinge of guilt as she stepped into the cabin and quietly closed the door behind her. It quickly disappeared when she considered the alternative, though. Breaking and entering was definitely preferable to wandering around the woods for the rest of the night. Hiking in the forest during the day was one thing, but doing it at night was completely different.

Even though she'd made enough noise to alert anyone to her presence when she'd broken the glass, she decided it might be a good idea to check and make sure the cabin really was empty before she went looking for a phone or raiding the fridge.

"Hello!" she called. "Is anyone here?"

No answer, just like before.

She sighed with relief. While she was planning on reimbursing the cabin's owner, it would have been really awkward to have to explain herself if he'd walked out of the back room right then.

Goldie looked around the cabin. In addition to the comfortable looking couch and matching chairs in the living room, there was also a coffee table and a bookcase filled with a mix of paperback and hardcover books. Though the room had definite masculine overtones, it still managed to pull off a warm and cozy vibe.

Her gaze went to the kitchen next. It was small, but the stovetop and microwave looked serviceable enough. She was more interested in the refrigerator, though. She only hoped there was something in it.

Considering how hungry she was, Goldie wanted check it out right then, but figured she should probably look for a phone first. Unfortunately, she didn't see one in the kitchen or the adjoining living room. Praying there was one in the back room, she hurried over to look inside, but all she found were three beds with matching nightstands and a dresser, as well as another bookcase. There was a small, adjoining bathroom, too.

So much for using the phone. Not that it would have done much good anyway. She could just imagine talking to the 911 operator. *Yes, I'm in a cabin in the middle of the woods. Can you send someone to come get me? No, I don't know where the cabin is. It's the one in the middle of the woods. Don't you have a listing for that address?*

Letting out a sigh, she walked back into the kitchen and over to the fridge. She held her breath as she pulled open the door, afraid she'd find nothing but a box of baking soda. While it wasn't what she'd call well-stocked, it wasn't completely bare. Along with a six-pack of beer and half a dozen bottles of water, there were several plastic containers of what had to be leftovers. Her stomach growled ferociously at the sight. She'd known she was hungry, but now that she was within arm's reach of food, she realized she was starving.

Goldie took out one of the containers and pulled off the lid. Inside was a reddish brown mixture of meat and beans that looked like it might be chili. She put it up to her nose and sniffed. Yup, it was definitely chili. Her stomach growling again, she opened the drawer closest to the fridge, looking for a spoon. It was full of various mismatched utensils and she had to rummage around until she found a spoon. Grabbing it, she dipped it in the chili and eagerly tasted it. The moment it touched her tongue, her whole mouth was engulfed in flames. Yikes! She liked spicy food, but that was stupid hot.

Putting the lid on the container, she placed it back in the fridge, then reached for the next one. She took off the top and peeked inside, then frowned. While the chili had been easy to identify, she couldn't say the same about whatever was inside the second container. It looked a little like oatmeal, but she'd never heard of anyone putting leftover oatmeal in the fridge. Deciding there was only one way to find out, she dipped her spoon in the thick, gooey mixture and took a taste, then immediately made a face. Whereas the chili was so spicy she could barely eat it, this had absolutely no flavor at all. She'd never tasted anything so bland in her life. It could have been wallpaper paste.

Closing the container, she put it in the fridge beside the chili and grabbed another from the fridge. After the first two, she was almost afraid to wonder what was inside this one. Praying it was something edible, she took off the lid and looked inside. From the chunks of beef and mix of vegetables, she decided it must be stew. She dipped the tip of her spoon in the brown liquid, then cautiously lifted it to her mouth. It wasn't too spicy or too bland, but just right, and she let out a moan of pleasure. In fact, it was so delicious she wanted to eat the rest of it standing right there in front of the fridge, but she suspected it would taste even better if she heated it up. With that thought in mind, she stuck the container in the microwave and turned it on.

While she waited for it to cook, Goldie grabbed a bottle of water from the fridge and took a long swallow as she looked around. She wondered who owned the cabin and when he might be back. The leftovers were obviously fresh, which implied he would probably be coming back soon. He might even be able to help her find her way out of the woods. If he wasn't too angry about her breaking into the cabin, of course. She wasn't too worried about that, though. She knew how to work a guy when she had to.

When the microwave dinged, she eagerly yanked open the door and took out the container, then sat down at the kitchen table to eat. She was right. The stew tasted even more delicious hot and she finished every bit of it.

Telling herself she'd wash out the container later, Goldie went into the living room and perused the bookshelf. Since it seemed like she was going to be spending the night, she might as well see if there was anything interesting to read. To her dismay, however, there was nothing but science fiction, spy thrillers, and mysteries, none of which were her thing. Crap, she'd been hoping to find a romance. Maybe there would be something better in the bookcase in the bedroom.

Goldie turned and headed toward the bedroom when the wood carvings on the mantel caught her eye. Curious, she walked over to take a closer look.

Three bears, each depicted doing something different. In the first one, the bear was standing in a river, fishing for salmon. She picked it up to take a closer look. While it was nice, the carving was a little too crudely done for her taste. Setting it down, she picked up the second wood carving. The bear in this one had his paw stuck in a beehive looking for honey. Although the carving wasn't as unsophisticated as the first bear, it didn't have enough detail for her. She put it back and picked up the third bear, admiring it first from one direction, then another. Unlike the other bears, which were shown in their natural habitat, this bear was sitting in a chair, carving another little bear out of wood. She smiled. Finely carved and richly detailed right down to the look of concentration on the bear's face, this one was just right. Whoever had carved it had obviously taken his time.

Still smiling, Goldie reached out to set it down on the mantle. She must have put it too close to the edge, though, because it fell off and hit the stone hearth before she could stop it. Chiding herself for being so clumsy, she bent down to pick it up and was horrified to see she'd broken one of the legs on the chair. She cringed as she carefully placed the carving back on the mantle, along with the chair leg. Something else she'd have to reimburse the owner of the cabin for, she supposed.

She stifled a yawn. Telling herself she should probably go to bed before she did any more damage, Goldie went into the bedroom and closed the door. She surveyed the three beds for a moment, wondering which one she should sleep in.

Shrugging, she chose the one closest to the door, pulled down the blanket, then sat down on the edge to take off her boots and socks. When she was done, she climbed into bed, only to discover it was so soft she sank into the middle of it. Good heavens, she'd probably smother to death if she tried to sleep in the darn thing.

Thinking there was no way the other beds could be as mushy as the one she was currently in, Goldie got up and went to the one on the other side of the room. She pulled back the blanket and sat down on that one, then groaned. Where the other bed was too soft, this one was so hard she thought it might actually be made of concrete. She was tempted to check under the sheet to see if she was right, but changed her mind. She was way too tired to care.

Yawning, Goldie got up and walked around to the third bed. Hoping it was more comfortable than the first two, she threw back the blanket and sat down. Not too hard or too soft, this one was just right.

Letting out a sigh of contentment, she pulled up the blanket and snuggled into the pillow. As she drifted off to sleep, she hoped the owner of the cabin didn't come back and find her sleeping in his bed. That would be really hard to explain.

* * * * *

Gregory shrugged into his shirt and buttoned it. If he'd been tired after chasing off those loggers, that was nothing compared to how exhausted he was now. Changing from a werebear into his human form took a lot out of him. He knew it did the same thing to Orson and Barrett. They probably shouldn't have shapeshifted after working that double shift, but the urge to run through the forest was always too powerful to resist. A little exhaustion was a small price to pay for the high they experienced from channeling their inner grizzly bear, though.

As he got into his SUV, he couldn't help but think back to when he'd first discovered he and his brothers were werebears. His mouth quirked at the memory as he started the engine.

He'd been fourteen when his father had sat him and his older brothers down for the talk. Figuring his father had been going to launch into the whole birds-and-bees routine, Gregory had been about to tell him Orson and Barrett had already filled him in, but to his surprise, his dad had told them a story about their great-great-great-grandfather Osborn Bauer.

According to Gregory's father, Osborn had been one of the early settlers in what was now Oregon. While out hunting one day, he rescued a young Indian woman from a grizzly bear. She was so impressed with his bravery that to show her gratitude, she bestowed a gift on him, giving him the ability to shapeshift into the same animal he just courageously confronted. Since then, every male in the Bauer family had had the ability to shapeshift into a grizzly bear.

Gregory, Orson, and Barrett had thought their dad was full of it, of course. So, to convince them, he changed into a huge grizzly bear right then and there. Gregory and his brothers had been so shocked all they could do was stand there and stare at him. When their dad had finally changed back, they barraged him with questions, all of which he'd patiently answered.

Since they were older, Orson and Barrett had been able to change into werebears before Gregory, and by the time he was old enough, he couldn't wait to experience it for himself. It had been as amazing as he had hoped. In fact, it was all his father could do to get him to change back into his human form. When he finally came down from the high after changing back, he was exhausted, starving, and horny as hell, all common side-effects of the transformation process.

It was the same, even after all these years. At that particular moment, he couldn't figure out if he wanted to take a nap, eat a horse, or find a woman to fuck. Since he wasn't currently seeing anyone, though, and there weren't a lot of women roaming around in the woods, he'd have to forget about the sex part of the equation for tonight and settle for satisfying his other basic needs instead.

As he followed Barrett's pickup down the winding access road, Gregory salivated over the thought of the leftover stew he'd stuck in the fridge earlier when he'd stopped by the cabin before going for a bear run. It was his favorite meal and he'd wanted to make sure he would have a big bowl waiting for him the moment he got back. He and his brothers hadn't been at the cabin for a couple weeks, so they would need to make a food run tomorrow, but for tonight that stew would do just fine.

Gregory pulled his SUV alongside Barrett's pickup in front of the cabin and cut the engine, then got out and headed for the front door. Halfway up the steps, however, he stopped when he saw the broken glass in the door. He stiffened, his werebear senses and years of police training taking over.

"What's up?" Barrett asked from behind him.

Gregory shot his brother a quick look over his shoulder. "Someone broke in."

"You're kidding, right?" Orson climbed the steps to stand beside Barrett. His mouth tightened as he took in the door. "Shit."

Gregory made no comment as he looked through the window and into the darkened cabin. In addition to his superior strength and agility, his night vision was as good in his human form as it was when he was a bear, and he could see the interior of the cabin as if there was a light on. It looked empty. That made sense, though. There wasn't much of value in the cabin, which meant any intruder wasn't likely to hang around for very long. But they would need to check anyway, just in case someone was hiding.

Glancing at Orson and Barrett over his shoulder, Gregory pulled his off-duty weapon and waited until they both did same, before he threw open the door.

Gregory stepped inside first, followed by Orson and Barrett. Since the cabin was small, there weren't many places to hide in the main part of it, so a quick look around told him the living room and kitchen area were clear. He sniffed the air. Damn, that had to be the most feminine scent he'd ever smelled. He looked over at Orson and Barrett to see that they'd picked on the same scent and were already putting their weapons away. Gregory kept his out for now. Just because the intruder was a woman, that didn't mean she wasn't dangerous.

He scanned the cabin, checking to see if anything was missing. His dark eyes narrowed as he caught sight of the plastic container and half full bottle of water on the kitchen table. What the hell?

Frowning, he walked over to the table and discovered the plastic container was empty. It didn't take a keen sense of smell to realize he was looking at what was left of the stew he'd been planning to devour. Dammit, what was he going to eat now?

"Someone's been in my chili," Orson said.

"My porridge, too," Barrett added.

Gregory looked up to see that his brothers had come in the kitchen and were now standing by the counter. He wasn't surprised the girl had passed up their food for his. Orson and Barrett both had shitty taste in food. "Well at least you have something let to eat. That same someone ate my entire container of stew."

Orson yanked open the fridge. "At least she didn't drink our beer."

"Do you think she's still here?" Barrett asked.

"I can't believe she'd be dumb enough to hang around, but I can tell you for a fact that the bedroom door was open when we left," Gregory said.

Orson obviously figured out where Gregory was going with that, because he slammed the refrigerator door and headed toward the bedroom. On the way there, however, he took a detour over to the fireplace.

"Whoever she is, she messed with our woodcarvings, too." He held up the bear Gregory had carved. "Looks like she broke the one you made."

Gregory clenched his jaw. He could overlook the woman eating his whole bowl of stew, but that bear had taken him hours to carve. Shoving his gun back in its holster, he tossed the plastic container on the table and strode toward the bedroom. He didn't bother to look at Orson and Barrett as he opened the door and walked in.

The moment he did, the feminine scent that hit him was so powerful and intoxicating, he immediately felt his cock begin to stiffen. Whoa. The woman was nowhere in sight, but he was sure she was still in there. And if her scent was any indication, then she was sexy as hell.

Gregory spotted the pair of hiking boots by Orson's bed. He glanced at his brothers and jerked his head toward the boots. They both nodded.

He looked around the room again. It was obvious from the way the blankets had been pulled down that the girl had tried out all three beds before she found one she liked. And from the looks of it, she liked his bed the most. He let out a snort of disgust. Why wasn't he surprised? She'd already eaten his stew and broken his woodcarving. Why not sleep in his bed, too?

"I think she was actually sleeping in my bed," Orson said.

"You're not the only one," Barrett muttered. "She's been in my bed, too."

Gregory almost laughed as he walked across the room to stand beside his own bed. His brothers' comments had an extremely familiar ring to them. Only this wasn't some fairy tale. This was breaking and entering.

"Obviously," he said dryly. "But I think she liked my bed more. And if I'm not mistaken, she's still here."

Even though the girl's sexy scent filled the small bedroom, he had no problem figuring out exactly where she was once he got close to the bed. Dropping to his knee, he looked under it and found himself gazing into the prettiest, clear blue eyes he'd ever seen. The fear in them was almost enough to make him forget everything she'd done and he was tempted to tell his brothers he was wrong and that she'd already left. But then he remembered how she'd helped herself to his stew, vandalized his property, and slept in his bed as if she owned the place. What she did was a crime and he couldn't look the other way, even if she was the most beautiful girl he'd ever seen.

So, he gave her his best no-nonsense, state-trooper glower. "I think you can come out now, don't you?"

Chapter Three

જી

Despite the authoritative tone in the man's voice, Goldie stayed where she was. She chewed on her lower lip nervously, wondering how she was going to talk her way out of this one. *Crap!* She couldn't believe he'd picked tonight to show up at the cabin.

Goldie had been startled out of her deep sleep by the sound of men's voices. Knowing she was in trouble, she had immediately jumped out of bed and looked for a place to hide. Thinking they would surely look in the adjoining bathroom for whoever had broken in, she had dived underneath the bed, hoping when they found the room empty, they would assume she'd already left. Of course, that was about the time she realized her hiking boots were still sitting on the floor right in plain sight. She'd just been debating whether to go get them when the door opened and by then it was too late. So, she'd just held her breath and peeked out as three pairs of booted feet entered the room, praying the men wouldn't find her.

They had found her, though. And from the way the man's golden brown eyes narrowed as he glared at her, it was obvious he definitely wasn't pleased she'd broken into his cabin. She was going to have to do some seriously fast talking to diffuse the situation.

From her place beneath the bed, she studied his face as she tried to come up with something to say. Even though he was clearly upset, with that dark hair, chiseled jaw, and wide, sensuous mouth, she couldn't help but notice he was extremely handsome. If she'd met a guy like him in a club, she'd be doing her best to get into his bed. Ironic that she'd ended up under it instead. She briefly wondered if she should try putting the moves on him, but then decided against it.

Trying something like that after breaking into his cabin wasn't likely to work. He probably wouldn't be receptive to her charms considering what she'd done.

"I'm waiting," he said.

Goldie let out a sigh of resignation and slowly began to wiggle out from underneath the bed. She'd been so worried about hiding she hadn't noticed how tight the space was when she'd darted under it earlier, but she practically had to low crawl out. She got to her feet with as much dignity as she could, then took her time brushing off her clothes. When she finally lifted her head, it was to find herself face to face not only with the gorgeous guy who had discovered her hiding place, but two more men who were just as attractive. Wow, if it wasn't for the whole breaking-and-entering thing, she'd be counting herself lucky right now. She was in a secluded cabin with three very hot guys. What more could a girl ask for?

Tall and broad shouldered like the man who had found her under the bed, they had the same dark hair and rugged features, and while their brown eyes didn't have the same touch of gold, they were equally as expressive. They bore such a strong resemblance to each other, she wouldn't be surprised if they were brothers. She absently wondered if there was a law against so many hunky guys being in one place at a time. If there wasn't, there should be, because the combined effect they were having on her was practically criminal. Her pulse was racing and she had a little quiver in her stomach. Then again, maybe it was just the fact she'd been caught hiding in their cabin.

Abruptly realizing they were all standing with their arms folded across their broad chests and looking at her expectantly, Goldie blushed. She reached up to nervously push back some long, blonde hair that had escaped from her ponytail.

"Th-this isn't what it looks like," she stammered.

The man who had found her under the bed lifted a brow. "Really? I think it's exactly what it looks like." He glanced at the man on his right. "Don't you, Orson?"

"Definitely."

He glanced at the man standing on his left. "Barrett?"

"Seems obvious to me."

The man turned his gold eyes on her again. As he lazily looked her up and down, she noticed his gaze lingered on the curve of her breasts and her long, shapely legs. So, was he a breast-man or a leg-man? It didn't matter. Either way, the way he was looking at her was starting to have an effect on her. Like he was imagining her naked.

"So, let's have it," he said. "What's your name and what are you doing here?"

"Goldie," she said, then after a moment, added, "Lockwood."

She only thought about giving him a fake name after the words were out of her mouth. It was too late now. Then again, with the way he was undressing her with his eyes, she was lucky she could remember her real name. She'd never met a man who could arouse her just by looking at her.

"That answers my first question, Goldie Lockwood. Now, tell us what you're doing here."

She hesitated, wondering if she should try to come up with some elaborate story to gain their sympathy, but then decided it would probably be better to just be honest. Something about the authoritative way these men were regarding her told her they would see right through whatever lies she made up anyway.

"I was out hiking and got lost," she explained. "I didn't bring any food or water with me and I was starting to get scared because it was getting dark. That was when I saw your cabin."

"So you just decided to break in?"

She felt her face turn red. "No, of course not! I knocked. Twice, in fact."

"And when no one answered, that's when you broke in," Barrett said.

Her color deepened. "Okay, okay. I did break in. But only because I thought you might have a phone."

"A phone?" Orson's brows drew together. "Wait a minute. Let me get this straight. You broke in because you were looking for a phone?"

She nodded sheepishly.

The man with the incredible golden eyes fixed her with a stern look. "So when you couldn't find one, you decided to vandalize the place instead?"

"Vandalize the place?" Goldie blinked. "What are you talking about? I didn't vandalize the place."

He arched a brow. "What about the woodcarving?"

"Oh. That. I picked it up to look at it and when I went to put it back on the mantel, it slipped." She caught her lower lip between her teeth and tried her best to look chastised, which wasn't very difficult. She did feel bad about breaking the woodcarving. She reached up to tuck her hair behind her ear again. "Look, I'm really sorry about breaking in. It was wrong."

"It's also a crime," Orson said.

Goldie's mouth went dry. Prison? He couldn't be serious. She wasn't a criminal. Her gaze went from Orson to the man with the gold eyes. "You're not really going to call the cops are you?"

His lips quirked. "Honey, we are the cops."

She eyed him skeptically, wondering if he was making that part up. Then he reached into the pocket of his jeans and pulled out a badge. *Oh crap.* He wasn't making it up. They were cops. Of all the cabins in the forest, she had to pick the one that belonged to three cops. "You're not going to arrest me, are you?"

"What do you think?"

She thought she was in big trouble. Even if by some miracle she didn't go to jail for breaking into their cabin, she'd still very likely lose her job if she got arrested. She gave him a pleading look, even more determined to talk her way out of this mess now. "Couldn't you just give me a ticket or something?"

"We don't give out tickets for that kind of stuff."

She formed her lips into a blatant pout. She hadn't met a man who could resist her pout. "Even if I pay for the broken window and promise never to do anything like this again?"

"Even then. It isn't as simple as paying for the window you broke. What you did was a crime and you have to be punished for it."

She wasn't sure why, but for some reason the way he said the words sent a delicious little shiver down her back. While he might be talking about carting her off to jail, the words took her mind in a completely different and much naughtier direction, one that involved him putting her over his knee and reddening her bottom.

What could she say? She was a girl who enjoyed a good spanking.

Between her legs, her pussy was already purring at the thought of one of the men doing just that. But did she dare say it aloud? She didn't know if it was a crime, but she didn't want to add attempted seduction of a police officer to her list of charges. On the other hand, it might be the only thing that kept her from getting arrested.

Of course, she'd have to figure out a way to get them to agree to it. She chewed on her lower lip. "Couldn't you just punish me yourself?"

His eyes narrowed suspiciously at her words, but she could see the spark of interest there. He was intrigued. "What would you suggest?"

She looked up at him from beneath lowered lashes. "Well...you could always...spank me."

He lifted a brow, clearly surprised. "Spank you? As in putting you over my knee and warming your bottom?"

Goldie nodded, trying not to look too eager at the idea. If the men knew she liked getting spanked, there was almost certainly no way they'd agree to it as an alternative form of punishment. No, instead she needed to look resigned to her fate.

"Yes, spank me," she said. "I've already apologized and said I'll pay you back for the window, but if you still think I need to be punished, then I suppose I'd rather get a spanking than go to jail."

"You would, huh?"

She nodded again, still careful to keep from appearing too enthusiastic. She had him hooked.

He said nothing, but merely regarded her with those captivating gold eyes, and she held her breath as she waited for him to make a decision. The longer he stayed silent, however, the more she began to think she'd misread him. She was just about to say something more to convince him when he glanced at the other two men.

"What do you say?"

Orson shrugged. "Works for me. It wasn't my woodcarving she broke."

"I don't have a problem with it, either," Barrett said. "She didn't eat my porridge."

Gold eyes swung back to her. "Okay, it's a deal. You get spanked and we'll call it even."

Relief coursed through her, along with a surge of excitement. She just knew he was going to give a great spanking. Her brow furrowed as a thought suddenly occurred to her. Just because he had done most of the talking that didn't mean he'd be the one who would do the spanking. What if he let one of the other guys do it? Of course, she'd still enjoy it, but she really wanted him to give it to her.

"So, which one of you is going to give me my spanking?"

Although she posed the question to all the men, Goldie looked at him when she spoke, silently willing him to be the one who volunteered.

His mouth edged up. "What do you mean, which one of us? We're all going to spank you."

Her eyes went wide. "All of you?"

He shrugged. "My brothers and I own the cabin jointly, so it's only fair."

"Gregory's right," Barrett said. "We should all get to spank you."

Goldie hadn't considered that scenario, but looking at the three hot guys in front of her, she had to admit the prospect of getting her bottom warmed by all of them was exciting. She'd never done anything like that before.

"Okay, I suppose you're right. I'll let all of you spank me." Just saying the words made her pussy quiver and she had to fight the urge to squeeze her thighs together. "Who wants to go first?"

She expected Gregory to step forward and announce he would spank her first, but instead it was Orson who spoke.

"Since I'm the oldest, I'll go first."

Goldie stifled a sigh. Guess she'd have to wait a little while longer to find out if Gregory was as good at giving a spanking as she suspected. When Orson led her over to the bed she'd been sleeping in, however, the feel of his hand on hers had her pulse quickening with anticipation. Suddenly, she could hardly wait for the oldest brother to spank her. He had really big hands.

As Orson sat down on the bed and expertly guided her over his knee, she shot Gregory and Barrett a quick look and saw that both men were eagerly watching the scene unfold. She wondered if they wanted to make sure their older brother did a good job spanking her or whether they were just satisfying their inner voyeurs. She hoped it was the latter because the idea of getting spanked in front of an audience was a huge turn-on, especially when that audience was made up of two gorgeous guys.

Reminding herself she wasn't supposed to look like she was enjoying this, Goldie tore her gaze away from the other men and stared down at the wood floor. She half expected Orson to tell her to push down her shorts, just so the spanks would sting more, but instead he placed a firm hand on the small of her back, holding her in place. Despite how much she liked getting spanked, she couldn't help but tense as she waited for the first smack. When it finally came, she gasped. *Ouch!* Now she knew why he hadn't asked her to push down her shorts.

She lifted her head to give Orson a pout over her shoulder. "That stung."

The corner of his mouth curved. "Spankings are supposed to sting. You're getting punished, in case you forgot."

"I know, but couldn't you at least give me a warm-up first? I have to get a spanking from your brothers, too."

His grin broadened. "Yes, you do. And by the time they each get you over their knee, your bottom will be very warm, trust me. Now, be a good girl and take your spanking. This was your idea, after all."

Though she gave him another pout, Goldie obediently turned around, but not before stealing a glance at Gregory and Barrett. From the amused expressions on their handsome faces, it was obvious they were enjoying themselves. She barely remembered to hide her smile as she dropped her gaze to the floor again.

"Ready?" Orson asked.

She nodded.

He lifted his hand and brought it down on her right cheek. Heat spread across her ass and she had to bite her lip to stifle a squeal. She barely had time to catch her breath before his hand came down on her bottom again, this time connecting with the opposite cheek. She thought her khaki shorts would offer more protection, but as Orson went back and forth from side to side, he might as well have been spanking her on the bare bottom. It didn't help that they were skimpy enough to expose a little cheek in that position or that his hand seemed to find that bit of skin every other spank or so.

She squirmed under each and every spank. But even though they stung fiercely, her pussy was throbbing and she almost let out a moan. Getting spanked always made her so hot that it was difficult to control herself. Luckily, Orson chose that moment to deliver a particularly hard smack so the sound she ended up making was more of a yelp than a moan. Not that she was complaining, though. Orson might be giving her a really hard spanking, but she loved it all the same. Her pussy was positively quivering with excitement now. She was going to be soaking wet by the time each brother got done spanking her.

She was just thinking she should probably protest a little more so they wouldn't suspect anything when Orson took her arm and gently put her back on her feet. Goldie automatically reached back with both hands to rub her tender bottom. Her ass cheeks felt like they were on fire underneath her shorts.

She was surprised he was already done and tried to hide her disappointment as she gave him an affronted look. "You gave me a very hard spanking."

"You deserved it." A smiled played about the corners of his mouth as he got to his feet. "Now maybe you'll think twice the next time you have the urge to break and enter."

Goldie opened her mouth to assure him she wouldn't be breaking and entering anytime soon, but Barrett interrupted her.

"My turn."

She whirled around to look at him in surprise. She had expected the brothers to give her a breather in between spankings, but apparently they were all impatient to have a go at her ass. She only hoped Barrett didn't spank quite as hard as his brother. While she'd enjoyed it, she thought it might be possible to have too much of a good thing.

Goldie waited for Barrett to put her over his knee the moment he sat down on the bed, but instead he gave her a lazy grin.

"Now that my brother has given you that warm-up you asked for, why don't you push down those little shorts of yours so I can give you a proper spanking?"

Her breath hitched, the command in his voice making her shiver. Next to a spanking, nothing got her going like a hunky guy with an authoritative voice. Goldie knew she should probably make a little bit of fuss about pushing down her shorts, but she couldn't get them down fast enough. Keenly aware of Orson and Gregory standing behind her, she unbuttoned her shorts and slid down the zipper. As she slowly wiggled them over her hips, she couldn't resist glancing over her shoulder at the two men. They were both staring at her panty-covered ass as if transfixed by it.

Pulse quickening, she stepped out of her shorts, then walked over to Barrett. He guided her over his knee, placing his hand on the small of her back just like his brother had done. As she squirmed around to find a more comfortable position, she felt her skimpy bikini panties ride up to expose even more of her ass cheeks and she blushed as she wondered if they were rosy from the spanking Orson had given her. If they weren't, she had the feeling they soon would be.

She held her breath as she waited for Barrett to begin. But when his hand finally came down on her ass, it felt like little more than a love pat. Well, maybe that was a bit of an exaggeration. The spank still stung, but not nearly as much as the ones Orson had given her. Maybe Barrett was starting out with lighter smacks since his brother had spanked her so hard.

As he continued to slap one cheek then the other, however, Barrett didn't spank her any harder. While what he was doing was still pleasurable, she wouldn't have minded some harder smacks mixed in every once in a while, especially since Orson had given her a very thorough warm-up.

"That's not too hard, is it?" Barrett asked.

Goldie was surprised by the question. He was supposed to be punishing her, after all. Though she wanted to tell him he could spank her harder if he wanted to, she caught herself just in time and instead shook her head in reply. She wasn't supposed to be enjoying this and she still had to get her spanking from Gregory. She had no idea how hard he might do it.

Besides, it wasn't like Barrett was doing a bad job of spanking her. The feel of his hand smacking against her bottom still had her pussy tingling like there was a vibrator down there. He had this little way of letting his hand linger on her ass between each smack, too, that just drove her crazy. He probably didn't even realize what he was doing to her.

She closed her eyes and tried not to moan as his fingers trailed over the sensitive skin exposed by her panties. Maybe suggesting they spank her hadn't been such a good idea. She was going to get all hot and bothered and not be able to do anything about it until she got home to her vibrator. She just hoped she could wait that long.

The temptation to grind against Barrett's jean-clad leg was almost too powerful to resist and she bit her lower lip in delicious agony. She was almost relieved when he finally pulled her to her feet. Although he hadn't spanked her hard, her bottom was still blissfully warm and she reached back to cup her ass with both hands.

She gave him a small smile as he stood up. "That wasn't so bad."

He shrugged. "I didn't want to spank you too hard. Like you said, you still have to take a spanking from Gregory, and since you ate his stew and broke the woodcarving he made, I figure he's probably going to warm that cute little backside of yours pretty good."

Hands still cupping her ass cheeks, Goldie spun around to find Gregory regarding her with amusement in his eyes.

"Barrett left out the part about sleeping in my bed."

She blushed. "So, I guess that means your brother's right about you warming my backside pretty good then, huh?"

His mouth quirked. "Honey, by the time I'm done spanking you, you're going to be on fire."

Heat pooled between her thighs at the promise in his voice. Something told Goldie he wasn't just talking about warming her ass. Could he possibly know how excited she was?

She waited for Gregory to take her hand and put her over his knee like his brothers had, but to her surprise he simply patted his thigh. He wanted her to climb over his lap of her own accord, she realized. When she didn't obey right away, he lifted a brow. Blushing, she stepped forward and submissively draped herself over his knee. Even though he'd already gotten a good look at her panty-covered ass when Barrett had spanked her, there was something very different about him doing it now that she was over his knee, and her color deepened as she felt his gaze on that part of her anatomy. Once again, she wiggled to get comfortable and felt a distinct and very sizeable bulge in his jeans. It looked like she wasn't the only one who was excited. The realization that she had made him rock hard turned her on almost as much as the spanking did.

Placing one hand on the small of her back, Gregory cupped her ass with the other. Goldie caught her breath. But instead of immediately spanking her like she thought he would, he gently caressed her bottom.

"You have the perfect ass for spanking, did you know that?"

She'd had guys tell her that before, but oddly enough none of them had ever done it while she'd been draped over their knee. The compliment warmed her all the way to the tips of her manicured toes. She looked over her shoulder at him. "Really? And just out of curiosity, what exactly makes my ass so perfect for spanking?"

Gregory made small, circular motions on her upturned bottom. "It's nicely toned, but yet still has enough of a sexy little jiggle to it when you get spanked. It also turns the most becoming shade of red I've ever seen."

"Is that important?"

"Definitely. Although your bottom is starting to lose some of the color from the spankings my brothers gave you."

Goldie's lips curved into a provocative smile as she forgot all about pretending she wasn't supposed to like getting spanked. "Maybe you should do something about that."

"Maybe I should."

Lifting his hand, Gregory brought it down on her right cheek with a firm smack. Goldie gasped, but the sound barely escaped her lips before his hand connected with her other cheek. Though not hard, the spanks still stung deliciously. She'd been right. Gregory had the perfect touch when it came to spanking.

She waited breathlessly for the next smack, but it never came. Instead, he went back to rubbing her ass cheeks. If this was his idea of punishment, she certainly wasn't going to protest. Though she might just come if he kept rubbing her bottom like that.

Then all at once, he stopped what he was doing and lifted his hand, smacking her on the right cheek again. He followed it up with another on her left cheek before moving back and forth from one to the other with an easy rhythm that made her think he'd definitely done this before. Heat engulfed her ass and she squirmed on his lap, unable to help herself. The move made her tummy rub against his hard-on and she wondered if it felt as good for him as it was for her.

She almost wished he would pull her off his lap and onto his hard cock, but the strong hand on her back kept her firmly in place as he continued to spank her. The smacks got a little harder each time and she forced herself to stifle a moan. God she loved a guy who could give a good spanking. And Gregory knew exactly what he was doing.

But then he suddenly stopped spanking her altogether. Instead of rubbing her tender cheeks like she thought he would, though, he hooked his fingers in the waistband of her bikini panties and pulled them down to mid-thigh. Although she'd been secretly hoping he would take them down, Goldie was still a little surprised by the move, and she lifted her head to look at him over her shoulder.

The corner of his mouth edged up. "You didn't think I'd pass up the chance to spank your bare ass now that I have you over my knee, did you?"

Goldie's pussy spasmed between her thighs. Oh yeah, he'd definitely done this spanking thing before. Wetting her lips, she turned back around. As she placed her hands on the floor again, it occurred to her that Orson and Barrett not only had a perfect view of her rosy ass cheeks, but of her pussy as well. The realization aroused her more than she would have thought possible and she knew she must be soaking wet. They had to see how excited she was.

Her thoughts were interrupted as Gregory chose that moment to start spanking her again. While her panties might be skimpy, they'd provided at least some protection and she was once again amazed at how much a spanking stung on the bare bottom. Goldie writhed around on his lap. The movement ground her clit against his leg and she closed her eyes. She didn't even try to stifle the moan that escaped her lips this time. What he was doing felt too damn good. And if he kept doing it, she was almost certainly going to come.

Gregory didn't keep doing what he was doing, though. Instead, he stopped spanking and gave her stinging ass cheeks a firm squeeze that felt so incredible it made her gasp aloud.

"Your ass is very red," he said softly.

Goldie could only moan in reply as he caressed her freshly spanked cheeks. His touch both soothed her tender skin and sent little shivers of pleasure rushing through her at the same time. Damn, he was good at this. She considered telling him as much when he slipped his hand between her legs and ran his finger over her wet pussy. She let out another moan. There was no use trying to hide how much she liked getting spanked now. He already knew she was excited.

"I think you're enjoying your punishment way more than you're supposed to," he observed.

She considered denying it, but at that moment, it was hard to think. All she wanted to do was spread her legs and beg him to slide his finger in her pussy. "Maybe."

But to her dismay, he took his hand away. "What do you think we should do about that?"

She didn't know if he was talking to her or his brothers. Oh God, she hoped he wasn't thinking of arresting her again. She needed to do something to distract him. Fast!

On impulse, Goldie pushed herself off his lap and allowed her panties to slide to the floor as she stepped between his legs. "How about this?"

She didn't wait for a reply, but bent her head and kissed him on the mouth.

Gregory reached around to cup her ass with his hands, pulling her closer as his tongue found hers. Goldie moaned and slid her hands in his silky hair. She could feel his shaft pressing against her thighs where it strained against the front of his jeans. With a cock that hard, she wasn't going to be getting arrested tonight. She might be getting fucked, but definitely not arrested.

Breathless from the kiss, she lifted her head to gaze down at him. The smoldering look in his eyes told her he wanted her as much as she wanted him. But there were two complications to consider—Orson and Barrett. She had an idea how to resolve that problem, but she wasn't quite sure how to bring it up.

Goldie had fantasized about a ménage before, usually imagining herself making out with the two hot actors on her favorite television show, but she'd never done anything quite so kinky in real life. She'd let all three brothers spank her. Could she let them make love to her, too?

She surveyed all three men. They looked like they wanted to just eat her up. And she definitely wanted to be eaten, among other things.

"Boys, I'm so excited that if I don't have sex I'm going to explode," she said. "The only question is if it's going to be with one of you or all of you."

Chapter Four

✂

Gregory's mouth quirked. "Normally, I'm not one to share, but I think tonight I just might make an exception."

His brothers grinned.

"We were hoping you'd say that," Barrett said.

Goldie had been hoping he'd say that, too. Although she'd really had her sights set on Gregory from the first moment she saw him, the opportunity to get busy with all three men was just too good to pass up. How many times in her life would she have the chance to sleep with three super-hunky brothers all at one time? Now the only question was which brother would go first. She was just about to ask when Gregory got to his feet and pulled her back into his arms. Her lips curved into a smile. Guess that answered her question.

As his mouth closed possessively over hers, Goldie looped her arms around his neck and melted against him. His hand slid up to cup the back of her head. A moment later, she felt his fingers gently tugging at her ponytail holder. When her long hair tumbled down her back, he buried his hand in it and tilted her back so he could kiss his way along the curve of her jaw.

Goldie completely forgot about his two brothers as Gregory slid his hands underneath her top and pushed it up. His fingers were warm against her skin and she caught her breath at the feel of them. At his urging, she lifted her arms over her head so he could take it off. Her satin bra quickly followed and a moment later, she was left completely naked before him and the two other men. Since Orson and Barrett were standing behind her, she couldn't see their reactions, but the predatory glint in Gregory's eyes as he took in her rounded breasts, slim waist, and long legs was enough to set her on fire.

"God, you're beautiful," he said, reaching out to lovingly cup her breasts in his hands.

Goldie wanted to thank him for the compliment, but all that came out was a moan as he found her nipples with his thumbs and began to play with them. She'd always had sensitive nipples, but tonight they seemed even more responsive than usual. Maybe it was the thought of the other two men watching them. Or maybe it was just that Gregory knew how she liked to be touched.

She clutched at his shoulders to steady herself and felt the muscles ripple and flex beneath her fingers. Wanting to see if he was as well built as it seemed, Goldie grabbed the bottom of his T-shirt and urgently pushed it up. Groaning, he reached over his shoulder to pull off his shirt. As his muscular chest and rock-hard abs came into view, all she could do was stare and try not to drool. She thought guys that ripped only existed in her imagination. What the heck was he doing working as a cop? With a body like that he should be posing for *Playgirl*.

Her gaze dropped to the bulge in the front of his jeans and suddenly she wanted all of him naked. Reaching out, she impatiently yanked open his belt, then hurriedly undid the buttons on his jeans. She shoved them down his muscular legs, then did the same with the boxer briefs he was wearing. When his hard cock finally sprang free, she gazed at it in feminine appreciation. He was big and thick and absolutely perfect, just like she knew he would be.

Goldie gave Gregory a sultry smile and dropped to her knees in front of him. Wrapping one hand lovingly around his shaft, she bent to lick the droplet of pre-cum from the tip. It tasted musky and sweet at the same time, and she made a soft sound of approval, savoring the flavor. As it lingered in her mouth, she closed her lips over the head of his cock and swirled her tongue round and round the velvety softness. The urge to take him deep right then was almost too much to resist and she had to force herself to go slowly. There was no need to rush. They had all night.

She tightened her hand around the base of his erection and gently cupped his balls with the other as she moved her mouth up and down over and over. When she finally lifted her head to look up at him, it was to find Barrett standing on one side of her and Orson on the other. Both men had taken off their clothes and were now as gloriously naked as Gregory. They were just as well muscled, too, she noticed. Not to mention equally well-endowed.

Goldie's pussy tingled as she imagined the picture she made kneeling before the three men and she squeezed her thighs together to ease the throbbing ache there.

She looked from one brother to the other, then up at Gregory. He was regarding her intently, as if waiting to see what she would do. Although she'd never been with three men at once, her next move seemed to come naturally to her. She wrapped one hand around Barrett's shaft and the other around Orson's, then bent her head to take Gregory's cock in her mouth again. Good thing she could multi-task so well.

Above her, Gregory let out a groan and slid his hand in her hair, guiding her movements. As she bobbed her head up and down on him, she moved her hands up and down on the other two men's cocks with the same steady motion. Their erections were already slick with pre-cum and her hands glided along them as easily as her mouth did on Gregory's shaft.

While she could have licked Gregory all night, she decided she should probably give each of his brothers some individual attention as well. Releasing Gregory's cock, she turned her head to the side to take Barrett's shaft in her mouth. He was longer and thinner than Gregory, she noticed, but just as tasty. She sucked on him greedily, allowing the head of his cock to tease the back of her throat before coming back up to nibble the sensitive tip. That earned her a groan from him as well and she couldn't help smile at knowing she was able to please both of them. Of course, she didn't want Orson to feel ignored, so she let Barrett's cock pop out of her mouth and turned to pay attention to his older brother. Orson's penis was shorter, but much thicker than Barrett's, and she had to open her mouth wider to accommodate him. As his pre-cum touched her tongue, she let out a little moan of her own. It was amazing how completely different one man could taste from another. Whereas Gregory's pre-cum was sweet and musky, Barrett's was kind of salty, while Orson's was sort of spicy. It was like a seminal smorgasbord and she couldn't get enough.

She moved back and forth from Gregory to Barrett to Orson over and over, trying out different oral techniques as she found what made each one of them groan loudest. Orson seemed to really like when she scraped the head of his cock with her teeth, apparently liking his oral sex a little rough. Barrett preferred when she used her hand in combination with her mouth, stroking his shaft in counterpoint to her tongue. Gregory, on the other hand, loved when she let his cock slide deep in her throat. She had to admit, she was partial to deep-throating a guy, so she enjoyed doing that the most. There was just something so powerful about the feel of a man's big penis sliding all the way down her throat.

As she moved from him to Barrett again, Gregory must have decided he needed to take a break because he kneeled down in front of her and cupped her breasts in his hands. Or maybe he was just paying her back for all the pleasure she'd given him. Goldie moaned around Barrett's cock as Gregory's mouth closed over one of her nipples. She'd imagined this same scene often enough in her fantasies, but the real thing was so much better. The sensation of one man making love to her breasts while she gave another a blowjob almost took her breath away.

Gregory swirled his tongue around the stiff peak, nearly driving her to distraction, and it was all she could do to concentrate on his brothers. Grasping Orson's cock more firmly in her hand, she rubbed her thumb over the head while she moved her mouth up and down on Barrett. He groaned in obvious pleasure and from the additional little spurt of pre-cum that came out, she realized he was close to coming. While she was more than willing to let Barrett come in her mouth right then, she decided she needed to pay some attention to Orson again. She didn't want thick cock of his to feel left out. Barrett was just going to have to hold off for a little while.

As she turned her attention to Orson, giving the head of his penis an extra firm nip with her teeth, Gregory turned his focus from one nipple to the other, suckling on it with such abandon that Goldie had to pause so she could let out a gasp of pleasure. She was so lost in what he was doing she barely remembered she was supposed to be stroking Orson's cock. She'd never had a man make love to her breasts like Gregory was and when he lifted his head a few moments later, she made a soft sound of protest. She hoped he wasn't finished because she really loved what he was doing. She turned to look at Gregory, intending to plead with him in the hopes he would continue feasting on her nipples, but when she saw his golden brown eyes practically glowing with desire, she completely forgot what she'd been going to say.

"Do you have any idea how hot you are?" he asked hoarsely.

He didn't give her a chance to answer, but instead closed his mouth over hers in an intoxicating kiss. Releasing Barrett and Orson, Goldie ran her hands up Gregory's smooth chest to clutch at his shoulders to steady herself. Gregory made a sound deep in his throat and gently grasped her arms, pulling her up he got to his feet.

Still kissing her, Gregory cupped her breasts in his hands and found her nipples with his fingers again. As he twirled and squeezed the sensitive buds, one of his brothers—she wasn't sure which—stepped up behind her and began to massage her ass cheeks with his hands. The feeling of being sandwiched between two rock-hard male bodies made her pussy throb and she was tempted to slide her hand down to touch herself. Before she could give in to the urge, however, a strong hand reached around to cup her sex.

Goldie moaned as fingers found her clit and began to make small circles around it. Whichever brother it was, he certainly knew his way around the female anatomy. The way his hard cock pressed against her ass wasn't half bad, either. Why the heck hadn't she ever made out with three guys before this? Because she'd never met three guys this damn hot before, she told herself.

As Gregory continued to tease and torment her nipples with his fingers, his mouth left hers to trail a path of kisses along the curve of her jaw and down her neck. She tilted her head to the side as much to give Gregory access as to see which brother was working his magic with her clit. Catching a glimpse of dark, wavy hair and a slightly crooked nose, she realized it was the middle brother, Barrett.

"Does that feel good?" he asked, his breath warm and moist against her ear.

She reached up to cup his cheek with one hand as the other found its way into Gregory's silky hair. "Mmm."

"Think I could make you come this way?"

She shivered as he pressed a kiss to the hollow behind her ear. "Why don't we try it and find out?"

Behind her, Barrett chuckled and moved his finger a little faster. Goldie dropped her hand to rest it on his muscular thigh and began to slowly rotate her hips in time with his finger. From the husky groan he let out, it was obvious he liked the way her ass was rubbing against his cock. She was just wondering if she might be able to make him come all over her freshly spanked cheeks when Gregory took one hand away from her breast to slowly slide it down her stomach and join his brother's between her legs. But instead of fighting over who would get to rub her clit, Gregory gently slid his finger in her pussy.

Goldie gasped in surprise, completely unprepared for the move. Since most guys weren't good enough at multi-tasking to both rub her clit and finger-fuck her pussy at the same time, she'd never had the opportunity to feel anything so amazing. The combined result of the two men's touch was mind blowing.

Gregory lifted his head to gaze down at her, his eyes glinting gold as he moved his finger in and out of her pussy. His fingers were very long and he was doing an absolutely incredible job of stroking her G-spot. Behind her, Barrett reached around with his free hand to cup one of her breasts, his finger moving round and round her nipple just like he was doing on her clit.

The sensation of so many hands doing so many unbelievable things to her body was almost too much and for a moment she wasn't sure if she could take it. But then she felt a distinctly familiar tingle around her clit and realized she was starting to come.

"That's right," Barrett whispered. "Go ahead and come for us."

Goldie couldn't have stopped herself from coming if she wanted to, which of course she didn't. Clutching Barrett's thigh in one hand and Gregory's shoulder with the other, she dropped her head back and moaned over and over as they brought her to orgasm. If the two men hadn't been pressed so tightly against her, she probably would have slid to the floor. But they held her steady as she rode out the long, powerful climax.

When she could finally see straight again, all she could do was collapse forward and lay her head on Gregory's chest. Dear God, that was amazing. And something told her the three men were just getting started.

As if to prove her right, Gregory tilted her head up with a gentle finger beneath her chin and kissed her long and thoroughly on the mouth before urging her back on the bed. Goldie lay back with a smile, eager to see what the men had planned for her. She found out soon enough when Gregory cupped the heel of one foot in his hand and carefully lifted her leg, then slowly kissed his way up the inside of it.

Goldie trembled as much from the feel of his warm mouth brushing the sensitive skin of her inner thigh as she did from the anticipation of what his tongue was going to feel like on her pussy. Despite just having had an orgasm a few minutes ago, she was hot, wet, and more than ready to come again. If she had her way, she'd be coming all night.

Gregory seemed to be in no hurry to make that happen, however. On the contrary, he appeared content to take his time getting to her pussy, pausing every few moments to lick and nibble everywhere else along the way.

She caught her lower lip between her teeth, panting excitedly as he edged closer and closer to the juncture of her thighs. She was just about to grab a handful of his thick hair and put his mouth where she so desperately wanted it when she felt him run his tongue along the slick folds of her pussy.

Goldie moaned, her fingers finding their way into his hair and holding him in place. Now that she had him where she wanted him, she wasn't letting him go anywhere. That didn't stop Gregory from continuing to tease her, though. Instead of focusing on her clit like she wanted him to, he slowly ran his tongue up one side of her pussy and down the other. But while it practically drove her insane, she had to admit it was the most delicious kind of torture. Deciding to stop being so impatient and just enjoy everything he was doing to her, she dropped her head back on the bed and found herself gazing up at Barrett and his very hard cock. He had come around the bed and was now standing over her. Mouth curving into a wicked smile, he wrapped his hand around the base of his shaft and offered it to her.

Pulse quickening, Goldie obediently opened her mouth and wrapped her lips around the head of his cock. She'd never given a blowjob in this position before, but as Barrett gently thrust in and out of her mouth, she decided she should definitely add it to her repertoire. It was sexy as hell to just lie there while a man slowly pumped his cock into her mouth. She felt submissive and powerful at the same time. Remembering how Barrett liked her to use her hand while licking him, she reached up and grasped the base of his shaft, letting him slide through her grip at the same time he fucked her mouth. From the way he was groaning, she didn't think he was going to be able to hold off for too long.

Focusing on one brother's cock while another was so expertly licking her pussy was more difficult than she'd thought, especially when Gregory began to make slow, little circles around her throbbing clit. She tightened her fingers in his hair as pleasure surged through her body and when he somehow found just the right spot with his tongue, she murmured her approval around Barrett's shaft.

As if Gregory's tongue on her clit wasn't enough to drive her wild, just then Orson climbed on the bed and began to play with her breasts. Tenderly cupping them in his big hands, he took first one nipple in his mouth, then the other, suckling on them as if he couldn't get enough. Every once in a while, he even nipped on the stiff, little peaks with his teeth. The two very different sensations were out of this world, and she let out a moan as she writhed on the bed.

She must have been moving too much for Gregory because he tightened his hold on her ass to keep her still as he lashed her clit faster and faster with his tongue. The combination of Gregory's magical mouth and Orson's exquisite touch ignited a firestorm between her legs and she found herself coming like crazy for the second time that night. Goldie clutched at the bed sheets, almost dizzy from the rush of sensations flowing through her. God, these guys were going to kill her with pleasure!

It wasn't until the last tremors of orgasm began to subside and she lay there trying to catch her breath that she remembered Barrett. While his cock was still in her mouth, she was embarrassed to realize she was no longer licking him. She eagerly started to get back to it, but he slid out with a rueful smile.

"I'm already close and watching you orgasm like that was almost enough to make me explode," he said. "I don't want to come yet, though."

Goldie wouldn't have minded making him and his brothers come more than once, but before she could make the offer, Gregory took her hand and pulled her into a sitting position, kissing her lingeringly on the mouth. The taste of her pussy on his tongue was heady and arousing and brought back the memory of how good his mouth had felt on her. When he lifted his head a little while later, she smiled up at him.

"You're very good at licking pussy, do you know that?"

He grinned. "I'm glad you think so."

"Oh, I definitely do." She reached down to wrap her hand around his hard cock. "But I think it's time I return the favor."

His grin broadened. "How could I refuse an offer like that?"

Laughing, Goldie rolled onto her hands and knees on the bed, then reached for his cock again. He was so perfect she was tempted to swallow all of him right away, but then she remembered how much he'd delighted in teasing her earlier. Telling herself turnabout was fair play, she slowly ran her tongue up his shaft from base to tip. She repeated the move twice more before the urge to wrap her lips around him was too much to resist any longer and she took him completely in her mouth.

The move elicited a groan from Gregory and she slid her mouth off his cock to give him a coy look.

"Does that feel good?" she asked.

He chuckled. "Very good. Don't stop."

"Stop?" She laughed. "I'm just getting started."

Goldie leaned forward to take him in her mouth again, but then hesitated when she felt the bed dip behind her. Curious, she glanced over her shoulder and saw that Orson had joined her.

"What about protection?" she asked, the thought just occurring to her.

"Since we're state troopers, we get tested all the time, so we're clean. Are you on the Pill?"

She nodded.

"Then we're good."

Giving him a seductive smile, she turned back to Gregory. She had just closed her lips over the head of his beautiful cock again when she felt Orson grasp her hips. A moment later, he began to rub the head of his erection up and down her very wet slit. He probably wanted to make sure she was wet enough to accommodate his thick shaft, but she definitely didn't have a problem with that. She was absolutely soaking. He must have figured that out, too, because seconds later, he slid all the way into her waiting pussy until his hips were pressing up against her ass.

She gasped as he filled her and automatically tried to move on his cock, but he held her hips firm and kept himself buried deep inside of her while he massaged her ass. Even though it had been a while since Gregory had finished spanking her, Orson's strong fingers brought the tingle right back. Between his hands on her ass and his large cock spreading her pussy, Goldie was close to another orgasm and the man hadn't even started fucking her yet. Unbelievable.

She took a deep breath and forced her attention back to Gregory's cock. Grabbing his ass in both hands, she dragged him closer so that his cock slid all the way down her throat. She remembered how much he loved her to deep-throat him and figured she could take him even deeper in this position. He slid his hand in her hair, holding her in place as he began to thrust in and out of her mouth with a hypnotic, smooth motion. She couldn't believe how easily the head of his cock slid down her throat. Maybe it was the position, or maybe his cock was just shaped perfectly for her. Whatever it was, she'd never been able to deep-throat a guy this easily.

Then Orson began to move in her pussy, sliding all the way out, then forcefully pulling her back against his hips every time Gregory thrust his cock into her mouth. The two strong men had their way with her, one firmly holding her hips as the other held her head, and she positively loved it. While Gregory kept his movements slow, though, Orson pounded into her harder and harder. The way his hips smacked against her ass almost made it feel as if he were spanking her at the same time he was fucking her. She'd never been so pleasured in her life and she couldn't imagine how she'd ever be able to go back to ho-hum sex after this.

Goldie tried to keep her orgasm at bay so she could come at the same time the two men did, but her pussy clearly had a mind of its own because she was quickly carried away on a tidal wave of ecstasy so powerful she had no choice but to stop licking Gregory's cock so she could scream out her pleasure. Orson knew how to draw her orgasm out, too, thrusting into her so the head of his cock pounded into her G-spot with the perfect rhythm, making her come over and over.

She was just getting her breath back and was about to start sucking on Gregory's member again, but he tightened his fingers in her hair, stopping her. She looked up at him curiously.

His mouth quirked. "I don't want to come just yet, either."

As Gregory stepped away from the bed, Goldie felt Orson slide out of her pussy and it occurred to her that he hadn't come either. Thinking maybe he wanted to hold off like the other two men, she glanced over her shoulder to look for him and saw Barrett climbing onto the bed behind her. Eyes locked with hers, he took hold of her hips and rubbed the head of his long cock along her pussy just like his brother had done before slowly sliding inside. Goldie moaned as he buried his shaft deep. It felt like he was touching her in a whole different place than Orson had. It was amazing how two men could make her feel completely unique sensations. Unique and earth-shattering, that was. If the brothers kept tag-teaming her like this all night, she was going to be a complete quivering mass of jelly before the sun came up.

Goldie caught her breath as Barrett got a firm hold on her hips. Hoping he'd take her just as hard as his older brother had, she turned back around to find Orson waiting for her, rigid cock in hand. Oh yeah, a girl could definitely get addicted to this. Lips curving into a smile, she leaned forward to take him in her mouth. As she wrapped her lips around the head, he threaded his fingers in her hair and began to fuck her mouth just like his youngest brother had. She'd never realized how much she liked having a guy take control while she performed oral sex on him before, but it was like all three of the brothers knew exactly what turned her on.

Out of the corner of her eye, Goldie caught sight of Gregory and realized he was following her every move. For some reason, knowing he was watching made what she and his brothers were doing even more erotic.

Wanting to put on a show for Gregory, she devoured Orson's manhood hungrily as she bobbed her head up and down. She made sure to occasionally let her teeth graze the sensitive tip, loving the way he groaned every time she did it. She also tenderly cupped his balls in her hand and massaged them in time with the rhythm of her mouth.

Goldie glanced over at Gregory to see if he was still watching and noted that not only was he glued to the action, but he was stroking his cock with his strong hand. Seeing him touch himself was so damn sexy she almost came just from that. She had never watched a guy jerk off before, but she decided it had to be the hottest thing she'd ever seen.

Behind her, Barrett must have felt her pussy spasm because he started slamming into her so forcefully it almost took her breath away. This time, however, she refused to be distracted from what she was doing with her mouth and kept sucking Orson's cock even as another orgasm ripped through her. If anything, she licked even harder, yearning to feel Orson's cum fill her mouth at the same time she was climaxing.

To her surprise, though, both men pulled out before coming, just as they had before. She'd never been with a man with as much stamina and willpower as these three brothers. They were likes forces of nature. Hopefully, the fact that they kept holding back meant they intended to make love to her some more. Goldie was almost breathless as she waited to see what they had planned for her next. The three men were incredibly creative when it came to pleasuring her and it made her wonder if they had done this before with another woman. As both Barrett and Orson climbed off the bed to be replaced by Gregory, however, she decided she didn't care if they had practiced this type of sexual maneuvering before. She was just glad they were so good at it.

His eyes hot with lust, Gregory lay back on the bed and beckoned her forward with his finger. Goldie eagerly obeyed. She was about to straddle him in the traditional girl-on-top position, but he grabbed her hips and spun her around so she was facing away from him before he gently pulled her down onto his cock. She let out a moan as his long, thick length slid inside her. *Oooh, baby*. This position certainly allowed him to poke her in entirely new and exciting places.

Eager to see what moving up and down on his shaft would feel like in this direction, Goldie arched her back and began to ride him reverse cowgirl. She'd read about this position in *Cosmo*, but she'd never done it. The movement sent little tingles of pleasure through her pussy every time the head of his cock touched her G-spot and she had to catch her breath. God, this was incredible. She could ride him like this for the rest of the night.

Gregory only let her have her way for a while, though. After a few minutes, he urged her to lie back on his chest. Goldie wondered how he was going to thrust in that position, but he managed quite well, pumping in and out of her with a slowness that left her breathless. It got even better when Orson settled himself between her spread legs and began to lick her clit as his younger brother's shaft slowly fucked her.

Goldie gasped as she felt Orson's mouth on her. After coming so many times already, she was afraid her clit would be too sensitive, but as he tenderly swirled his tongue round and round the plump flesh, she was both surprised and relieved to discover she wasn't overly sensitive at all. In fact, her clit seemed primed and ready for another orgasm.

Just as she settled back against Gregory's chest again, though, Orson stopped licking her. Confused, she lifted her head to protest, but the words disappeared as Barrett bent to take his older brother's place. Barrett's mouth felt different than his brother, but still amazing. Satisfied, she lay back with a soft sigh of contentment.

Orson and Barrett continued to take turns licking her clit as Gregory pumped into her pussy. As one pleasurable sensation after another washed over her, she couldn't resist doing her part to get herself off. Reaching up, she cupped her breasts in her hands and played with her nipples, squeezing and tugging at them urgently. Her every touch sent shockwaves through her body and she lost herself in how good it felt.

Goldie tried to keep track of which brother was between her legs without lifting her head to check, just so she could see who brought her to orgasm, but after a while, she gave up. All she knew was that coupled with what Gregory was doing, they were both driving her crazy.

As if somehow magically knowing she was on the edge of coming, Gregory began to drive his hard cock deeper and deeper into her pussy at the same time one of his brothers began to lash her clit faster and faster with his tongue. Goldie squeezed her breasts harder and cried out as yet another climax burst through her. With nothing in her mouth to silence her this time, the sound echoed around the room as she came over and over.

By the time she could manage a coherent thought again, she lifted her head to see which brother she had to thank for that wonderful lick, but both men were standing there with equally self-satisfied grins on their handsome faces. Maybe they'd both done it. Was that even possible?

Before she could decide on an answer, Gregory wrapped his arms around her and rolled onto his side so she could slide off his still-hard cock. She fell back on the bed, breathing hard. Finally she pushed herself up on an elbow and smiled at him.

"That was amazing," she said softly.

He bent to kiss her. "You're the one who's amazing."

Goldie blushed at the compliment and would have thanked him, but he was already kneeling beside her and offering his cock. Realizing he wanted her to give him another blowjob, she lay back and wrapped her hand around his shaft only to pause when Orson got into bed, kneeling on the other side of her. With a smile, she reached for his cock and gave it a gentle tug, pulling him a little closer. Once both men were positioned above her, she ran her tongue up first one cock, then the other. Pulling them even closer together, she held their erections tip to tip so she could lick both of them at once. Deciding that was fun, she made as if to do it again, but was momentarily distracted by Barrett lifting her legs high in the air and placing them on his shoulders as he plunged himself deep in her pussy.

Moaning her approval, Goldie turned her attention back to the two magnificent cocks on either side of her head. While concentrating on them completely was still hard to do when she was being fucked so fiercely, she was getting much better at multi-tasking. Holding their erections so close they were touching, she alternated between running her tongue up both of them simultaneously and giving each of them some one-on-

one time. Even when she focused on one brother, though, she rubbed the other's shaft with her hand. She was going to make them come this time, she promised herself. Taking two big, hot loads of cum in her mouth at the same time was going to be another new thing for her, but she had no doubt she was going to love it.

Of course, it was a little more difficult to focus once Barrett began to really fuck her hard and she started to orgasm. But she determinedly kept licking both men's cocks even as she moaned out her pleasure. To her dismay, however, all three men once again backed away before they could come.

Goldie was so completely sated she felt like purring like a kitten. She couldn't imagine there was a sex position they hadn't tried, so now the only thing left to do was make these three studs come. But apparently Gregory had another position in mind because he lay back on the bed and pulled her onto his rock-hard cock. Okay, so maybe they hadn't done the traditional girl-on-top position. That was one of her favorites. How could she have forgotten?

Goldie was tempted to sit up and ride Gregory like that so she could show off her breasts, but his sensuous mouth was too inviting to resist and she had to lean forward to kiss him.

He groaned and cupped her ass in his hands, urging her up and down on his shaft. She complied, her tongue tangling with his as her fingers found their way into his hair. She was so into him she completely forgot about the other two men until she felt a gentle finger glide along the opening of her anus. With a startled little gasp, she dragged her mouth away from Gregory's to look over her shoulder and saw Barrett kneeling on the bed behind her. Although he said nothing, there was a questioning look in his dark eyes. Realizing he was waiting for her permission before he went any further, she gave him a small smile. She'd never had anal sex before, but had always wanted to try it. She decided there was no better way to experience it than with a hunk like Barrett. She couldn't help but wonder how he was going to slide in her ass without any lube, though. But then she felt him run a finger along her slick pussy and realized she was wet enough to provide her own lubricant.

Her pulse quickening with excitement, Goldie turned back around to find Orson standing beside the bed with his cock just in reach of her eager mouth. As she bent over to wrap her lips around him, she was aware of Gregory's eyes on her. Knowing he was watching her give another man a blowjob sent a quiver through her and she wondered if he got as turned on by it as she did. She'd have to remember to ask him later. Right now, she was too busy enjoying herself.

Behind her, Barrett gently slid his finger in her anus and she moaned around the cock filling her mouth. She expected him to immediately pull back out, then lube up his shaft and plunge right in, but instead he tenderly moved his finger in and out a few times, helping her relax completely and making little tingles of pleasure course through her. If his finger felt that good, she could only wonder how much more amazing his cock would feel.

Fortunately, she didn't have to wait long to see if she was right. A moment later, he pulled his finger out and she felt the head of his penis against the puckered opening. Despite how excited she was, she couldn't help stiffening a little anyway.

Gregory ran his hands over her ass. "Relax, baby."

Goldie wondered how Gregory had known she was tense, but then realized she'd probably clenched her pussy around his cock. Taking a deep breath, she forced herself to relax and lean forward a little more. As soon as she did, she felt Barrett slowly slide in her ass inch by incredible inch. She'd never dreamed having a man there could feel so amazing. It was almost like her ass was having one long, continuous orgasm.

She gasped around Orson's cock, unable to believe how breathtaking it felt to have her mouth, her pussy, and her ass filled at the same time.

All three men started moving slowly, as if they knew she needed to get used to so many different sensations. It was more than just the physical aspect of what they were doing, though. There was something psychologically intoxicating about being so completely possessed by these men, pleasing them as much as they were pleasing her.

Soon, though, their slow movements weren't enough for her, and she couldn't resist the urge to grind her hips back against Gregory and Barrett, silently begging them to take her harder. They must have picked up on her need because both men began to pound into her more forcefully. Even Orson started to push his cock into her mouth faster. All she could do, all she wanted to do, was hold on for the ride.

Goldie instinctively knew that this time there would be no pulling out, this time all three men were going to come inside of her. That image, as much as the pleasure the men were giving her, was enough to make her start to come. That's when the three men really began to fuck her good, making her almost pass out as she came harder than she ever had in her life. When they all exploded inside her at the same time, Orson's creamy cum flooding her mouth while Barrett and Gregory filled her ass and her pussy, it was like she'd been transported to another plane of existence. It was more than an orgasm, it was like she was in heaven.

Goldie was only vaguely aware of Barrett and Orson sliding out of her, then stumbling across the room to fall into their own beds. With a sigh, she collapsed on Gregory's chest. As she lay there, she realized his cock still throbbed inside her pussy and she found herself slowly grinding against him, drawing out the last few quivers of orgasm. His cum felt so unbelievably warm inside her that it overpowered every other sensation she was feeling right then. She couldn't explain why, but she was so glad it had been Gregory who had come inside her pussy.

As Gregory wrapped his strong arms around her, she smiled and closed her eyes. She was never going to forget this night. When she'd broken into the cabin, she'd never imagined she would end up having sex with the three hunkiest brothers she'd ever seen or that it would be the most extraordinary erotic experience of her life.

While having her first moresome had been fantastic in and of itself, Goldie decided Gregory was the one who had made the whole thing perfect. She had a feeling it was more than just sexual attraction between them. Even though she'd had sex with all three men, she had really only felt a spark with him. Not just a simple I-can't-wait-to-have-sex-with-you-again kind of zap, but a tingly I-want-more-than-a-one-night-stand kind of electricity.

But how could she and Gregory possibly see each other again when she'd just had a torrid orgy with him and his two brothers? That wasn't the way normal relationships started. She let out a sigh. Oh well, she supposed she was just going to have to settle for what was likely to be the most wonderful sexual event of her life and just be satisfied with that.

As she drifted off to sleep, however, she still couldn't help wishing there could be more between them.

Chapter Five

ॐ

When she woke up the next morning, Goldie was half afraid last night's wild orgy had been nothing but an erotic dream. However, finding herself draped over Gregory's muscular chest, she realized it hadn't been her imagination at all.

With a smile, she tugged the blanket more tightly around her and snuggled closer to him. He must have pulled it up sometime during the night, she thought, and was touched by the gesture. Since a big, rugged guy like him obviously wouldn't have gotten cold, he must have grabbed the comforter for her. Thoughtful and great in bed. What more could a girl ask for?

Careful not to wake Gregory, she lifted her head and looked over at the other two beds. Much to her surprise, they were empty. Thinking his brothers must be in the outer room, she turned to put her head back down on Gregory's chest and found him regarding her from beneath half-closed eyes.

She gave him a rueful smile. "Sorry. I didn't mean to wake you up."

The corner of his mouth curved. "You didn't. I've been up for a while."

"Oh." She reached up to tuck her hair behind her ear. "You should have woken me up."

"I thought about it, but you looked so adorable sleeping, I didn't want to disturb you."

She felt her face color at the compliment. She'd never had a guy tell her she was adorable. She was even more amazed he could think so after the torrid sex she'd had with him and his brothers. She caught her lower lip between her teeth and chewed on it for a moment before glancing casually over at the other beds. "Where are your brothers?"

Gregory reached up to tuck her hair behind her ear again when it fell forward. "They took off about an hour ago."

She looked at him in surprise. "They did?"

His mouth quirked. "I imagine they probably figured we'd want some time alone."

"They did?" She had certainly wanted to spend some time alone with Gregory, but how could they have possibly known that?

"Yeah. They might not look like it, but my brothers can be rather perceptive now and then," he said as if reading her mind. Then he grinned. "You want to take advantage of the privacy?"

Goldie didn't want to read too much into Gregory's off-handed comment, but it sure sounded like he was as interested in her as she was in him. While she hoped she was right, she didn't want to say something foolish and end up ruining the mood, so she instead she mentally bit her lip and bent to kiss him.

Gregory let out a groan and buried his hand in her hair, his tongue engaging hers in an erotic slow dance that made her sigh with pleasure before he drew her bottom lip into his mouth to gently suckle on it. Damn, the man sure knew how to give a kiss. That's when she realized she'd never kissed either of his brothers the whole time she'd been having sex with them. Had they somehow known she was hooked on their younger brother?

All rational thought disappeared, however, as Gregory's tongue found hers again. He slid his free hand over the curve of her hip and along her midriff to cup her breast. Her nipple immediately pebbled in response to his touch and she moaned when he took the sensitive little bud between his thumb and forefinger and gave it a firm squeeze. With a chuckle, Gregory kissed his way down along the curve of her jaw and down her neck.

Moaning, Goldie clutched at his shoulders and arched against him. He gave her nipple another squeeze before releasing her breast to slide his hand down her tummy to the downy curls between her legs. Whatever protest she'd been going to make when he stopped playing with her breast was forgotten as her pussy began to purr. She couldn't believe she was ready for more sex after that session last night, but apparently Gregory had that effect on her.

He ran his finger teasingly along her folds. "You're already wet, do you know that?"

She moaned. "You tend to do that to me."

He kissed his way back up her neck until he found her lips again. "I'm glad to hear it."

She opened her mouth to reply, but all she could do was catch her breath as he thrust his finger deep in her pussy and began to wiggle it back and forth. It occurred to Goldie that she should probably give him some manual stimulation in return, but Gregory had already slid his finger out and was pulling her on top of him. She smiled as she felt his hard cock pressing against her pussy. Based on his morning wood, he obviously didn't need any more stimulation.

Lifting herself up, she braced her hands on his chest, then slowly lowered herself onto his hard cock. She'd never been with a man who fit her so perfectly or so completely before and she closed her eyes for a moment as she savored the feel of him inside her. When she opened them again, she found Gregory watching her, a mix of desire and something else she couldn't quite name on his handsome face. For one wild moment, she wondered if he felt the same connection between them she did. While she longed to ask, now wasn't exactly the time for such serious talk. Actually, now wasn't the time for talk at all.

The urge to ride up and down on him right away was difficult to resist, but she decided she didn't want to rush their joining. If she and Gregory went their separate ways after this morning, then she wanted to make this last as long as possible.

Her lips curving into a smile, Goldie lifted her hand to her mouth and deliberately licked her finger, then slowly slid it down her stomach to the soft thatch of curls between her legs. Lying back on the pillows, Gregory's eyes just about glowed with excitement as she began to make lazy, little circles on her clit. She'd touched herself in front of other men, but there was something about doing it for Gregory that made the whole thing even hotter.

Wanting to really put on a sexy show for him, she leaned back to give him a better view of both her breasts and her pussy, then slowly rotated her hips in time with her fingers. The position pushed out her breasts, allowing her rosy nipples to peek out from between her long, blonde tresses, and she reached up with her free hand to take one in her thumb and forefinger and give it a firm squeeze. Little tingles of pleasure went through her and she automatically moved her finger faster on her clit. She threw back her head and lost herself in the moment, letting the excitement between her legs build higher and higher until she felt she couldn't contain it anymore.

"That's it, babe," Gregory urged. "Make yourself come while I watch."

The husky reminder she had an audience was enough to push Goldie over the edge. Her breath coming in quick pants, she closed her eyes and let her fingers take over, moaning in ecstasy as wave after wave of pleasure washed over her. She didn't stop until she had coaxed every last little bit of orgasm from her clit, then all she could do was collapse against Gregory's chest.

"Do you have any idea how sexy that was?" he asked in her ear.

Goldie smiled, but could only manage a soft groan in reply. That must have been enough for Gregory because he cupped her ass cheeks in his hands and began to move her up and down on his rigid cock. Her pussy clenched tightly around his shaft each time he thrust and she clung to his shoulders with a breathy little cooing sound. She buried her face in his neck, ready to be swept away by another orgasm when Gregory suddenly rolled her onto her back so that he was on top.

As he braced himself with a hand on either side of her head, Goldie felt positively engulfed by his powerful body. It made her feel feminine and sexy and she murmured her appreciation against his mouth as he bent to capture hers in a searing kiss.

Holding onto his muscular shoulders with both hands, Goldie wrapped her legs around him, pulling his cock inside her as deep as it would go. Gregory made a sound deep within his throat, but instead of thrusting right away, he held himself still, just pulsing inside her. When he finally began to thrust, it was with such tenderness and such slowness that it almost brought tears to her eyes.

Goldie lifted her hips to meet his, matching the rhythm he set thrust for thrust. Whoever said the missionary position was dull and boring had obviously never had sex with Gregory. But while it was beyond pleasurable, she still needed more.

"Harder," she demanded. "Fuck me harder!"

Gregory obeyed, pumping into her so hard and so fast it made the headboard bang against the wall.

"Yes!" she breathed, lifting her hips to meet his thrusts. "Just like that! Don't stop! Please don't stop!"

He didn't, not until she threw back her head and screamed her pleasure loud enough for the entire forest to hear. The moment she did, he buried his face in her neck and drove his cock deep in her pussy. His hoarse groan of release was more like a growl in her ear and for some reason, the primal sound sent her completely into orbit.

It was a long time before Gregory lifted his head and when he did, it was to kiss her tenderly on the mouth.

"That was a whole 'nother level of pleasure," she said softly.

He rested his forehead against hers, his mouth curving into a grin. "I would definitely have to agree with you."

Rolling onto his side, Gregory pulled her into his arms and held her close. Goldie smiled and snuggled against him. She would have been content to stay there all day and thought Gregory might have been, too, if it wasn't for the loud growl coming from her stomach.

At his raised brow, she blushed. "Sorry. I guess I must be a little hungry."

His mouth quirked. "I guess so. I'd offer you something to eat, but someone broke in last night and ate all my stew." When her color deepened at his teasing, he chuckled and tilted her chin up to give her a kiss. "However, I happen to know this great diner nearby that makes the most amazing breakfast, if you want to check it out."

Her pulse skipped a beat. Apparently this was going to be more than a one-night stand. Maybe a relationship with Gregory could work after all. She smiled. "I'd love to."

He grinned. "I was hoping you'd say that."

As they got dressed and left the cabin a little while later, Goldie couldn't help but think that while the workweek might have ended crappy, the weekend was starting out just right!

Goldie glanced at Gregory as they walked to his SUV. "I really am sorry about the window and for breaking the woodcarving you made." Her mouth curved. "What is it with you guys and bears anyway?"

He slipped his arm around her. "I'll tell you about it sometime."

MR. RIGHT-NOW

෪

Dedication

&

With special thanks to my extremely patient and understanding husband, without whose help and support I couldn't have pursued my dream job of becoming a writer. You're my sounding board, my idea man, my critique partner, and the absolute best research assistant any girl could ask for! Thank you for talking me into finally taking the plunge and submitting to Ellora's Cave.

Trademarks Acknowledgement

&

The author acknowledges the trademarked status and trademark owners of the following wordmarks mentioned in this work of fiction:

Abercrombie & Fitch: Abercrombie & Fitch Company

Cosmo: Hearst Communications, Inc.

Seattle Mariners: Baseball Club of Seattle, L.P.

Victoria's Secret: V Secret Catalogue, Inc.

Chapter One

ഇ

Always the bridesmaid, never the bride. Wasn't that how the saying went? Well, it sure the heck fit her, Kate Gentry thought. Since graduating from college eight years ago, she'd been a bridesmaid eight times and had the dresses in her closet to prove it. After the last time, she told herself if one more friend asked her to be in their wedding party, she was turning them down. Of course, she couldn't very well keep that promise when it was her best friend in the whole world doing the asking. Which was why she was on a ferry heading from Seattle to San Juan Island to be maid of honor at the upcoming nuptials.

For all her grumbling, though, Kate would never have dreamed of turning Rachel down when the other girl asked her to be in the wedding party. While she might have rotten luck when it came to men, Kate was thrilled Rachel was marrying the man of her dreams. Not only was Rachel's fiancé good-looking and successful, but he treated her like a princess. Seeing the couple together gave Kate hope there was a guy just as wonderful somewhere out there for her. All she had to do was find him.

Kate leaned on the railing and propped her chin on her hand as she looked out over the water at the Cascade Mountains. Why the heck did all of her friends find Mr. Right while she got stuck with one loser after another? Okay, maybe "loser" was the wrong word. The men she'd gone out with were all very nice. Unfortunately, none of them were interested in marriage. Or maybe they just weren't interested in marrying her.

Sighing, she let her gaze wander over the deck below. It was deserted except for a tall, dark-haired man standing by the railing. He had his back to her, so she couldn't see his face, but from his broad shoulders, sculpted biceps, and great butt, she was willing to bet he was handsome. With a body like that, he had to be. It'd be a crime if he wasn't. She wished he would turn around so she could see if she was right.

As if he'd somehow read her mind, the man turned to face her direction. He leaned back, casually resting his elbows on the railing behind him. Kate blinked as she took in his straight nose, chiseled jaw, and wide, sensual mouth. It was just as she thought. He was gorgeous. In fact, he was so good-looking it made her wonder if he was a model and there was a photo shoot going on for a magazine or something down on the lower deck. She could definitely picture him in an ad for Abercrombie & Fitch. She scanned the deck for a camera crew, but she didn't see one. If anything, Mr. Tall, Dark, and Perfect seemed to be all alone down there.

Kate chewed on her lower lip thoughtfully, wondering if she should go down and casually run into him. It wouldn't be the first time she did it to meet a guy. Who knew? Maybe he lived in Seattle, too. They could go on a couple dates, develop a deep meaningful connection, and be coming back to San Juan Island to get married themselves by this time next year.

Her gaze lingered on the man for another moment before she turned away from the railing and went back inside. Quickly making her way over to the stairs, she hurried down to the lower deck and out the double doors to the front of the ferry. When she got there, however, the handsome hunk was nowhere in sight.

Frowning, she turned around to look through the windows to see if she could spot him inside, but to her dismay, she didn't see him anywhere.

"Damn," she muttered.

Wasn't that just her luck? She finds a gorgeous guy and loses him before she can even talk to him. Oh, well. He was probably married anyway. Or gay. The good ones were always one or the other.

Tucking her long, ash-blonde hair behind her ear, Kate walked over to the railing and looked out at the mountains again. Though not nearly as interesting as the hot guy she was eyeing earlier, the view was still breathtaking. She didn't think she'd ever get tired of seeing the lush, green trees and snow-topped mountains. The ferry was certainly a great way to see it all. After the wedding, maybe she should come up here on her own for a vacation.

The cool breeze coming off the sound whipped at Kate's hair and she reached up to tuck it behind her ear again. Although she would have preferred to stay on deck and enjoy the view, she knew if she didn't get out of the wind soon she'd be a mess by the time she got to San Juan Island. Since the rest of the wedding party would probably already be there, she didn't want to show up looking like she'd spent the afternoon in a wind tunnel. Besides, she thought as she made her way across the deck and back inside, maybe she'd run into that gorgeous guy. God, he'd look so damn good in a tux.

Much to Kate's disappointment, however, he was nowhere to be found. She kept an eye out for him anyway, hoping he might make an appearance at some point before the ferry arrived at San Juan Island, but he didn't. When the boat neared the dock a little while later, Kate finally gave up on the notion of running into him and went down to the lower deck where the vehicles were parked. She made her way along the row of cars until she came to hers, then got in and waited along with everyone else while the passengers without vehicles disembarked.

Once Kate got off the ferry, it was a short drive through the small town of Friday Harbor to the inn where her friend's wedding was being held. Though Kate had never been to the hotel before, she'd read about it in several magazines and according to them, it was one of the premier wedding venues in the Pacific Northwest. As she drove up the winding driveway, she could see why. With its panoramic windows, sleek-looking architecture, and well-manicured grounds, it was absolutely beautiful. She could just imagine the pictures of her own wedding party on the front lawn. She and her husband would pose right by that cute, little fir tree near the deck. It would be so romantic.

Kate glanced at her watch as she crossed the hotel lobby to the main desk a few minutes later. According to the detailed schedule of events Kate had helped Rachel plan for the weekend, the bridal party was supposed to be getting together for drinks at the poolside bar in twenty minutes. Although she knew she'd be cutting it close if she went up to her room and changed after checking in, she really didn't want to show up in jeans and a funky graphic-print T-shirt.

Once in her room, Kate unpacked as fast as she could, but after one look in the mirror, she decided she needed to redo her makeup. Between hurrying to catch the ferry and braving the wind to find that guy, she was a mess. By the time she was dressed and ready, she was already fifteen minutes late for the start of the get-together. Catching sight of her reflection in the mirror on the wall as she made her way to the pool area, however, she decided being a little late was worth it. The flirty little slipdress and high-heeled sandals she'd changed into accentuated her slender curves and made her legs look a mile long. She didn't like making her friends wait, but she never knew when she might meet her future husband, so she always liked to look her best.

Rachel and the rest of the bridal party were sitting at a table on the far side of the patio and Kate quickly made her way over to them. Spotting Kate, her slender, dark-haired friend squealed excitedly and immediately jumped up to greet her with a hug. The other girls did the same, each one taking turns putting their arms around her and giving her a big squeeze. Kate couldn't help but laugh. It was wonderful to have all of her friends together in one place like this. Though they all lived within a couple hours of Seattle, they didn't get together nearly as much as she would like. They had met during their freshman year in high school and been close friends ever since. Along with Rachel, the other girls—Kristen, Heather, Briana and Melanie—were like the sisters she never had.

"Come on and sit down," Rachel said, patting the chair beside hers. "Did you just get in?"

"About thirty minutes ago. I wanted to unpack and change before I met up with everyone." Kate looked around for Rachel's fiancé as she sat down. "Where are Bob and the rest of the guys?"

The other girl waved her hand. "At the bar. They went to get us drinks, but I think they got sidetracked by the baseball game on the television."

Kate laughed. "Typical."

"Speaking of guys," Heather said, looking around. "Where's Jason?"

Kate made a face at the mention of her ex-boyfriend. "I broke it off with him a couple of weeks ago."

Heather's pretty brown eyes went wide. "You did? Why didn't you tell us? What happened? He seemed so perfect for you."

Around the table, Kate noticed the rest of the girls looked just as surprised to hear she'd called it quits with her most recent boyfriend. All except Rachel. Kate had told her the day after it had happened, but hadn't got around to mentioning it to the others. It was kind of embarrassing, really. She'd been going on and on for months that Jason was The One. Then again, she thought every guy she went out with was The One. Until she figured out he wasn't.

She shrugged. "I thought he was perfect, too, at first. But after a while, it was obvious there was something missing. I don't think he was really marriage material. Which is why I'm really not all that upset about breaking up with him."

Across from her, Kristen sat back with a frown. "He wasn't marriage material? What the heck does that mean? He was good-looking, funny, had a great job, and according to you, dynamite in the sack. You'd only been going out with him for four months. I don't see the problem."

Kate should have known Kristen wouldn't see the problem. She and her husband John had gone out off and on for years before they suddenly decided to get married. That concept didn't make sense to Kate. Either a guy was The One or he wasn't. And if he wasn't, then why waste her time with him? To Kate, it always seemed like Kristen had just settled for John. Her husband was nice and all, but how magical could their relationship be if they'd been able to date other people in between? Of course, Kate would never say anything like that to her friend.

"The problem was that I could never see our relationship transitioning to marriage, no matter how long we went out," Kate said, then added, "Actually, I'm not sure if the word marriage was even in his vocabulary. I didn't want to waste my time with him anymore."

"Kate, you're crazy," Briana said. Petite and slightly plump, she had curly red hair and a smattering of freckles across her nose. "Going out with a guy is never a waste of time if you're having fun with him." Her brow furrowed. "You did have fun with Jason, didn't you?"

Kate almost laughed. "Sure I did. I wouldn't go out with a guy if I didn't. He just really wasn't what I was looking for in a husband."

"Ah, the infamous checklist," Melanie said, her blue eyes teasing.

Around the table, the other girls nodded as if in agreement and Kate felt her face color. "What checklist? I don't have a checklist."

"Don't even try to deny it," Melanie said. "We've all known about it forever. It may not be in writing, but it's the one you came up with senior year in high school. You know, the one you used to figure out which guy you wanted to take you to the prom? As I remember, you started at the beginning of the school year and mentally crossed off a guy's name whenever he got a bad grade on a math test or showed up late to class too many times in a row. By the time prom rolled around, you came up with one guy in the whole senior class who fit your criteria and because you were afraid he might take someone else, you asked him to the dance."

Kate blushed even more at that. She'd always been very organized and methodical when it came to doing something, so coming up with the checklist of criteria to help her figure out which guy she wanted to take her to the prom seemed like the most efficient way to go about it. She hadn't realized her friends knew about it, though. "That was prom. I don't use a checklist now."

"Sure you do," Melanie insisted. "You used it all through college. You never dated a single guy you didn't think was worthy of marriage. You never had one drunken hookup or ever banged a guy just because he was on the football team. You evaluated every guy against your checklist back then and you still do now. You might have changed some of the things on it since then, but you still use one."

"Okay, so maybe I do," Kate admitted. "But everyone has one."

Melanie let out a snort. "Not like yours."

Kate shrugged. "I just have high standards, that's all."

Melanie laughed. "The problem isn't your high standards. It's your single-minded focus on finding the perfect husband." She leaned forward to rest her arms on the table. "Let me ask you something. When was the last time you went out with a guy simply because he was hot and you thought he'd be good in bed?"

Kate opened her mouth to answer, but then closed it again when she couldn't come up with an example.

"See? Either it was so long ago you can't even remember or you've never done it at all," Melanie said. "Which proves my point."

Kate eyed her warily, feeling like this was some kind of intervention. "What point is that?"

"That you have to forget about your stupid checklist," the other girl said. "It's okay to stop looking for Mr. Right and just have fun with Mr. Right-Now every once in a while."

Kate was silent as she mulled over her friend's words. Considering Melanie was married to a great guy, that approach had obviously worked for the other girl, but it wasn't Kate's style. She didn't go out with men unless she thought they had long-term potential. What was the point of hooking up with a hot guy for a night of amazing sex if it didn't eventually lead to marriage?

"Melanie's right," Briana said. "You can't expect every guy you go out with the be The One. I sure as heck didn't think I was going to marry Tom when we first started dating. I just knew I liked spending time with him because we had fun together. I wasn't even thinking about marriage, but when he proposed, I realized I'd actually fallen in love with him." She grinned. "It helped that he's great at oral sex, of course. It's possible that was actually the deciding factor."

Kate laughed at that last part along with everyone else, then shook her head. "Okay, I admit being great at oral sex is high up on my checklist, but I don't see the casual approach working for me."

"That's the point," Kristen said. "You're not supposed to go into that kind of relationship expecting anything. That's why they're so much fun. For once, give yourself permission to have a no-strings-attached fling with a hot guy just for the fun of it."

Beside Kate, Rachel grinned. "That's a great idea! In fact, you can start this weekend."

Kate looked at her in surprise. "This weekend?"

Rachel nodded. "No time like the present. And you know what they say, 'what happens on San Juan Island, stays on San Juan Island.'"

Kate gave her a wry look. "I don't think I've ever heard anyone say that."

"Well, they should. Besides, I have the perfect guy for you to have a fling with. Bob's best man, Dawson McKenna."

"You're kidding, right?" Kate asked. "I've never even met him."

"Which is why he's the perfect guy to have a no-strings-attached fling with. After this weekend, you won't ever have to see him again, which means you can be as wild and uninhibited in bed as you want."

Kate shook her head. "You can't honestly expect me to sleep with some guy I don't even know."

"Did I mention he's handsome, smart, and has an absolutely gorgeous body?" her friend asked.

"You left that part out," Kate said dryly. "But if he's handsome, smart and has an absolutely gorgeous body, then why is he still single?"

Rachel shrugged. "I don't know and I don't care. Neither should you. You're not looking to marry the guy, remember? You're just looking to have a good time with him."

"I don't know, Rachel..." Kate began.

"Honey, believe me, if I wasn't already so in love with Bob, I'd be all over Dawson and his six-pack abs," Rachel told her.

"God, yes," Melanie agreed.

"Same here," Briana said.

"I'd do him," Heather chimed in.

"Me, too," Kristen added, then sighed. "But since we're all married, or about to be, we'll just have to live vicariously through you."

Kate narrowed her eyes at the other girl. "So, by doing the best man, I'd be doing all of you a huge favor, is that what you're saying?"

Kristen grinned. "Exactly. As a matter of fact, I think it might be one of your duties as maid of honor."

"Uh-huh." Kate sighed. "Look, I know you all mean well, but I'm just not the kind of girl who has a weekend fling with a guy."

"Even if he is as ridiculously hot as Dawson McKenna?" Kristen asked.

"Even then," Kate insisted.

Beside her, Rachel exchanged looks with the other girls, then nodded. "Okay, okay, we won't push you. But you might want to change your mind after you meet Dawson."

Kate didn't think so and would have told her friend as much, but Bob and the rest of the men were already on their way over to the table, which effectively put an end to the girl talk. Curious to get a glimpse of this hunk her friends thought was so droolworthy, she was casually trying to get a look at him when she recognized the gorgeous guy from the ferry in their midst. He had exchanged the jeans and T-shirt for a pair of khaki pants and a button-up shirt, but there was there was no mistaking those ruggedly handsome features. She blinked in surprise. Mr. Tall, Dark, and Perfect was the best man?

She glanced at Rachel curiously, hoping her friend would give her a conspiratorial wink to let her know if he was the best man or not, but the other girl was smiling up at her fiancé. "We were beginning to think we'd have to send out a search party."

Bob chuckled as he handed her a glass of white wine. "We were watching the game. We figured you'd be so busy talking that you wouldn't notice we were missing."

Rachel gave Kate and the other girls a knowing look. "What did I tell you? Good thing the Mariners aren't playing this weekend or we'd be getting married in front of a big-screen TV."

Although Kate laughed along with everyone else, she couldn't keep her gaze from going back to Dawson McKenna.

He was even more gorgeous up close. On the ferry, she hadn't been able to tell what color his eyes were, but now she saw they were the most intriguing shade of golden brown and fringed with dark, sooty lashes. This guy was so good-looking, it should be illegal.

Beside Kate, Rachel glanced her way. "Kate, this is Dawson McKenna, the best man. I think I might have mentioned him to you. Dawson, my maid of honor, Kate Gentry."

He flashed her a smile. "The maid of honor. Then this must be for you." He held out a glass of wine. "Bob mentioned you'd come outside while we were at the bar, so we figured we should get you something, too. Hope white wine is okay?"

Though Kate was vaguely aware of the glass in Dawson's hand, she was so mesmerized by his voice, she couldn't seem to make herself reach out to take it. When Rachel and the other girls were going on about how hot the best man was, they forgot to mention his voice was as sexy as the rest of him. She couldn't remember ever feeling heat pool between her thighs at the sound of a man's voice. Damn, with a voice as deep and velvety as his, Dawson could probably read to her from the dictionary and her pussy would be purring like she was a cat in heat.

Kate absently wondered if the only reason she was so hot and bothered by this guy was because her friends had gone on and on about how beddable he was. Had they planted a subliminal suggestion?

She didn't realize how long she'd been sitting there gazing up at Dawson until Rachel nudged her foot underneath the table. Abruptly aware of the amusement on the other girls' faces, Kate blushed. Well, what did they expect? They were the ones who made a big thing about what a hunk Dawson was in the first place. It wasn't her fault they'd been right.

Ignoring them, Kate returned Dawson's smile and reached out to take the glass. "White wine is perfect. Thank you."

Rachel said, "I was just reminding the girls we're playing croquet tomorrow. We're going to be in teams of two, so I thought maybe you and Kate could pair up, Dawson. Is that okay with you?"

Kate stifled a groan. So much for Rachel not pushing Dawson on her. She couldn't be angry with her friend, though. Like Kristen said, Dawson was ridiculously hot. Maybe having a fling with him wouldn't be such a bad thing. Good heavens, how could she even be thinking of doing that? Weekend flings were not her style.

"Fine by me." He lifted a brow. "Kate?"

For some reason, her name sounded provocative on his tongue, and between her thighs, her pussy quivered. She barely managed to resist sliding her hand between her legs to touch herself as she gave him a nod. "Sounds good." She looked up at him from beneath lowered lashes. "Though I do have to warn you, I've never played croquet before."

He gave her a sexy smile. "I have. I can show you a few things, if you want."

Kate's pulse quickened at the suggestive words. While she kept trying to convince herself she didn't do casual sex, her mind was telling her something completely different. Right now, she was imagining all the wicked things she wanted Dawson to show her and none of them had anything to do with croquet.

Underneath the table, Rachel nudged her foot again. Kate pretended not to notice as she sipped her wine.

As if apparently satisfied with her efforts to get Operation Get-Kate-Laid in motion, Rachel changed the subject, talking about the rest of the events she had planned for the weekend. Though Kate joined in the conversation, her gaze kept straying to Dawson. Every time it did, she caught him looking her way and their eyes would inevitably meet, sending little shivers of sexual excitement through her body. She didn't know why Dawson was having such an effect on her. It wasn't like she'd never been around a good-looking guy before. She just usually didn't spend the time mentally undressing them and fantasizing about all the ways she'd like to have sex with them, like she was doing now. Again, it must be all that talk with her girlfriends about having a weekend fling. It was making her think all kind of lusty thoughts.

As she took another sip of wine, Kate studied Dawson from underneath her lashes, letting her gaze wander over his wide shoulders and broad chest. Regardless of her earlier protests, the thought of having a fling with him was definitely tempting. But could she really let herself go enough to have a fun-filled weekend of meaningless sex if a long-term relationship wasn't even on the table? She wasn't sure.

Kate felt her resolve slip a little more when Dawson's leg brushed hers as he sat down next to her at the table in the hotel restaurant a little while later. Just feeling the heat of his body that close to her was enough to make her knees weak. She could only imagine what it would be like for their naked bodies to be intertwined.

Maybe her girlfriends had the right approach after all. Maybe she did need to stop looking for Mr. Right and have fun with Mr. Right-Now. At least for this weekend. Trouble was, she didn't know how to go about it. How did one proposition a guy for a weekend of meaningless sex anyway? She was better at twenty questions and checklists than come-on lines and sexual innuendos.

Figuring she should at least say something to him so he wouldn't think she was a wallflower, Kate glanced at Dawson as she placed her napkin on her lap. "So, how do you and Bob know each other?"

Not exactly a sexy come-on line, but it was the best she could do at the moment.

Dawson took the menu the waitress handed him before answering. "We went to college together."

"Oh. Are you an architect too, then?"

He shook his head. "No, I'm a civil engineer for the city of Seattle."

She nodded. "Which means you build roads and bridges and things, right?"

The corner of his mouth edged up. "I don't actually build them, I just design them. I leave the hard work to someone else."

She laughed. "I don't know about that. Using all that complicated math seems pretty hard to me. I'm lucky I can balance my checkbook."

He chuckled, the sound a deep, sexy rumble that made her feel warm all over. "What about you? What kind of work do you do?"

"I work for an advertising agency in Seattle," she said.

"You live in Seattle, too? Small world. Are you in the marketing side of advertising or do you work in the art department?"

"Marketing."

"Do you like it?"

Her lips curved into a smile. "Most days."

Kate supposed talking about their respective careers wasn't very high up on the list of ways to seduce a man, but as Dawson told her about the current project he was working on while they had dinner, she discovered she liked listening to his voice too much to care. Besides, she still found plenty of ways to flirt with him while they talked, like lightly touching his arm or brushing her leg against his underneath the table.

It was then that Kate realized she was no longer thinking in the abstract about having sex with Dawson. Damn, she really wanted to get him into bed. After the initial shock of that stunner wore off, another thought occurred to her. If she was trying to let Dawson know she wanted to sleep with him, she was doing a really crappy job of it. While he certainly seemed to enjoy talking to her, she didn't think he was picking up on any of her come-get-me signals. If she was serious about wanting this guy to take her to bed, then she was going to have to be a little bit more obvious with her desires.

Taking a deep breath, she slipped her hand underneath the table and rested it lightly on his upper thigh. Then she licked her lips seductively and gave him her best sultry look as she told him about the latest ad campaign she was working on. From the way his eyebrow rose, she could tell Dawson had finally picked up on what she was trying to tell him. He leaned in a little closer and slipped his own hand under the table to run his fingers up and down her bare thigh. His touch immediately sent electric sparks dancing along her leg. She smiled. *Now we're talking.*

By the time Rachel and Bob announced they were going to call it a night, Kate was getting a lot more forward than she ever had in her life. As they talked, she let her fingers trail all the way up Dawson's leg until they were dangerously close to his cock before moving back down to his knee and doing it all over again. From the look in his eye, she had no doubt he was enjoying their foreplay just as much as she was.

"And remember," Rachel added as she pushed in her chair. "Croquet starts promptly at noon tomorrow on the back lawn, so don't be late."

Around the table, the other couples began pushing their chairs back and getting to their feet as well. Kate reluctantly did the same. She would have rather stayed there at the table with Dawson and seen where their wandering hands would lead. Their friends were all leaving to go to their rooms, though, and it would look odd if she and Dawson sat there alone. So if she wanted to continue getting frisky with him, she was going to have to find another place to do it.

She was reaching for her purse as Rachel came up to her.

"You and Dawson certainly hit it off," the other girl said. "I knew you would."

Kate looked around for Dawson, worried he might overhear and think Rachel was trying to set them up, but he was standing a few feet away talking to Bob. "You were right," she told Rachel, trying to make her voice sound as casual as possible. "He's very nice."

"Nice. Uh-huh. Don't think I didn't see where your hand was going during dessert. You are so busted, girl." Rachel reached into her purse and dug around. A moment later, she pressed something into Kate's hand. "Here. You might need this."

Kate looked down to find a condom packet in her hand. Afraid Dawson might see it, she quickly closed her fingers around it. She gave her friend an incredulous look. "You carry these around in your purse?"

Rachel grinned. "I'm like the boy scouts, I'm always prepared. And now you are, too."

Kate shook her head. "I won't need it."

Rachel shrugged. "Better to have it and not need it, than need it and not have it. And trust me, I think you're going to need it."

Kate opened her mouth to reply, but her friend had already turned away. Short of running after the other girl and shoving the condom in her hand, Kate had no choice but to put it in her purse.

Rachel looped her arm through her fiancé's. "Ready to go have mad monkey sex?" she asked teasingly.

Bob's blue eyes danced with amusement. "Race you to the elevator."

Though Kate couldn't help but laugh as the couple practically ran from the restaurant, her gaze was wistful as she followed them. She'd never been that eager to be alone with any of the men she dated.

Dawson walked over to stand beside her. "Do you want to go to the bar for a drink?"

Kate hesitated. The bar was certainly much more intimate than the restaurant, so it would be the perfect place to carry on what they'd been doing underneath the table earlier. That would certainly be fun, but if she was really going to do this, why waste time in the bar? She caught her lower lip between her teeth, then tilted her head a little to the side and gave him what she hoped was a sexy look.

"Or we could just go up to your room and raid the minibar instead," she suggested softly.

Dawson's golden eyes went molten. "Even better."

Holy crap, she'd done it. She'd just propositioned a guy for sex. Okay, maybe it wasn't quite that blatant, but it was obvious Dawson knew exactly what she meant. She felt so proud of herself she almost did a little cheer right there.

His room was on the fourth floor just like hers, but because the elevator stopped on every floor in between to let people on and off, it seemed to take forever to get there. Now that Kate had made the decision to sleep with him, she was impatient to get his clothes off and see if he was as well built as she thought. Being in the close confines of the elevator only made her hotter for him. By the time they got to his floor, she was ready to push him up against the wall and get busy right there. She actually might have done it, too, if she wasn't afraid they'd get arrested for public indecency. She almost laughed. Wow, she was better at being naughty than she'd thought.

His hotel room was an exact replica of hers, right down to the fireplace and hot tub. It was the king-size bed against the wall that caught and held her attention, however. As she took in the fluffy pillows and white goose down comforter, she pictured herself rolling around on it with Dawson, their naked bodies entwined as they engaged in hot, sweaty sex. Just the idea started a really nice purr between her legs.

"The minibar is probably pretty limited, but I'm sure we can find something," Dawson said as he tossed his key card on the dresser. "What can I get you?"

Images of her and Dawson still running through her head, Kate turned to face him. She couldn't believe she was actually going to go through with this. Before she could change her mind, she set her purse down on the bedside table and walked over to loop her arms around his neck. She hadn't realized how tall he was downstairs, but now she had to tilt her head back to look up at him.

"Maybe we should forget about having a drink and test out the mattress instead," she suggested softly. "I hear they're very comfortable."

Surprise flickered in his eyes for a moment, but he rested his hands lightly on her hips all the same. "Kate Gentry, are you seducing me?"

"I might be," she admitted. "But only if it's working."

He chuckled. "Oh, it's definitely working."

She smiled up at him. "Then in that case, I'm definitely seducing you. I figured since we're both obviously attracted to each other, we should hook up for the weekend."

She tried to make the words sound casual, but inside, her heart was pounding like crazy. She didn't know if it was from excitement or nerves, though. Maybe it was a little of both. She'd never actually seduced a man like this. And the words "hook up for the weekend" had certainly never, ever come out of her mouth before.

He lifted a brow. "Hook up? As in casual sex, no strings attached?"

Clearly he was way more familiar with this type of thing than she was. She nodded. "Exactly. Once the weekend is over, we get on the ferry and go our separate ways. No muss, no fuss."

He pulled her closer, his mouth curving into a sexy grin. "That works for me."

She should have tried this whole seduction thing long before this. She was better at it than she'd thought. Kate didn't reply, but instead leaned in and kissed him.

Dawson's mouth was gentle, his tongue slow dancing deliciously with hers. He deepened the kiss with a groan, one hand sliding in her long hair to tilt her head back so he could completely take possession of her mouth. She sighed and melted against him, her hand wrapping around the nape of his neck.

His hard cock pressed against her tummy, evidence of his arousal, and her pussy quivered with desire. God, this was going to be so good.

She dragged her mouth away from his to look up at him. Gaze locked with his, she put her hands on his chest and urged him back onto the bed with a firm little push. He went without protest, the corner of his mouth curving into a smile.

Without a word, Kate reached behind her and unzipped her dress. Rather than pushing it down right away, though, she slowly let it slide over her breasts, then took her time wiggling it over her hips. She'd never done anything as sexy as a striptease for a man before, but as Dawson's hot gaze followed her every move, she decided she liked it. She felt empowered, like she had permission to do things she wouldn't normally do. Probably because she had no expectations where Dawson was concerned. The weekend was just about having fun and some seriously hot sex with a gorgeous guy. She didn't have to worry about whether he would respect her in the morning.

Dawson's gaze caressed her from head to toe, lingering on her satin-covered breasts for a moment before moving over her skimpy panties and long legs. Squeezing her legs together to ease the sudden throbbing in her pussy, Kate bent to slip off her high-heeled sandals.

"Leave them on," Dawson commanded softly.

Kate hesitated for a moment, but then straightened. She could do that. It made her feel like one of those models from Victoria's Secret.

Stepping over her dress, she slowly made her way to him, careful to add a little extra wiggle to her walk. Positioning herself between his legs, she slid her hand in his silky, dark hair and bent to kiss him. This time, she was the one in charge and she plunged her tongue into his mouth to take possession of his.

Dawson cupped her ass cheeks in his hands, giving them a firm squeeze through her panties as he kissed her back. Kate murmured her approval against his mouth. She loved it when a guy paid attention to her ass.

Dragging his mouth away from hers, he trailed hot kisses along the curve of her jaw and down her neck. His breath was warm and moist on her skin, and she shivered, clutching at his shoulders to steady herself. Dear God, if his mouth felt this good on her neck, she couldn't wait to see what it felt like on other, even more sensitive parts of her body.

As if reading her mind, Dawson moved lower to press a kiss to the top of her breasts. Beneath her bra, her nipples hardened, straining at the satin covering them, and she let out a husky moan. She twisted her fingers more tightly in his hair and guided his mouth where she wanted it to go. He let her take charge, moving his lips and tongue over the slope of her breast, then dipping into her cleavage.

She closed her eyes and let out a sigh. She liked the sensation of being in control. It was a new experience for her.

Eager to continue to explore her newfound assertive side, Kate gently pulled his head away and gazed down at him with a wicked smile. "You're way too overdressed."

His mouth quirked. "We should do something about that then."

Her smile widened. "I will."

As she reached out to unbutton his shirt, she had to resist the urge to tear it open and send buttons flying everywhere. But undoing them slowly was just as much fun. Kind of like unwrapping a Christmas present.

Dawson leaned back on his elbows as his shirt parted to reveal a smooth, muscular chest and washboard stomach. She caught her breath at the sight. She'd seen some nice abs before, but his were positively lickable.

Kate caught her lower lip between her teeth, her gaze roaming over his bare chest. Did she dare?

Bending over, she shoved his shirt off his shoulders, then wrapped her hands around his muscular arms and slowly kissed her way down his chest. She paid special attention to his nipples as she went, teasingly flicking her tongue over them before taking each one in her mouth and gently suckling on the stiff little peaks. He let out a husky groan that made heat pool between her legs.

She moved lower, alternately kissing and nibbling her way down his rock-hard abs until she came to his bellybutton. Once there, she hesitated. She went out with a lot of guys in her search for Mr. Right, but she'd never done anything as bold as undo their belt and take off their pants. She was used to being more passive, figuring that was what men liked in a potential wife. But this weekend wasn't about acting shy or demure. It was about letting herself go and just enjoying some hot, steamy sex.

Kate lifted her gaze to find Dawson regarding her expectantly. Lips curving into a slow smile, she gave him a seductive look as she ran her hands down his chest. Grabbing his belt, she roughly tugged it open, then slowly lowered the zipper on his khaki pants. When he lifted his hips so she could take them off, her eyes went a little wide at the sizeable bulge in his boxer briefs. Apparently, he was well built everywhere. This weekend was looking better and better by the second. Yanking his pants the rest of the way off, she playfully tossed them across the room. He wasn't going to need them for a while.

Impatient to see if he really was as well endowed as he looked, she hooked her fingers in his underwear and yanked them down. When his hard cock sprang free, all she could do was stare in appreciation. He was bigger and thicker than any guy she'd ever been with. This was like winning the lottery, only better. She wasn't going to have to pay taxes on this big boy.

Throwing his boxer briefs over her shoulder, Kate dropped to her knees in front of him and slowly ran her hands up Dawson's muscular thighs. She didn't know why, but being on her knees like this between a guy's legs was incredibly arousing.

She was so mesmerized at the sight of his gorgeous erection moving slightly in time to his pulse that she could have spent the whole night just like she was. But then she changed her mind. Why just look when she could touch all she wanted? She reached up to wrap her hand around him and almost moaned at how he filled her hand. He had the most beautiful cock she'd ever seen. Suddenly, she wanted to have him in her mouth, wanted to possess every glorious inch of him.

Between how hot she was for him and how tasty he looked, she was tempted to take all of him in her mouth at once, but she'd always been the type to savor her dessert and she had the feeling he was definitely going to be worth savoring. Besides, she had no reason to rush. They had all night.

She bent and ran her tongue over the glistening bead of precum on the head of his shaft. It was sweet and musky, and she let out a little moan of pleasure at how delicious he tasted. Wanting more, she closed her lips over the tip and slowly began to move her mouth up and down. As she did, she was rewarded with even more of his precum as the silky liquid rolled over her tongue.

Dawson groaned and slid his hand in her hair, gently guiding her movements. Kate liked the feel of his fingers there. While she liked being in control, she didn't mind relinquishing some of it now. In fact, it gave her pussy a little extra quiver when he pulled her mouth down further on his shaft.

She took him a little deeper with each bob of her head until he was touching the back of her throat. Then she took him just a little bit deeper, letting the head of his cock slide down even more. Dawson groaned again, louder this time.

Kate cupped his balls in her other hand, gently massaging them as she moved her mouth up and down. She occasionally allowed him to slip deep into her throat again, but mostly she just swirled her tongue around the head. She didn't want him to come too quickly, after all. She had another place she wanted his big, thick cock sliding into before that happened.

Satisfied she had teased him to complete hardness, she let Dawson's cock slip out of her mouth with an audible sound.

He lifted a brow. "You didn't have to stop."

"I'm not stopping." She smiled. "On the contrary, I'm just getting started."

Looking at him from beneath lowered lashes, Kate got to her feet and reached around to unclasp her bra. Remembering how much of a turn-on it had been to reveal her body inch by inch when she'd slipped out of her dress earlier, she slid off first one strap, then the other, careful to keep her arms crossed over her breasts. On the bed, Dawson was leaning back on his elbows watching her, his stare hungry. She caught her lower lip between her teeth and slowly lowered her arms, allowing her bra to fall to the floor.

Dawson's sharp intake of breath was audible in the big room and Kate felt herself blush. She had to fight the urge to cover her breasts at the suddenly predatory look on his face. She was a modern, empowered woman, for this weekend at least, and modern, empowered women were not shy in the bedroom. With that in mind, she hooked her thumbs in her panties, then slowly wiggled them over her curvy hips and let them slide down her legs.

"God, you're beautiful," Dawson breathed.

Other men had told Kate she was beautiful, but coming from Dawson, the compliment warmed her to the tips of her toes. She moved to take off her shoes, but then remembered his earlier command and decided to leave them on. There was something very naughty about wearing nothing but a pair of high heels during sex.

She stepped out of her panties and was just about to walk over to the bed when she remembered the condom in her purse.

Dawson must have seen her hesitate. "There's a condom in the bedside table."

Kate opened the drawer to find a box of condoms sitting there. Obviously, he came prepared. As she tore off one of the foil packets, Rachel's earlier comment came back to her and she found herself wondering if Dawson was ever a boy scout. She'd have to remember to ask him, she thought as she handed the packet to him.

She'd never really paid much attention when a guy put on a condom, but watching Dawson roll one on was an erotic experience all its own. When he was done, he pushed himself back on the bed and gave her a sexy look.

Eager to finally have him inside her, Kate climbed on the bed and straddled his legs. Gazing into his eyes, she rubbed the slit of her pussy against the head of his cock for one, long teasing moment before slowly and deliberately lowering herself onto him. He was hot and hard, and she gasped as his length filled her. It was as if he was made for the sole purpose of pleasuring her.

Dawson put his hands on her hips. "Ride me."

Kate didn't need to be told twice. Placing her hands on his chest, she began to slowly move up and down on his cock. Each time she came down on him, she rolled her hips, squeezing him tightly with her pussy.

"Damn, that feels incredible," he rasped. "Don't stop."

She smiled. "I wouldn't dream of it."

Keenly aware of him watching her through half-closed eyes, Kate lifted her hands and cupped her breasts as she continued to move. Her nipples hardened even more at her touch and she gave them a firm little pinch between her fingers.

Beneath her, Dawson shifted his hands to grip her ass and slowly began to thrust his hips in time with hers. The move drove his cock deeper and deeper inside every time he pumped, and she let out a little moan. God, that felt amazing. It was like he was finding places inside her she never even knew existed. Then again, considering how big he was, it was entirely possible he was touching her in places she'd never been touched before.

She leaned forward to kiss him, her mouth closing over his hungrily. His tongue met hers halfway, claiming it for his own, and she sighed with pleasure.

With a groan, Dawson tightened his hold on her ass and rolled them both over so that he was now the one on top. Kate blinked up at him in surprise, breathless from their kiss.

"That was a neat move," she said.

He chuckled. "I've got plenty of them."

She smiled. "I bet you do."

But the words came out muffled as Dawson bent his head to kiss her again. Kate reached up to loop her arms around his neck, her fingers finding their way into his thick hair as she wrapped her legs around him to pull him in even deeper. As soon as she did, he began to move inside her. She undulated beneath him, automatically lifting her hips to meet his.

"Harder," she begged. "Fuck me harder!"

At her words, Dawson buried his face in her neck and pumped into her harder.

"Oh yeah," she moaned. "Just like that."

Every thrust pushed her closer and closer to orgasm, and she tightened her fingers in his hair as she felt herself nearing the edge. When she finally went over the precipice, the pleasure that coursed through her was so intense she screamed loud enough for the whole hotel to hear.

Despite how vocal she was, though, she still heard Dawson's hoarse groans in her ear as he found his own release. Knowing he was coming just as hard as she was made it that much better.

Kate was still floating down to earth when Dawson rolled over onto his back a few moments later, taking her with him. She snuggled into the curve of his arm and rested her head on his chest. Why the heck hadn't she ever had sex like that before? Maybe because she'd never let herself be so uninhibited. She had certainly never dropped to her knees and given a guy she just met a blowjob or asked a guy to fuck her harder, that was for sure. Well, maybe she should have been doing those things all along because that was the most mind-blowing sex she'd ever had in her life.

She lifted her head to gaze at him. "That was amazing."

His mouth twitched. "The weekend's just getting started. You haven't seen anything yet."

Chapter Two

✺

Dawson woke up the next morning to find Kate draped over his chest, fast asleep. Her full lips were slightly parted and it was all he could do not to bury his hand in her long, silky hair and tilt her face up to his so he could kiss her. But she looked so cute sleeping that he didn't have the heart to wake her. Much to the dismay of his cock, which was rapidly hardening. He stifled a groan and lay back on the pillow again.

When he had agreed to be his friend's best man, Dawson expected to have to fend off every single woman desperately looking to find herself a husband at the wedding. Instead, he'd met a woman who wasn't interested in anything more than a weekend fling and some casual sex. He'd never known a woman who was so sexually liberated and sure of herself. Not to mention so beautiful or so damn hot in bed. They'd stayed up all night making love and only fallen asleep as the sun was coming over the horizon.

He had been attracted to Kate the moment he'd laid eyes on her last night. Tall and slender, she had curves in all the right places and the sexiest pair of legs he'd ever seen. Simply put, she was perfection on sky-high heels. While he was honored Bob asked him to stand up for him at his wedding, Dawson had to admit the prospect of hooking up with Kate Gentry for the entire weekend made putting on the uncomfortable tux he had to wear a whole hell of a lot more bearable.

Dawson turned his head to look at Kate again. Telling himself one little touch wouldn't wake her up, he gently brushed her hair back from her face. She stirred at the feel of his fingers on her cheek, then snuggled against his chest like it was a pillow as her arm tightened around him. A moment later, her eyes fluttered open and she blinked up at him sleepily.

He gave her a lazy grin. "Sorry. I didn't mean to wake you. But you looked so beautiful that I couldn't help myself."

She let out what sounded like an embarrassed laugh and he was surprised to see a rosy blush coloring her cheeks. "I'm pretty sure I don't look beautiful first thing in the morning, but thank you for saying so anyway."

Dawson slipped his finger beneath her chin and tilted her face up to his. "I'm just being honest."

Kate looked like she wanted to protest, but he silenced her with a kiss. He slid his hand in her hair, ready to plunder her mouth with his tongue, when a loud growl interrupted him. She pulled away to give him a sheepish look.

He chuckled. "I guess that means you're hungry."

She blushed again. "Sorry. I'm always starving in the morning."

"Don't be. I'm pretty hungry myself." Though not necessarily for food, he added silently when the sheet covering them slipped a little to give him a tantalizing glimpse of Kate's breasts. "Why don't I order us room service? I think I saw a menu around here somewhere."

Dawson didn't wait for an answer, but instead threw the sheet back and padded naked to the desk on the other side of the room. Grabbing the room service menu, he turned around to find Kate propped up on one elbow in bed, eyeing him unabashedly as she chewed on her lower lip. He didn't know how it was possible for a woman to look so demure and so wanton at the same time, but somehow Kate managed. Damn, it was sexy as hell.

Walking over to the bed, he climbed in beside her and held the menu so they could both read it.

"So, what'll it be?" he asked.

She scanned the menu for a moment, then looked at him. "Just some fresh fruit, I think."

He lifted a brow. "That's it?"

"And some whole wheat toast with peanut butter. Oh, and coffee."

"No eggs or pancakes or anything?"

She shook her head. "Nope."

Dawson had a feeling she might change her mind once she saw how good his plate of pancakes looked, but he didn't say anything. He discovered he was right fifteen minutes later when Kate dipped her finger in his maple syrup and licked it off her finger. The move probably wasn't meant to be seductive, but inside the pajama bottoms he'd put on to answer the door, his cock went rock-hard. Of course, that could have something to do with the fact that she was sitting in bed completely naked with nothing but a small bowl of fresh fruit in her lap. The sight was so damn distracting he didn't know how he managed to eat. Not that he was complaining. He couldn't think of a better way to start the day than having breakfast in bed with a woman as sexy as Kate.

Dragging his gaze away from her perfect female form, he stuck a piece of pancake with his fork and dipped it in some syrup, then held it out to her with a grin. "Syrup always tastes better on something."

She smiled, eyeing the fork. "It does, huh?"

He pushed the fork a little closer, trying to tempt her. "It does."

Laughing, Kate leaned forward to close her full, pouty lips over the fork. Just as she did, syrup dripped off the pancake to land squarely on her rosy red nipple. Dawson didn't know which image was more provocative and quickly decided it was a tossup.

"Ooops," she said.

She gave him an embarrassed look and reached for a napkin, but he stopped her.

"I'll get it." He gave her a grin. "I'm the one who made the mess after all."

Setting the half-finished plate of pancakes on the bedside table, he shifted on the bed until he was above her, then bent and slowly swirled his tongue round and round her nipple until he got every last little bit of syrup. When he was done, he drew the stiff peak into his mouth and suckled on it. Kate whimpered and buried her fingers in his hair, holding him in place as he made love to first one beautiful breast, then the other.

Giving her nipple one last flick with his tongue, Dawson lifted his head to give her a grin. "I was right. Syrup does taste much better when it's on something."

Kate laughed. "Even my nipples?"

"Especially those," he said, bending his head to kiss his way down her taut tummy.

"I don't think you got any syrup down there, Dawson," she teased.

He paused mid-kiss to look up at her. "You sure about that? Your pussy is very sweet."

Her eyes went a little wide at that and she blushed.

The corner of his mouth curving into a smile, Dawson picked up the bowl of fruit in her lap and set it on the bedside table before going back to what he'd been doing. The muscles of her stomach flexed in response to his kisses as he moved lower. Even though the scent of her arousal drew him like a drug, he couldn't resist pausing to dip his tongue in the hollow of her bellybutton. Above him, he heard Kate catch her breath and he swirled his tongue around the opening once more before trailing kisses down her tummy to the juncture of her thighs.

Kate spread her legs invitingly and he gently parted her perfect pink lips with his fingers so he could run his tongue along her slick folds. Her juices weren't just sweet, they were intoxicating, and he groaned in appreciation. The urge to bury his face between her legs and devour her pussy was so strong it was all he could do to hold himself back. When he went down on a woman, however, he liked to take his time making her come.

With that in mind, Dawson teased her folds with his mouth before dipping his head to plunge his tongue into her wetness. Kate moaned and lifted her hips off the bed, her hands grasping his head.

"Mmm," she breathed.

He pushed his tongue in a little deeper, then leisurely ran it up her folds until he came to her plump, little clit. He closed his lips over the nub, suckling on it gently before slowly swirling his tongue round and round.

Kate's fingers tightened in his hair. "Oh yeah. Right there."

As he lapped at her clit, Dawson slid his hands around to cup her ass cheeks, holding them firmly. She rotated her hips in time with his movements, grinding against him while he licked her over and over. He could do this all morning.

"Oh God, don't stop," Kate moaned. "You're going to make me come."

His mouth quirked. Apparently, it wasn't going to take all morning. Kate was like a firecracker with a very short fuse. All he had to do was light it and watch her go off.

Dawson tightened his grip on her ass and moved his tongue faster, licking her more firmly as he focused directly on her clit. Kate writhed beneath him, her hips undulating wildly, her cries of pleasure filling the room as she came.

He continued to lick her clit until he was sure he had coaxed every ounce of orgasm out of her, then he licked her some more. Only when she moaned and tugged gently at his hair, did he stop.

Giving her clit one more gentle flick with his tongue, he lifted his head to see her gazing down at him sleepily, her pretty green eyes half closed, full lips parted. He thought it just might be the sexiest sight he'd ever seen.

Pressing a gentle kiss to the inside of her thigh, Dawson leaned back and stripped off his pajama bottoms, then reached for a condom packet on the nightstand. He quickly sheathed his cock, then took Kate's hand and gently tugged her onto his lap. She instinctively seemed to know what he was looking for because she straddled his legs and slowly lowered herself onto his shaft and wrapped her legs around his back.

Kate was tight and wet and ready for him, and Dawson let out a low, throaty groan of appreciation as her heat enveloped his cock. He'd never been with a woman who had a more perfect pussy.

She sighed and lifted her arms to drape them around his shoulders. He wrapped his own around her and pressed a kiss to the side of her neck. She arched against him and pulled him close as she began to slowly ride up and down on him. The sitting position he was in allowed his cock to go as deep as possible and each time she moved, she rotated her hips so that her pussy clenched tightly around his shaft. The sensation, along with her husky, little moans of pleasure, had him dangerously close to the edge and he had to focus all his efforts not to explode right then.

It didn't help that Kate had started riding him faster. Dawson slid his hands down her back to cup her ass cheeks. But instead of slowing her down like he'd meant to do, he found himself urging her to move even faster.

She obeyed, bouncing up and down on him wildly. There was no holding back now even if he wanted to and the moment he heard Kate cry out that she was coming, it was like the dam holding his orgasm at bay burst. Dawson buried his face in the curve of her neck and let out a hoarse groan of release as he climaxed.

Dawson could have stayed like that all day, his arms wrapped around Kate, his cock nestled deep in her pussy, but to his dismay, she stirred a few minutes later and pulled back in his arms, her eyes wide.

"Oh no! We're supposed to meet everyone out on the lawn at noon to play croquet."

He groaned. Damn, he'd forgotten about that. "What time is it?"

"Ten 'til."

"Then that gives us ten minutes to get down there."

She looked at him as if he were insane. "I can't get showered and dressed in ten minutes."

He shrugged. "So we'll be a little late."

"Try a lot late." She climbed off him and hopped off the bed. "And because we're both going to be late, everyone will know we've spent the night together."

Dawson frowned as he watched her grab her dress off the floor. "Is that a problem?"

She gave him an exasperated look as she slipped into the dress. "Yes! I mean, no! I mean..."

He got up and walked across the room to put his arms around her. "Look, just relax, okay? If you'd rather everyone not to know we're sleeping together, I'll get dressed and go downstairs ahead of you."

Kate blinked up at him, her green eyes wide as if she was stunned by the suggestion. "No, of course not. Don't be silly. I'm not embarrassed to be seen with you."

His mouth twitched. "I'm glad to hear it. Then go get changed and I'll meet you at your room in fifteen minutes."

She went up on tiptoe to kiss him on the mouth. "Make it twenty."

Dawson chuckled as she slipped her feet into her shoes, then grabbed her bra and panties off the floor and shoved them into her purse. Knowing she was naked underneath that sexy little dress had his cock hardening all over again and it was all he could do not to say the hell with croquet and take her back to bed. But it was his best friend's wedding. Besides, he and Kate had the whole weekend to make love.

Smiling at him over her shoulder, Kate picked up the half-eaten bowl of fruit from the bedside table and darted out the door.

Seeing Kate make off with the bowl of fruit reminded Dawson he hadn't finished his pancakes, so he quickly wolfed down the rest of them, then went into the adjoining bathroom to take a shower. As he stepped under the spray a few minutes later, he thought of how much more fun the mundane activity would be if Kate was there with him. Then again, maybe it was better she went to her own room to get ready because if she stayed to shower with him, they'd never make it downstairs.

Pushing the images of all the x-rated things he and Kate could be doing from his mind, Dawson ignored his hard-on and finished showering. When he was done, he quickly toweled off, then pulled on jeans and a T-shirt before heading to Kate's room.

When she didn't answer his knock right away, Dawson thought she might still be in the shower, but a moment later the door swung open. Kate had changed into a tank top and a short, flirty skirt that showed off her long legs, and he let his gaze linger on them appreciatively.

"You're early!" she said.

His mouth quirked. "Only a few minutes. You look great."

She lazily looked him up and down. "You look pretty good yourself."

"Ready to go?"

"Almost. I just have to finish my makeup. I'll be right back."

"Take your time," he said, but she was already hurrying into the bathroom.

Kate left the door ajar and as Dawson wandered across the room to stand by the fireplace, he caught a glimpse of her through the opening. As he watched, she leaned closer to the mirror to put on her lip gloss. He'd seen other women apply makeup, of course, but there was something unbelievably erotic about the way she ran the glossy pink applicator over her lips and he found himself fantasizing about having that shiny mouth wrapped around his cock. He stifled a groan as he felt his jeans tighten in the crotch.

Turning away from the bathroom, he walked over to the door leading out to the balcony and gazed out at the harbor. While he'd lived in the Seattle area his whole life, he'd never been to San Juan Island, but he had to admit it was beautiful. He'd heard there were some great places to kayak. He wondered if Kate liked to kayak. He'd have to remember to ask her.

When she walked out of the bathroom a few minutes later and announced she was ready to go, however, kayaking was the last thing on Dawson's mind. All he could think about was making love to Kate again.

Telling himself they'd better get out of there before he succumbed to the urge, Dawson gave Kate a smile and walked across the room to open the door for her.

When he and Kate walked out onto the back lawn a few minutes later, the croquet game was already in full swing. At their approach, Rachel and the other girls smiled broadly, as if they knew exactly why they were late.

"And where have you two been?" the bride asked, a teasing twinkle in her eyes.

Color rushed to Kate's cheeks. "I...um...we were..."

"It was my fault," Dawson said when her voice trailed off. "I thought we were supposed to meet you on the front lawn of the hotel. Kate wanted to ask one of the staff where you were, but I insisted we were in the right place. Turns out I was wrong and she was right. You know guys. Never can ask for directions."

As everyone laughed, he glanced at Kate to see her looking at him gratefully.

Rachel exchanged what he was sure was a knowing look with the other girls. "Uh-huh," she said. "Well, you figured it out just in time because it's your turn. Go grab some mallets and stop holding all of us up."

Dawson would have gotten one for Kate, but when he started to head over to where the mallets were, she fell into step beside him.

"You didn't have to do that," she said softly.

He grinned. "Sure, I did."

She smiled. "Well, I'm not sure if they believed you, but thank you anyway."

"You're welcome." He picked up one of the mallets and handed it to her. "Come on, let's go show 'em how the game is played."

Kate laughed. "I would if I knew how. I've never played croquet before, remember?" She hefted the mallet. "Looks dangerous."

He grabbed a mallet for himself, then gave her a wink. "Any implement can be dangerous if you don't know how to use it."

She looked up at him from beneath lowered lashes. "I take it that means you're an expert at using your implement then?"

His mouth quirked. "I think you already know the answer to that one."

Taking her hand, he started over to where their friends were waiting. Someone had already placed a colorful croquet ball at the starting pole for them and he led Kate over to it.

She gazed down at the big colored ball and the pole planted in the ground for a moment, then gave him a curious look. "So, I just whack the ball with the big wooden hammer?"

He chuckled, watching as she leaned over the ball like a golfer would. "Something like that, but your form is a little off. Here, let me show you."

Dawson supposed he could have just demonstrated the proper form using his own mallet, but it was much more fun to wrap his arms around her from behind and guide her through the motion. He took his time showing her how to swing the mallet back and forth between her legs, not because he thought she wouldn't catch on, but because it made her sweetly curved ass rub against his groin.

Off to the side, Rachel eyed them with amusement. "This looks like it's going to take a little while," she said to the rest of the wedding party. "Maybe we should just play through and let them catch up later."

"That okay," Dawson heard John say. "We can wait."

"No, we can't," Kristen told her husband. She grabbed his arm and urged him in the direction of his own colored ball. "They'll catch up in a bit."

A few moments later, Dawson found himself alone with Kate, or as alone with her as he could with the other couples all within earshot. He couldn't help but notice everyone seemed to be looking at them out of the corners of their eyes.

Kate turned her head to smile at him. "Guess they must think I'm a slow learner."

His mouth edged up. "We'll soon fix that."

As he spoke, Dawson reached his arms around Kate again and guided her through the swinging motions a few more times. God, he liked the feel of her ass rubbing against his cock as she leaned over. And the way her silky hair brushed his cheek as she moved wasn't half bad, either. Focusing on the fundamentals of croquet was going to take a lot more concentration than he'd originally thought.

"Now, for the first part," he said, his mouth close to her ear. "The objective is simply to use your mallet to whack the pole so that the ball rolls through the first wire hoop over there."

She half turned her head to give him a flirtatious look. "Are you sure it's okay to go right for the pole like that?

Shouldn't I start off with the balls...I mean ball...and work my way up to the pole?"

Dawson couldn't help but notice she was doing a whole lot of unnecessary wiggling with her ass as she spoke. Not that he or his cock minded. In fact, if she kept doing it, he wasn't going to need a croquet mallet to play the game.

"We are talking about croquet, right?" he asked softly.

"Of course." She blinked at him with innocent green eyes. "What else would we be talking about?"

He felt a grin tug at the corner of his mouth. "I just wanted to be sure. To answer your question, yes, you always start off by giving the pole a good firm whack."

Kate shrugged. "Okay, if you're sure."

She took a tentative swing at the start pole and missed.

"Hold on a second," she said, turning her head to look at him again. "I don't think I'm doing this correctly. It doesn't feel right."

Dawson stifled a groan as she pushed her ass more firmly into his crotch. "Feels like you're doing it right to me."

"I don't think so," she insisted. "I mean, what kind of grip should I use on the shaft of my mallet? Should it be firm or loose?"

Inside his jeans, his cock was hardening to new and painful proportions. He couldn't help but wonder if she knew the effect her words were having on him. "I've always preferred a rather firm grip myself."

She gazed down at the mallet she was holding as if considering that. "But if I hold it too firmly how will I slide my hand up and down the shaft? I am supposed to move my hand up and down the shaft as I move it between my legs, right?"

Damn, she was good at this. She acted like she didn't have a clue what she was talking about with her innuendos, but she was driving him crazy.

"Oh, you definitely need to slide your hand up and down the shaft," he said. "But it's all in the technique. Your grip shouldn't be too firm or too loose."

She sighed and turned her head to look at him. "This is much more complicated than I thought. Maybe you better demonstrate how you handle your own. I wouldn't want to do it wrong."

He lifted a brow. "So you like to watch, huh?"

Her lips curved into a seductive smile. "Uh-huh."

"Well, if you're a good girl, maybe I'll give you a private demonstration later. Right now, we need to concentrate on croquet."

She gave him little pout. "But I thought we were concentrating on croquet."

"Right." His mouth quirked. "You know, if we don't catch up to everyone else soon, they're going to come see what's taking us so long. Though I think they'll figure it out pretty quick when they see the bulge in my jeans."

"It is sort of a giveaway, isn't it?" Kate laughed. "Who knew croquet could be such a turn-on?"

Not him, that was for damn sure. The last time he played the game was at his grandfather's birthday party and it definitely wasn't this much fun. Then again, he didn't have a sex kitten like Kate flirting with him the whole time, either.

She tightened her hold on the mallet and gave the pole a stout whack. Her ball rolled halfway toward the first wire hoop, then stopped.

"Not bad," he said as she stepped to the side so he could take his turn.

Dawson didn't often put aside his competitive nature, but for some reason he found himself striking the pole with his mallet more gently than he normally would. As a result, his croquet ball gently rolled to a stop behind hers.

Kate's next swing sent her ball rolling across the grass and into the side of the hoop hard enough to nearly knock the metal wicket down. She caught her lower lip between her teeth and gave him an embarrassed look.

"Ooops," she said.

Hurrying over to the metal hoop, she bent over to straighten it, giving him a sexy shot of leg as she did. She took her time getting the wicket perfectly set and as he watched her gorgeous ass wiggle from side to side, he began to think she knocked over the hoop on purpose just to torture him. When she stood up a few moments later to give him a sultry smile over her shoulder, he decided he was right. Minx.

From that point on, any thought he and Kate might actually come from behind and win the game disappeared. Every time she smiled or laughed, his cock got hard all over again and his concentration went out the window, something that allowed Heather and her husband Eric to win easily. That was okay with Dawson. Flirting with a sexy woman like Kate was better than winning at croquet any day.

She smiled up at him as she put her mallet away. "You're a very good teacher. I can now play croquet with confidence."

He chuckled. "There are a lot of things I could teach you."

She lifted a brow. "Oh really? Like what?"

Dawson was just about to lean close to whisper in her ear when Rachel appeared beside them. She gave him an apologetic look.

"Sorry to interrupt, but I need to borrow Kate for a minute," she said. "Wedding stuff."

The girl didn't wait for a reply, but instead grabbed Kate's arm and whisked her away and over to where the other women were standing.

"You can put your tongue back in now."

At the sound of Bob's voice, Dawson turned to see his friend standing beside him. He was so focused on Kate, he hadn't heard the other man come over.

"What are you talking about?" he asked.

The other man laughed. "Come on. You're practically drooling."

Dawson opened his mouth to deny it, but then decided he'd only be wasting his time. He and Kate had probably been putting on quite a show during the croquet game. Anyone watching could tell there was something going on between them.

"You didn't tell me Rachel's maid of honor was so beautiful," Dawson said.

Bob shrugged. "She was going out with someone up until a couple weeks ago. I didn't think she'd be available."

Dawson considered that. "Were she and this guy serious?"

"Kate doesn't go out with a guy unless she plans to get serious about him."

Dawson frowned. That didn't sound like the Kate he knew. "Really? We agreed to hook up for the weekend, no strings attached."

The other man looked surprised at that, then his brow furrowed. "No kidding? Well, I guess that means she doesn't think you have any long-term potential or something."

"Thanks a lot."

"No offense, dude. Besides, nothing wrong with a getting a little somethin' somethin' from a beautiful woman, no strings attached. You should consider yourself lucky."

Dawson did, but in the back of his mind couldn't help but wonder what it was about him that made Kate think he wasn't worth more than just a weekend lay.

* * * * *

"So," Rachel asked excitedly, "what did you think?"

Kate almost laughed at the eager looks on her friends' faces. "About croquet? It's a lot more fun than I thought."

Rachel's brows drew together. "Very funny. I'm not talking about croquet and you know it. I'm talking about your night with Dawson."

Kate lifted her chin. "How do you know I spent the night with him?"

"Because it's written all over your face," the other girl said. "You look like the cat that licked the cream."

"Not to mention other, more delectable parts of a certain best man's anatomy," Kristen added.

Kate blushed.

"And if that didn't clue us in, the way you two were all over each other when we were playing croquet would have," Heather grinned. "I was thinking of telling you and Dawson to get a room, but then I remembered you already have one. Whose room did you spend the night in anyway?"

Kate shook her head. "You girls are awful. Okay, if you must know, we spent the night in his room."

Her friends squealed in unison.

"Well, don't keep us in suspense," Briana said. "How was it? Is Dawson as good in bed as he looks?"

Kate's lips curved into a slow smile. "Better."

"How much better?"

Her smile widened. "Let's just say we were still going when the sun came up."

More squeals.

"Now aren't you glad you took our advice?" Rachel asked.

Kate's gaze strayed to where Dawson stood talking to Rachel's fiancé and she let out a little sigh of contentment. "Yeah, I am."

"Whatever it is you're thinking, Kate, stop right there," Rachel ordered.

Kate turned to look at her friend in confusion. "What are you talking about?"

The other girl folded her arms and fixed Kate with a pointed look. "I recognize that wistful little tone in your voice. You're thinking about what a wonderful husband Dawson would make."

"No, I wasn't!" Kate protested.

Rachel arched a brow. Beside her, the other girls were looking just as skeptical.

"I wasn't," Kate insisted. "But now that you mention it…"

"Don't even go there," Rachel warned. "This weekend is about having a fling with a seriously hot guy, remember? You're not allowed to think of Dawson as anything more than a walking, talking sex toy. Got it?"

Kate wanted to protest, but then realized Rachel was right. If she tried to turn Dawson into yet another Mr. Right, she was only going to mess up what was probably the best sex she'd ever had in her life. "Okay, you're right. I got it."

"Good," Rachel said. "Now pretend we've been talking about wedding stuff. The guys are coming over."

Kate turned to see the men heading in their direction and her pulse quickened at the sight of Dawson. Their croquet game had gotten her all hot and bothered and even though they'd made love a few hours ago, she was eager to jump into bed with him again. From the sexy look he sent her way as he came to stand beside her, she suspected he felt the same.

Standing so close to Dawson made concentrating on conversation extremely difficult, especially since he casually slipped his arm around her waist. Kate was just trying to come up with some way for them to make a graceful exit when Rachel mentioned the sunset whale watching cruise the bridal party was going on that evening.

Kate felt Dawson lean close and put his mouth to her ear. "What do you say we skip the whale watching cruise and spend the rest of the day in bed?"

His breath was warm on her skin and she shivered with anticipation. As the maid of honor and best man, she and Dawson should really go on the cruise, but she had the feeling Rachel and Bob would understand.

Her lips curved into a smile. "Sounds like a plan."

Kate turned her attention back to the rest of the bridal party just as Rachel suggested they all go inside to get something to eat. As everyone started toward the big double doors on the patio, Kate caught up with Rachel.

"Dawson and I are going to skip the whale watching cruise, if that's okay," she said to her friend.

Rachel grinned. "Staying here to wax the dolphin instead, huh?"

Kate felt her face color at the risqué words. She quickly darted a glance over her shoulder to see if Dawson had heard, but to her relief, he was talking to Bob and didn't seem to be paying attention.

The other girl laughed. "Relax, Dawson didn't hear. And of course, it's okay. You two have fun." She winked. "Don't do anything I wouldn't do. Then again, there's not much I wouldn't do."

Kate just laughed. Sometimes her friend could be incorrigible.

"Ready?" Dawson asked, coming up beside her.

Eager to finally be alone with him again, she nodded. She'd been hoping they'd have the elevator to themselves, but another couple hurriedly stepped inside just before the doors slid closed. Telling herself she could wait a few more minutes, Kate forced herself to stand there patiently while the elevator took them to the fourth floor. When it came to a stop, she and Dawson quickly darted out the doors and practically ran down the hall to his room.

Once inside, Dawson urged her back against the wall and covered her mouth with his. The kiss was hot and demanding, and Kate let out a little moan of approval as she wrapped her arms around his neck.

He kissed his way along the curve of her jaw and down her neck. "You've been driving me crazy all afternoon, you know that?"

She cooed as his mouth found the curved of her shoulder. "I have?"

He braced one arm against the wall and lifted his head to gaze down at her, his eyes smoldering with desire. "You know very well you did. Rubbing that gorgeous ass of yours against my cock. I was hard the whole time."

She gave him a coy look. "I don't know what you're talking about. I was just playing croquet."

He chuckled, sending a sexy shiver running down her back. "Sure you were. You're such a bad girl."

"Me?"

"Uh-huh. And you know what happens to bad girls, don't you?"

She didn't know where this little game they were playing was going, but she liked it anyway. "What?"

He leaned in closer. "They get a spanking."

She blinked up at him in surprise. Had she heard right? "A sp-spanking?"

He nodded. "A spanking. Right on that sexy little ass."

Dawson didn't wait for a reply, but instead took her hands in his and backed toward the bed. Kate's pulse skipped a beat as she realized what he had in mind. She was both excited and a little nervous at the prospect.

When they stopped beside the bed, she caught her lower lip between her teeth and gazed up at him from beneath her lashes. "I think I should tell you that I've never been spanked before."

He lifted a brow, clearly surprised by that. "Never? With an ass as cute as yours?"

She shook her head. She'd heard of other couples doing it, of course, but it had just never come up with any of the men she went out with. Even if it had, she wasn't sure she would have done it. She'd always assumed good girls didn't do kinky stuff like that, at least not with men they were looking to marry. But she wasn't looking to marry Dawson, which meant she didn't have to be a good girl. And from what she'd seen so far, being a bad girl was a lot more fun anyway.

Suddenly realizing he might have taken her confession to mean she didn't want to try it, she let her lips curve into a slow, naughty smile. "But you're right. I have been a very bad girl. I should definitely be spanked," she said, then added more softly, "But only if you promise not to spank me too hard."

His mouth quirked. "Just hard enough to make your pussy wet."

Kate caught her breath. Something told her she was going to like getting spanked. That didn't stop her pulse from racing wildly as Dawson sat down on the edge of the bed. Taking her hand, he guided her over his knee so that she was lying half on the bed. The position was surprisingly comfortable and she let out a little sigh as he began to gently rub her upturned bottom through her skirt.

"Do you like that?" he asked softly.

She rested her head on her arms. "Mm-hmm."

He gave her ass a squeeze. "How about this?"

She moaned in reply, only to let out a startled little gasp when she felt a sharp smack on her right cheek.

"Owww!"

"Too hard?" he asked.

Kate thought a moment. While the smack stung, it didn't really hurt. In fact, it was actually kind of pleasant. And if the delicious tingle between her thighs was any indication, then her pussy liked it too.

She lifted her head to look at him over her shoulder. "No. You can spank me harder, if you want."

He chuckled. "You really are a bad girl, aren't you?"

Her lips curved. "You bring it out in me."

Blushing at the words, Kate quickly turned and put her head back down. Had she really just said that? She didn't have time to think about it because Dawson was spanking her again.

He smacked first one cheek, then the other, working back and forth with an easy rhythm that soon had her ass stinging all over and her pussy getting very wet. Kate didn't know why getting spanked was such a turn-on, but she decided there was something extremely hot about a sexy guy holding her down and smacking her ass. Especially when that guy was Dawson.

Abruptly, Dawson stopped spanking her and went back to massaging her ass again. Her bottom seemed more sensitive now that she'd just been spanked and she gasped as he squeezed her bottom.

Dawson chuckled and ran his hand over the curve of her ass and down the backs of her thighs before sliding underneath her skirt to push it up. Kate felt her face color as he exposed her tiny bikini panties. It was silly to feel shy, especially since he'd already seen her in a lot less clothing, but there was something about being over his knee with her ass on display and ready to be spanked that made the whole thing even seem naughtier.

Kate held her breath, waiting for him to continue with her spanking, but he surprised her by rubbing her panty-covered ass before sliding his hand between her legs and running his finger along the silky material.

"Your panties are getting wet," he said softly.

She closed her eyes and murmured something unintelligible as his finger glided over her.

"Maybe I should slip my fingers underneath this sexy little scrap of nothing and slide one of them inside your pussy," he suggested. "Or…"

When he hesitated, she lifted her head to look at him over her shoulder, hoping he was thinking the same thing she was. "Or?"

His mouth quirked. "Or maybe I should spank you some more first."

Actually, she was thinking he could just slide his hard cock in her pussy instead, but she wouldn't mind having her bottom warmed a little bit more. She opened her mouth to tell him as much, but he was already lifting his hand to smack her on the ass. The skimpy panties she was wearing didn't offer nearly as much protection as the skirt and she gasped in surprise as heat spread over her skin. Dawson delivered a second smack to the opposite cheek before falling into the same back and forth pattern he had before. He moved slowly from side to side, spanking one cheek, then the other. Despite how much Kate liked it, she couldn't help squirming each time his hand connected with her bottom. The spanks really stung!

Which was why she was torn between relief and dismay when he stopped spanking to massage her poor ass cheeks. Her skin was tender to the touch and she let out a sigh as he made small circular motions with his hand. A moment later she felt him slip his fingers into the waistband of her panties and slowly lower them to mid-thigh.

"You have the most perfect ass I've ever seen," he breathed.

Though Kate blushed, she was immensely pleased he liked her ass so much. She knew there was a reason she did all that Pilates.

After a compliment like that she expected Dawson to treat her bottom to a massage, but instead she felt a sharp smack on her right cheek, followed by another on the left. A minute ago she hadn't thought her panties provided much protection, but now she realized how wrong she'd been. Getting spanked on the bare ass stung a whole heck of a lot more. And as crazy as it seemed, she loved every minute of it. She liked it even more when Dawson changed things up and gave her cheeks a firm squeeze after each smack. Then he did something that completely wowed her. He stopped spanking her to press his lips to her freshly spanked ass.

His mouth felt cool on her red-hot flesh and Kate caught her breath as the stubble on his jaw rubbed against her sensitive skin. She'd never had a man put his mouth there before, but as Dawson kissed and nibbled his way from one cheek to the other, she decided it felt so exquisite she might have to ask him to do it several more times before the weekend was over.

Still kissing her ass, Dawson slipped his hand between her legs and ran his finger along the folds of her pussy. Kate sighed and spread her legs further, giving him complete and total access to her womanly charms. He took advantage of that, finding her clit with his finger and making slow, languorous circles around the plump nub.

Kate moaned and rotated her hips in time with his movements, grinding against his hand as he played with her clit.

She was just starting to think she might come when Dawson stopped what he was doing. She opened her mouth to protest, but all that came out was another moan as she felt him slide his finger deep inside her pussy. Oh yeah. That worked, too.

Dawson moved his finger in and out, fucking her slowly with it as his tongue found the hollow right above her ass. Kate clenched the bed sheet in her fists, pushing back into his hand.

"Faster," she begged. "Move your finger faster."

Dawson obeyed, wiggling his finger in and out of her wetness more quickly. As good as what he was doing felt, she yearned for something else right now.

She craned her neck to give him a pleading look over her shoulder. "I need you inside me. Now!"

Desire in his eyes, Dawson slid his finger out of her pussy, then took her arm and gently pulled her to her feet. Although her ass didn't sting nearly as much as it had a few moments ago, Kate automatically reached around to cup her cheeks in her hands as she watched Dawson hurriedly unbutton his jeans and put on a condom. Much to her surprise, her bottom was still warm to the touch and she couldn't resist giving it a firm squeeze.

"Turn around and sit down on my cock," Dawson commanded softly.

As Kate turned around, her panties fluttered to the floor and she wondered if she should take off the rest of her clothes, but then decided to leave them on instead. There was something very exciting about having sex with their clothes on, like they were so hot for each other, they didn't even want to take the time to undress.

Lifting her skirt, Kate positioned herself over Dawson's shaft and slowly lowered herself onto his hard length. He grasped her hips, holding her in place while his cock pulsed inside her. She placed her hands on his muscular thighs and leaned back against his chest as he pressed a kiss to the side of her neck.

"Is this what you wanted, my cock buried deep inside you like this?" he asked, his voice deep and husky in her ear.

She closed her eyes and let out a sound that was half sigh, half moan. "God, yes!"

He kissed the side of her neck again. "Ride me."

Kate did as he told her, moving up and down on his shaft with a slow, steady rhythm that pushed him deep into her pussy each time.

160

Dawson gripped her hips, controlling her pace when she started to move faster. "Nice and slow, just like that."

Kate didn't know if it was the position or not, but every time she came down on him, his cock came into contact with her G-spot, sending little ripples of pleasure through her. Knowing the sensation would be even more intense if she came down on him harder, she began to move faster. Each time she did, her tender ass cheeks smacked against his hard thighs, making it feel like she was getting spanked all over again, which only doubled her pleasure.

Suddenly remembering Dawson had wanted her to ride him slowly, she was half afraid he might rein her in like he had before, but instead of trying to control her pace, he went with it, thrusting his hips up to meet her every time she came down on him.

Kate clutched his thighs with her hands and leaned forward, bouncing up and down on him wildly as he pumped his cock into her. Each thrust pushed her a little closer to orgasm and when she finally toppled over the edge into ecstasy, she let out one long continuous scream of pleasure that seemed to echo around the room.

Behind her, Dawson tightened his hold on her hips and pulled her back hard against him, letting out a low, hoarse groan as he found his own release.

Afterward, Dawson wrapped his arms around her, holding her against his chest. "You're amazing, you know that?"

She smiled and wrapped her arms around his as he hugged her close. "You're pretty amazing yourself."

As she leaned back into him, Kate realized she wasn't just talking about the sex, either, though that was certainly off the charts. She'd never felt so comfortable so quickly or clicked so completely with a man in her life. While part of her thought that was wonderful, another part wondered why it was happening with a guy she'd already decided she was only going to hook up with for the weekend.

Chapter Three

ॐ

Kate and Dawson spent the rest of the day in bed, which was something she'd never done with any of the other men she dated. She just never had the desire to laze around in bed after having sex with any of them. Then again, the sex had never been as good with them, either.

Not that she and Dawson had sex the whole time, of course. They also spent a good portion of the day simply lying in each other's arms talking about everyday ordinary stuff like family and work and what they both liked to do in their free time. Like her, Dawson was a Seattle native, but whereas she was an only child, he had an older brother to get into trouble with, and she laughed as he told her one funny story after another about the mischief the two of them had gotten into growing up. While she didn't think tales of her own childhood were nearly as amusing, she still managed to entertain him with stories about all the things she and her friends had done. All the while they were laughing, Kate had to swear him to secrecy. She didn't want the other women to know she'd broken the sacred girl-code by revealing all the embarrassing stuff they'd done. If she'd stopped to think about it, Kate might have censored what she said a little bit more, but Dawson was so easy to talk to that she found herself sharing things with him she'd never told another guy.

In fact, she and Dawson talked so much while they were lying there in bed that Kate didn't think they could possibly come up with anything more to talk about over dinner. When they went out to the balcony later that night after room service came, however, she discovered she was wrong. As the conversation continued to flow without any of those uncomfortable silences, she realized how much she and

Dawson had in common. They liked the same kind of movies, they listened to the same music, they even liked to hang out at a lot of the same clubs in Seattle.

Without even meaning to, she found herself mentally running through her checklist as they ate and putting a check mark beside each thing she came to. She was more than halfway through the list when she abruptly remembered she wasn't supposed to be sizing up Dawson as a potential husband. This thing with him was a weekend fling and at the end of it, they would go their separate ways. They had both agreed to it. That was getting more and more difficult to remember, though, especially when he was shaping up to be the most perfect guy she'd ever met.

Kate took a sip of wine, eyeing him over the rim of the glass as he casually leaned back in his chair. Even if she wanted to explore their relationship further, she couldn't. She was the one who had made the rules about this being a no-strings-attached affair. Heck, she'd practically spelled it out in big, block letters for him. She couldn't simply change her mind in the middle of things, no matter how much she might want to. Dawson would think she was a complete nutcase. She was just going to have to settle for enjoying their little fling while it lasted.

Afraid Dawson would notice she'd suddenly zoned out, Kate forced herself to stop being introspective and focus on what he was saying. He was talking about the latest summer blockbuster, which he'd recently seen and liked.

Kate groaned at the name. So much for liking the same movies. "Oh God, I hated that movie."

Dawson looked at her incredulously. "You're kidding. It's one of the best action movies of all time."

She laughed. "I should have known you'd like all that stuff blowing up."

He chuckled. "I'm a guy. It's in my DNA."

She shook her head. *Men.* As long as a movie had special effects and things exploding, they didn't need something as unimportant as a storyline getting in the way.

Taking another sip of wine, she leaned back in her chair. He did the same, stretching his legs out in front of him. Even though he was wearing pajama bottoms, she could still see the outline of his muscles. God, he had great legs. Unable to help herself, she slowly ran her bare foot up his leg, following the muscular curve of his calf underneath the material. As she did so, the complimentary hotel robe she had on parted slightly to reveal even more of her leg and she felt heat pool between her thighs as his predatory gaze slowly ran up and down her silky skin.

"Maybe we should go inside and finish our wine in front of the fireplace," he suggested.

Her lips curved. "You must have read my mind."

Picking up his glass, Dawson got to his feet and opened the sliding glass door for her. Kate stepped inside and walked across the room to sink down on the faux bear skin rug in front of the fireplace. Since it was a gas-burning one, all Dawson had to do was turn it on before joining her on the floor. He set his glass down, then leaned close to gently kiss her on the mouth.

Kate closed her eyes and parted her lips, her tongue meeting his halfway and tangling with it eagerly. He tasted like the wine they'd had with dinner, but was more potent and intoxicating than any drink could ever be, and she willingly surrendered to him, tilting her head back so that he could plunder her mouth more completely.

She ran her hands up his bare chest and over his shoulders, sighing in appreciation as the muscles flexed and bunched beneath her fingers. She absently wondered how many times a week he had to work out to look like he did. At least twice, maybe more, she surmised, letting out a little moan as she pictured his gorgeous body all slick with sweat after a hard workout.

But then all thought fled her mind as Dawson reached down to untie the sash on her robe. When it fell open, he pushed it off her shoulders and cupped her naked breast, his thumb and forefinger finding her nipple and giving it a firm little squeeze. Kate gasped as he dragged his mouth away from hers to kiss his way along the curve of her jaw and down her neck.

She arched her back, offering her breasts to him. But instead of moving his mouth lower, he lifted his head to gaze down at her. His eyes were molten gold in the firelight and she caught her breath at the heat she saw in their depths. She'd never had a man look at her with such desire before. She was so mesmerized she didn't even realize he'd moved his hands until she felt him slide the belt of her robe from the loops.

She stared at it in confusion. "What are you doing?"

He didn't answer, but instead put her hands together and wrapped the sash around her wrists.

Kate's eyes went wide as realization dawned on her. "Oh," she murmured, watching in fascination as he looped the belt around her wrists again, then expertly tied a knot. That answered the question as to whether he was a boy scout or not. Then again, maybe not. She was pretty sure they didn't teach Bondage 101 in the boy scouts. She stifled a little giggle at the thought.

Dawson lifted his head and gazed into her eyes for a moment before swooping down to cover her mouth with his again. This time, he wrapped his arm around her and urged her back onto the fur rug. When she was completely lying down, he took her bound wrists and gently placed them above her head, then leaned close and put his mouth to her ear.

"I'm going to kiss every inch of your beautiful body and while I do, you're going to keep your hands right where they are," he said softly. "Is that understood?"

She shivered at the command in his deep voice. "Yes," she whispered.

He pressed his lips to the hollow behind her ear. "Good. Because if you don't, then I'll stop what I'm doing, even if I'm in the middle of licking your sweet pussy. You wouldn't want that, would you?"

Kate moaned in reply, instinctively squeezing her thighs together and squirming beneath him. She'd never let a guy tie her up and have his way with her before, but the idea of playing the submissive and Dawson being completely and totally in charge turned her on like crazy.

Shifting above her, Dawson began to slowly trail a path of warm kisses down the curve of her arm. While she was careful to keep her arms where they were, Kate couldn't help but wiggle against her bonds a little, just to see how secure they were. Although they weren't tight, they weren't loose enough for her to free her hands, either. That realization got her even more hot and bothered and she found herself almost wishing Dawson would forego his exploration of her body and just go straight for her pussy instead. As he paused to lick and nibble on the inside of her elbow, however, she had to admit that getting him there was going to be half the fun.

She giggled as his lips brushed the inside of her arm, unable to help herself.

He lifted his head to look at her. "Does that tickle?"

"A little," she admitted.

"Really? Makes me wonder where else you're ticklish."

Giving her a wolfish grin, he lowered his head to continue kissing his way down her arm. Kate turned her head to the side, hoping he would stop to nibble her neck a little. He did, much to her delight.

Kate sighed and tilted her head back as he placed a series of light, little kisses along the curve her jaw. She parted her lips in anticipation, but instead of covering her mouth with his, Dawson teased her lips with featherlight kisses that made her tingle all over. She moaned and squirmed beneath him, wanting to grab a handful of hair and pull him down for a real kiss, but afraid if she disobeyed his command and moved, he would make good on his words and stop what he was doing altogether. She definitely didn't want that.

So she forced herself to be good and stay where she was. Which really wasn't all that difficult because despite her desire to grab him and kiss him, she rather liked his teasing. But she could only be patient for so long.

"Kiss me," she begged as he lightly traced her lips with his again. "Please."

He chuckled, capturing her lips and ravishing her mouth thoroughly and completely.

As she kissed him back, Kate once again had to fight the urge to hold him there. But she knew the penalty if she did, and so she lay there obediently when Dawson dragged his mouth away from hers a few moments later to slowly kiss his way down her neck so he could focus his attention on her breasts.

Cupping them gently in his hands, he took one nipple between his thumb and forefinger, then bent his head to close his mouth over the other. Kate gasped as he suckled on the pebbled tip. Her nipples were always sensitive, but there was something about being tied up that made the sensation seem more intense and arousing. Maybe it was the feeling that Dawson could do anything he wanted to her and she'd be powerless to stop him. That was an illusion, of course. She knew Dawson would never do anything she didn't want him to do. It was just part of the fantasy, and she definitely got off on it.

Dawson swirled his tongue round and round her nipple with a kind of methodical slowness that left Kate panting for breath. Although she thought she might actually go insane from such exquisite torture, that didn't stop her from opening her mouth to protest when he lifted his head. Realizing it was only so he could do the same to the other nipple, she let out a little sigh of contentment instead. God, he had a talented mouth.

When Dawson released that nipple several long, delicious moments later, she thought he might go back and treat the first one to a repeat performance, but he slowly kissed his way down her stomach. Any complaint she might have had disappeared as soon as she figured out where he was heading. As much as she adored having her breasts touched, she loved having her pussy licked even more.

Rather than head straight there, though, Dawson stopped on the way to make teasing little circles around her bellybutton with his tongue before dipping it inside the little indentation. Kate caught her breath at the sensation. She'd never had a guy pay any attention to that part of her anatomy before and she was surprised at how sexy it was. In fact, she liked it so much she almost protested when he stopped and moved lower. Between her legs, her pussy tingled in anticipation and she quickly forgot about her bellybutton.

Instead of licking her pussy right away like she thought he would, however, he kissed his way down her leg. Damn, he was good at this teasing stuff. His hair tickled her skin, making her shiver, and she wiggled a little on the fur rug as much from that as from frustration. While what he was doing was extremely pleasurable, it was also complete torture, and she had to stifle a moan.

When Dawson got to her feet, he leaned back on his heels and gazed down at her. "You look sexy as hell, do you know that?"

Although she knew it was silly to feel shy at the words, especially after all the sex they'd had, Kate felt herself blush anyway. Maybe it was the blatant desire in his eyes that made her face suffuse with color. Or maybe it was the fact that she was submissively lying there with her hands bound, completely exposed to his hungry gaze. The image of what she must look like naked on the fur rug in front of the fireplace suddenly made her tremble.

But while being naked and on display for Dawson was a total turn-on, Kate was impatient for him to hurry up and go down on her. She was about to tell him as much when he bent and slowly began kissing his way up her other leg. She stifled a groaned. He was determined to tease her until she went completely mad, wasn't he? By the time he reached her inner thigh, she was sure she was going to scream in frustration if he didn't put his mouth where she so urgently needed it.

"Stop teasing me and lick my pussy," she demanded.

Dawson lifted his head to look at her, his eyes teasing. "You do like to be in charge, don't you? Maybe I should remember to gag you the next time I tie you up."

Kate flushed, torn between the way her pulse was racing at the idea of being not only bound for his pleasure but gagged as well, and the notion he was already planning on tying her up again.

Bending his head, Dawson pressed one more gentle kiss to the inside of her thigh, then cupped her ass in his hands and ran his tongue up the slick folds of her pussy. Kate moaned and strained at the fabric holding her captive. The urge to grab his head and put his tongue exactly where she wanted it was almost too much to take. And yet knowing she couldn't made what he was doing even that much better.

Dawson must have sensed her need because a moment later she felt his tongue on her clit. He flicked the sensitive nub with quick, light caresses before making lazy, little circles round and around it.

"God, you taste so good," he rasped, swiping her pussy with his tongue before focusing his attention on her clit again.

Kate arched against him with a moan, balling her hands into fists above her head. "Oh yeah, just like that," she breathed. "Don't stop!"

He tightened his grip on her ass cheeks and began to lick more deliberately, his tongue firm and insistent on her clit. The sensation was so intense that Kate wanted to scream, but her cries were trapped in her throat as she felt her orgasm beginning to build. He had teased her for so long that she was about to explode already. The sensation started right at her clit, then gradually spread through her entire body until she was trembling all over.

She writhed beneath him, moving her head from side to side and struggling at the bonds that held her prisoner as she screamed in ecstasy as he continued to lap at her clit. Then all at once, the pleasure got to be too much and now more than before, she wanted her hands free so that she could pull Dawson's mouth away. But held captive by his command not to move, she was powerless to do anything except ride out the waves of her climax as one orgasm after another coursed through her body.

Dawson didn't stop licking her until he had wrung every ounce of pleasure from her and when he was done, all Kate could do was lie there and try to catch her breath. She wasn't sure he could top the cunnilingus he'd given her that morning, but the pussy licking he'd just given her had to be the best oral sex she'd ever had in her life. He may well have ruined her for any other man she was ever going to be with.

Pressing his lips to her inner thigh, Dawson sat back on his heels with a lazy grin and held out his hand. Kate placed her bound hands in his and let him pull her into a sitting position, moaning with pleasure as he covered her mouth with his in a possessive kiss.

When he pulled away a few moments later to untie her hands, she let out a little sigh of longing as she watched the ends of the belt slip from her wrists.

"You didn't have to untie me so soon, you know," she said softly. "I liked being your captive."

He lifted a brow, his eyes glinting in the firelight as he regarded her. "Is that so?"

She nodded.

His mouth curved into a slow smile. "Then maybe I should tie you up again."

She returned his smile with a sexy one of her own. "Maybe you should."

"Turn around and put your hands behind your back," he ordered softly.

Pulse racing, Kate got to her knees and turned away from him, obediently putting her hands behind her back and crossing them at the wrists. A moment later, she felt Dawson wrap the belt around her wrists and pull it snug, then tie it in a knot. When he was done, he came around to stand in front of her.

Kate looked up at him, waiting breathlessly for him to say something, but he didn't speak. Instead, he just held her gaze with his and shoved down his pajama bottoms until he was standing before her gloriously naked, his cock hard, the head glistening with precum. In the glow of the flames, he looked like some conquering warrior about to ravish his captive slave. She'd thought lying on the rug with her hands tied above her head had been hot, but it paled in comparison to being on her knees in front of him with her hands bound behind her back.

Holding on to the base of his shaft with one hand, Dawson slid the other in her long hair and gently tilted her head back so that he could rub the head of his cock against her parted lips. That little taste wasn't nearly enough and she opened her mouth wider, silently begging him to let her have more. But he just continued to run the tip of his shaft back and forth over her lips, teasing her as effectively as he had when she was lying on the rug and he'd been exploring her body with his mouth.

To her relief, Dawson took pity on her and allowed her to wrap her lips around the head of his cock. She eagerly tried to take more of him in her mouth, but his hand tightened in her hair, keeping her where she was. Deciding two could play at this game, she swirled her tongue over the tip, then glided it up and down the sensitive skin on the underside of his shaft. He only let her tease him like that for a few moments, however, before finally giving in and letting her take more of him in her mouth.

Kate moaned in appreciation, sucking on him greedily as he guided her head up and down on his hard length. She was used to controlling the pace when she gave a guy a blowjob, but she couldn't do that with her hands tied behind her back, which was a huge turn-on. She had no idea she'd like being so submissive.

Each time he fucked her mouth, he went a little farther until he was deep in her throat. When she felt the head of his cock slide down the back of her throat, she swallowed, taking him even deeper. Above her Dawson groaned.

Sliding his cock out of her mouth, he stood gazing down at her, his eyes smoldering and hungry.

"Do you have any idea what you do to me?" he asked hoarsely.

She studied his glistening shaft for a moment before giving him a sultry smile. "I can guess."

Kate waited for him to slide his cock in her mouth again so she could make him come, but he surprised her by wrapping his hands around her arms and gently pulling her to her feet. She opened her mouth to ask what he was doing, but the words were muffled as his came down possessively on hers. His erection was hot and hard where it pressed against her tummy and she moaned into his mouth as her pussy throbbed between her legs. She needed him inside her. Now!

Dawson must have felt the same sense of urgency because a moment later, he dragged his mouth away from hers. She barely had time to catch her breath before he spun her around and gently pushed her face down on the bed. Kate's breath hitched. She'd had sex doggy-style before, but she had a feeling the position was going to be even hotter with her hands tied behind her back.

"Spread your legs for me," Dawson commanded softly.

Kate obeyed, going up on tiptoe as she did so. Behind her, Dawson grasped her hips in his hands and positioned his cock at the opening of her pussy. She waited breathlessly for him to enter her, but instead he ran the head up and down her wetness.

She moaned, though whether in pleasure or protest, she wasn't sure. Maybe it was a little of both. While she loved what he was doing, she desperately needed to have that big, thick cock of his inside her. When he finally did stop teasing her and slid into her pussy, she cried out in relief.

Dawson didn't thrust right away, but stood unmoving, his cock nestled deep. She could feel him pulsing inside her, like a beast waiting to be unleashed, and she gasped when he slowly began to pump in and out.

Wanting him to move faster, Kate tried to rock back against him, but with her hands bound behind her back, she couldn't get enough leverage and so she was forced to let him control the pace. The reminder that he was in charge and she was his willing submissive was enough to drive her completely wild, and she moaned into the bedding as he moved inside her.

Kate wasn't sure how it could get any better, but then Dawson lifted his hand and gave her a hard smack on the ass that made her gasp. She tensed, waiting for him to spank her again, and when he didn't, she lifted her head to give him a pout over her shoulder.

"You didn't have to stop," she said.

His mouth quirked. "So, you liked being tied up and spanked, huh? You're more of a bad girl than I thought."

Despite all the kinky stuff they're already done that night, Kate still blushed, and she quickly turned back around before Dawson could see the color suffusing her face. As his hand came down on first one ass cheek, then the other as he continued his slow thrusts, she forgot all about being shy, however, and gave herself over to the pleasurable sensations.

"Harder," she begged.

"Spank you harder?" he asked, is voice deep and husky. "Or fuck you harder?"

"Both," she moaned.

Dawson did as she asked, pumping his cock into her forcefully each time his hand connected with her already stinging ass.

"Oh yeah," she breathed. "Don't stop! Don't stop!"

Dawson definitely didn't stop. He kept spanking her and fucking her harder and harder until she thought they might actually move the bed across the floor. Damn, she'd never been fucked this good in her life.

All at once, Dawson stopped spanking her to grip her hips in both hands. Kate was too close to orgasm to complain, though, especially since he started thrusting into her even harder. That was enough to send her into orbit and she cried out in ecstasy as her pussy spasmed around his cock. Being tied up like she was made her orgasm seem even stronger. Behind her, she heard Dawson let out a hoarse groan and knew he was coming with her.

Kate could have stayed bent over the bed with Dawson inside her all night long, which was why she let out a little sound of protest when he finally pulled out of her. A moment later, she felt him untie her hands and gently pull her to her feet. Taking her in his arms, he kissed her long and hard on the mouth.

When he lifted his head to gaze down at her, his eyes were twinkling. "Was that good?"

She smiled up at him. "Babe, we left good behind a long time ago. That was on a whole 'nother level of pleasure that Webster's would have a hard time describing."

He chuckled. "Let's see if we can do even better this time."

Without another word, he swung her up in his arms and set her down on the bed, then joined her.

Chapter Four

ɞ

The next morning, Dawson would rather have stayed in bed with Kate all day, preferably exploring her love of bondage a little bit more. But since they hadn't had breakfast with everyone else the day before, they both reluctantly decided they should join the rest of the wedding party down in the hotel restaurant. They didn't want the bride and groom thinking they were completely blowing off the wedding festivities.

"Any idea what's on the agenda today?" he asked as he pushed in her chair when they got to the restaurant.

She glanced at him as he sat down beside her. "A digital camera scavenger hunt, I think."

Dawson groaned inwardly. He'd forgotten about that. Running around San Juan Island with a digital camera trying to find a tree with a yellow bird in it wasn't exactly his idea of fun, but if he was partnered up with Kate again, then he was all for it. As the bride's mother went over the rigid list of rules while they were finishing breakfast a little while later, however, he was beginning to rethink that idea. Not only did the woman act like a drill sergeant, but from the way she was talking, it sounded like they weren't going to get finished with the game for hours. One glance at Kate told him she was thinking the same thing.

He leaned over to put his mouth close to her ear. "What do you say we blow off the scavenger hunt and do some sightseeing instead?"

She smiled. "Sounds like a plan. Just don't make it obvious."

Thinking that was probably wise, Dawson decided it was easier to take the neatly typed list of unusual items they were supposed to hunt for when Rachel's mother handed it to him. If anyone asked afterward, he and Kate could explain they hadn't managed to find even one item on the list. Once they got outside, everyone was in such a hurry to go their separate ways, it was easy for him and Kate to go off and do their own thing.

Since the hotel was within walking distance of the harbor, they didn't bother grabbing Dawson's SUV, but instead followed the historical walking-tour path in that direction. They stopped in various shops along the way, as well as a few art galleries Kate dragged him into. Although he wasn't really much for artsy stuff, he had to admit he enjoyed watching Kate "oooh" and "ahhh" over the work done by the local artists. Her exuberance for the simple pastime was infectious. As she leaned close to get a better look at an Inuit-inspired sculpture, smiling as if she'd found the next Mona Lisa, he concluded Kate was the type of person who could make doing anything fun.

Spotting a coffee shop on Cannery Landing, they decided to go inside and grab a cup before heading over to check out the shops by the waterfront. By the time they came out of the last one a few hours later, Dawson was shopped out, but was still glad he'd suggested doing the tourist thing nevertheless.

"Since we didn't go whale watching the other night, do you want to grab a picnic lunch from one of the restaurants and go up to the state park?" he asked as they walked down the steps and onto the sidewalk. "I heard the guy in the bookstore tell some tourists it's the best place to see them from land."

Kate looked both surprised and a little confused at that, and for a moment he thought she might not want to do it, but then she smiled. "I'd love to."

When they got to Lime Kiln State Park a little while later, he and Kate checked out the lighthouse first before finding a secluded spot on the cliffs where they could have lunch and see the killer whales. As they ate their turkey sandwiches and watched the graceful orcas breach and spyhop in the water below, Dawson couldn't help but think that it felt more like he and Kate were dating rather than having a weekend fling. While he knew that was a slippery slope to go down, especially since she'd made it clear she wasn't looking for a relationship, he found himself trying to figure out the best way to bring up the subject of continuing their relationship when they got back to Seattle.

"Ever been kayaking?" he asked after a moment.

She nodded. "I went a few times in college."

"Did you like it?"

She laughed. "Not at first, but once I got the hang of it, I did."

He chuckled as he imagined her doing what a lot of beginners did, which was paddle the kayak in a circle. He picked up his bottle of water and took a swallow. "It's too bad we'll be leaving in a couple days. I hear they have some great kayaking whale watching tours. It would have been fun go."

Dawson tried to make his voice as casual as possible, hoping Kate would give him the opening he was looking for by suggesting they should come back and go kayaking sometime, but instead she mumbled something that could have been agreement or not before looking away. He frowned. Well, he supposed that answered his question. Kate couldn't have made it any clearer that she wasn't interested in having anything to do with him after this weekend.

As she gazed out at the ocean, her expression was unreadable, and he hoped he hadn't made her uncomfortable. He was about to apologize when she pointed out a killer whale slapping his tail against the water below them as if he'd never even spoken.

Dawson was relieved when Kate leaned back against him after they finished their sandwiches a little while later. He was glad to see he hadn't ruined the mood. His cock, which immediately got hard as she settled herself between his spread legs, was equally grateful. It might have been nice to think about seeing her in the future, but if all he had was right now, then he wasn't going to complain.

Kate turned her head to smile up at him teasingly. "Is that a spyglass in your pocket or are you just happy to see me?"

He chuckled. "I'm definitely happy to see you. In fact, maybe you can do something about that when we get back to the hotel."

She gave him a flirtatious look. "Or I could do something about it right now."

He lifted a brow, surprised, but aroused at the same time. "Here?"

She shrugged. "Why not? There's no one around."

That was true enough. The park was practically deserted. He was about to tell Kate he was game if she was, but she had already turned around to kneel between his legs. Tugging open his belt, she slowly unbuttoned his jeans, then shoved down his boxer briefs just enough to free his hard cock. Giving him a sexy smile, she wrapped her hand around the base, then leaned forward to slowly run her tongue up the entire length before taking the head in her mouth.

Dawson groaned as her long hair fell forward to brush against his thighs. Her mouth was warm and soft as she moved up and down on him, and he groaned again as she gently cupped his balls in her other hand. Damn, she was good at giving a blowjob.

"Oh yeah, baby," he breathed. "Just like that."

Kate moaned and swirled her tongue over the tip of his shaft before going down on him again. She took him a little deeper each time until the head was finally touching the back of her throat. Then she swallowed.

Dawson sucked in a breath. *Daaaaaaammnn!* He'd never met a woman could do that.

Sure he was going to blow right then, he tightened his hand in her hair. "I'm already close."

At his words, Kate immediately moved her mouth back up his shaft to a place that kept him on edge but not in danger of exploding. She slowly bobbed her head up and down over and over, sometimes pausing to swirl her tongue over the sensitive tip, sometimes nipping a little with her teeth, sometimes deep throating him.

While Dawson liked to think he had at least a modicum of self-control, what Kate was doing felt too incredible to hold back for long and before he knew it, he was shooting a load of hot cum into her mouth. She moaned around his cock, swallowing it all, then carefully licking him clean until she was sure she got every last little bit. When she was done, she ran her tongue over her lips and smiled up at him.

"Wasn't that more fun than waiting until we got back to the hotel?" she asked as he buttoned his jeans.

He bent over to kiss her on the mouth. "Much."

Dawson would have kissed her again, but the sound of footsteps on the gravel path caught his attention. Brow furrowing, he turned his head to see a park ranger coming toward them. Shit. He hoped the man hadn't seen anything. He didn't think the bride and groom would appreciate bailing their maid of honor and best man out of jail.

But to Dawson's relief, the ranger just gave them a nod and a smile. "Great day for whale watching. A lot of orcas out there. Did you see any of them blow?"

Kate glanced at Dawson, then smiled at the ranger. "One just blew a couple of seconds ago, actually. He was a big guy, too."

The park ranger might have thought she was talking about killer whales, but Dawson knew exactly what she was referring to and he had to stifle a laugh. Her comment got the park ranger talking, though, and he ended up spending the next half hour telling them about the pod of whales that frequented the local waters. While the information was interesting, Dawson wanted to be alone with Kate and he was glad when the other man finally left. Once he was out of earshot, Dawson and Kate burst into laughter.

"Good thing he didn't come by a few minutes earlier or I would have been right in the middle of going down on you," Kate said.

Dawson ran his hand up her bare leg, his fingers brushing the hem of her khaki shorts. "Speaking of which, I still owe you for that amazing blowjob. What do you say I return the favor when we get back to the hotel?"

She smiled. "I say that's a wonderful idea. But unfortunately it'll have to be after the rehearsal dinner."

"That's tonight?"

She nodded. "Of course it's tonight. The wedding's tomorrow, remember?"

Actually, he'd forgotten, and the reminder only made him more aware of the fact that the weekend was coming to a close. Which meant their weekend fling was coming to an end, too. That was really too bad because he was going to miss Kate Gentry. He only wished she felt the same about him.

* * * * *

By the time she and Dawson got back to the hotel, they had just enough time to shower and change before they had to meet the rest of the wedding party down on the bluff overlooking the marina for the rehearsal. To Kate's relief, no one mentioned their little disappearing act, though Rachel and the other girls gave her and Dawson knowing smiles.

Rachel wanted to make sure the wedding was absolutely perfect, so she made everyone practice over and over until she was satisfied they had it right. Which meant a lot of standing around while Rachel made up her mind. Which in turn gave Kate a lot of time to think about what Dawson said up at the state park that afternoon.

Was that whole thing about going kayaking his subtle way of telling her he wanted to continue seeing her when they got back to Seattle? Although she wanted to believe it was, she'd never known a guy to be subtle. So she had interpreted his casual comment as a gentle reminder that they had agreed to have a no-strings-attached weekend, just in case she had read more into their picnic than he had intended. She hadn't known what to say, which was why she had just muttered something noncommittal.

Of course, now that she had time to stand around and think about it, she couldn't keep from replaying their conversation over and over in her head to see if she'd gotten the message right. All that did was confuse her even more. She was almost positive he wanted everything to come to a nice, tidy finish at the end of the weekend, but a part of her wasn't sure. Then again, that part could just be wishful thinking. God, she wished she'd never put that stupid no-strings clause in her proposition that first night. If it wasn't for that, she'd probably be well on her way to planning her own wedding right now, at least mentally. As she took Dawson's arm to follow the soon-to-be bride and groom down the aisle a little while later, she let herself imagine for just a moment that she and the handsome man at her side were rehearsing for their own wedding.

"You know," he said softly, "I could be licking your pussy right now instead of walking up and down this aisle over and over. How many times is this anyway?"

Kate ignored the tingle between her thighs and forced herself to focus on the question. "I'm not quite sure. Ten, I think."

He groaned. "Well, if Rachel announces she wants to do it again, I say we make a run for it."

Kate laughed. "I think she might notice."

Luckily, though, Rachel decided they'd all practiced enough and suggested they go inside and have a drink before dinner. Everyone sighed with relief at that, including Kate. She was eager to be alone with Dawson.

"And where did you two run off to this morning?" Rachel asked, sidling up to Kate in the bar the moment Dawson went to get them something to drink.

"We went on the scavenger hunt like everyone else," Kate said.

Her friend laughed. "Sure you did."

Crap. She never was a good liar. "Okay, you caught us. Dawson and I didn't go on the scavenger hunt. We went sightseeing instead."

Rachel lifted a brow. "I'd think after two days, you'd have seen all the sights his room has to offer. Or did you spend the day in yours just for a change of scenery?"

Kate shook her head. "We didn't spend it in either. We had a picnic lunch at Lime Kiln State Park, then sat on the cliffs and did some whale watching."

"Sounds romantic, but that naughty look on your face tells me that wasn't the only thing you did up there."

"Well, no. I gave him a blowjob while we were there, too."

Rachel's eyes went wide. "You didn't! Right out in the open?"

Kate blushed and nodded. "I did! I couldn't help myself. Besides, there wasn't anyone around. Well, the park ranger came by, but I was finished by then."

"He almost caught you?" Her friend grinned. "You're crazy. I don't blame you a bit, though. Dawson's a hot guy."

Kate sighed. "And amazing in bed. Not to mention creative."

"Creative, huh?"

"Very. Though maybe kinky might be a better word."

Rachel looked even more surprised at that than she did at hearing Kate and Dawson had gotten busy at the state park. She took a step closer. "Kinky? Do tell."

Kate looked around to make sure no one was standing close enough to overhear. Even so, she lowered her voice. "Well, when we went up to his room after playing croquet yesterday, he gave me a spanking. Then last night, he tied me up."

"Damn, that is kinky." Rachel sighed. "Okay, I'm officially jealous."

Kate looked at her friend in surprise. Rachel was getting married tomorrow. What could she possibly be envious about? "Jealous? Why?"

"Because Bob and I never do anything that kinky in bed."

Kate found that hard to believe. Next to Kristen, she would have thought Rachel was the most likely to experiment with a guy in bed. "You don't?"

Rachel shook her head. "No, but that's going to change."

"Well, if it makes you feel any better, I never did anything that kinky either until I slept with Dawson," Kate said.

Rachel smiled. "I knew having a weekend fling with him would be a good idea."

At the reminder, Kate wondered if she should get Rachel's take on what Dawson had said that afternoon, but then she changed her mind. Her friend would probably only lecture her again. Besides, Dawson was coming over with their drinks.

Giving him a smile, Kate took the glass of wine he'd brought her and forced herself to stop overanalyzing things and just enjoy being with Dawson. She'd figure out what he meant later.

Although dinner with her friends was as much fun as it always was, she was impatient to be alone with Dawson again and was glad when he suggested they make their escape after dessert. Telling everyone to have a good night, they left the restaurant and took the elevator upstairs. Once in his room, he pulled her into his arms and kissed her.

"What do you say we try out the hot tub?" he asked when he lifted his head.

Kate had never made love in a hot tub before, but according to *Cosmo*, it was a totally erotic experience. Her lips curved into a smile. She was having a lot of erotic experiences with Dawson, she noticed. "I'd love to."

He grinned. "I was hoping you'd say that. Why don't you grab us some towels from the bathroom and I'll get the tub going."

It must have taken Kate longer to put her hair up and get the towels than she realized because when she came out of the bathroom, Dawson had already stripped off his clothes and was waiting for her in the hot tub, arms outstretched on either side of him.

He gave her a lazy grin. "Aren't you going to get undressed and join me?"

Kate smiled as she set the towels down. If she knew Dawson, he probably got the hot tub filled in record time just so he could sit back and watch her take her clothes off. As she reached back to undo the zipper on her dress, she remembered what a rush it had been to give him a show the other night and her pussy tingled between her legs.

If the way Dawson's gaze swept over her body as she slowly undressed was any indication, then he was just as captivated now as he'd been the first time she'd done her striptease for him. As she stepped into the hot tub and immersed herself in the warm water, Kate couldn't help feeling a little thrill of excitement at knowing she turned him on.

Dawson took her hand and tugged her close to capture her lips in a long, drugging kiss that had her melting against him. With a sigh of pleasure, she wrapped her arms around his neck. Underneath the water, his hand cupped her breast. Her nipple stiffened at his touch and she moaned against his mouth as he grasped it between his thumb and forefinger and gave it a squeeze. *Cosmo* hadn't been wrong. His touch felt completely different in the water.

Drawing her bottom lip into his mouth, he suckled on it gently before trailing kisses along the curve of her jaw. Kate arched against him, letting her head fall back as he continued kissing his way down her neck and along the curve of her shoulder. She would have liked him to continue moving down her body, though she wasn't exactly sure how he'd manage it in the hot tub without drowning. Not unless he could hold his breath for a really long time, of course. But Dawson got around that little problem. Putting his hands on her waist, he easily lifted her up and sat her on the edge of the tub. Now, why hadn't she thought of that?

Dawson must have mistaken the look of wonder on her face for one of surprise, because his mouth twitched. "I did promise to return the favor for that incredible blowjob you gave me today, remember?"

Oh yeah, she remembered. Her lips curved. "Not only do I remember, but I've been waiting impatiently for you to make good on that promise. My pussy has been wet the entire day."

"Show me," he commanded.

Considering she'd just been in the hot tub, she was obviously wet, but as she spread her legs wide, Kate felt the unmistakable creaminess of her arousal. That was the kind of wetness she was talking about.

Dawson groaned. "You are wet, aren't you?"

She grinned. "Told you I was."

Kate leaned back on her hands and propped one foot on the tile, expecting him to bend forward and dive right in, but instead he leaned back against the opposite wall of the tub and stretched his arms out on either side of him.

"Show me where you want me to lick you," he ordered softly.

She caught her lower lip between her teeth, hesitating. She'd masturbated before, of course, but never in front of a guy. However, the idea of touching herself while Dawson watched excited the hell out of her.

Keeping her gaze locked on his, Kate lifted her hand and provocatively slid her finger in and out of her mouth to get it nice and wet before slowly running it up and down the slick folds of her pussy. "I want you to lick me here."

On the other side of the hot tub, Dawson followed her movements as if mesmerized, and she felt a rush at the knowledge that she held such power over him.

She made her way down to her opening and dipped her finger inside. "And here."

Dawson inhaled sharply.

She slid her finger out and glided it along the folds until she came to her clit. Once there, she made small, lazy circles around it. "And most especially here." She gave him a slow, sexy smile. "Think you can remember all of that or should I demonstrate again?"

His mouth quirked. "I think I've got it, but why don't you do it again, just to make sure."

Kate laughingly obeyed. When she slid her finger in her mouth this time, though, it was wet with her arousal, and she let out a moan at the musky flavor. As she ran her finger up and down her slit, she wondered if getting turned on by the taste of her own juices made her extra kinky or not. As she slipped her finger deep into her pussy a moment later, she decided she didn't care if it did make her extra kinky. She liked it.

She also liked the way her finger felt inside her and couldn't resist giving it a little wiggle before pulling it out to rub her clit. The plump little flesh tingled beneath her touch, evidence of how excited she already was, and she found herself moving her finger round and round much longer than necessary for demonstration purposes.

"You're not going to make yourself come, are you?" Dawson asked.

Kate opened her eyes to find him regarding her with a teasing expression on his handsome face. She blushed, but while she slowed her movements, she didn't take her fingers away. "No, of course not."

"Good. Because as sexy as watching you touch yourself is, I've been waiting to nibble on your pussy all day."

Pushing away from the wall of the hot tub, Dawson crossed the distance between them until he was kneeling between her legs. Kate took her fingers away from her clit without protest. While touching herself always brought her to orgasm, it didn't compare to the magic Dawson could work with his tongue.

He put his hands on her thighs and gave her what could only be called a wicked grin. "Let's see if I have the sequence right."

She opened her mouth to tell him that whatever sequence he followed was fine with her, but he had already bent his head to slowly run his tongue along the folds of her pussy and all that came out was a sigh.

"You wanted me to lick you here, right?" he asked.

"Mmm," she breathed.

He moved lower to tease the opening of her pussy. "And here?"

She gasped as he plunged his tongue into her. "Oh yeah, right there."

He moved back up the folds to flick at her clit with his tongue. "And here, too, isn't that right?"

She moaned. "Most especially there."

He chuckled softly, then let out a husky groan as he buried his face between her spread thighs and began to repeat that same sequence over and over again.

He teased her so long she thought she was going to go insane. He never gave her clit more than a couple of flicks with his tongue before moving back down her folds. He probably knew how close she was and wanted to keep her on the edge.

Then just when she was about to start begging for release, he turned his attention to her most sensitive place and began to lap hungrily at her clit.

Kate threaded her fingers in his hair, wanting to make sure he wasn't going anywhere this time. But when Dawson thrust his finger deep in her pussy and began to move it in and out as he licked her, she knew he was done teasing her.

Her climax washed over her like a tidal wave, picking her up and taking her with it until she was dizzy from the ecstasy of it. When it finally subsided, she opened her eyes to find Dawson gazing up at her, a lazy grin on his face.

"Was that how you wanted me to lick your pussy?" he asked.

She leaned forward to kiss him long and hard on the mouth, her taste there arousing her all over again. "That was exactly how I wanted you to lick my pussy." She glanced down to see the head of his hard cock poking out from beneath the bubbles and she reached into the water to wrap her hand around him, her lips curving into a smile. "I see I'm not the only one who enjoyed that."

He groaned at her touch. "I need to be inside you."

"Really? I would have never guessed."

"Really."

She kissed him again. "Then you'll have to catch me first."

Before he could ask what she meant by that, Kate scooped up a towel, jumped to her feet, and ran for the bedroom. Behind her, she heard a deep chuckle followed by water sloshing in the tub as Dawson hurried after her. Giggling, she raced across the room, heedless of the mess she was making on the carpet. She'd almost reached the bed when a strong arm caught her around the waist.

"Gotcha!" Dawson growled, his soft voice sending delicious shivers coursing through her as he pulled her back against his chest.

Kate laughed. "Guess that means you get to slide that hard cock of yours inside me."

He pressed a kiss to her ear. "Guess it does."

Taking the towel from her, he slowly and methodically dried her off. Kate couldn't help but notice he paid particular attention to her breasts, pussy, and ass cheeks, none of which were all that wet to begin with. Not that she was complaining, of course.

"You have the sexiest ass I've ever seen," he said as he ran the towel over the curve of her bottom yet again.

She glanced over her shoulder at him. "Do you really think so?"

He tossed the towel on the floor and ran his hand over her derriere instead. "You sound surprised."

She shrugged. "It's just that no other guy has ever complimented my ass before."

"Then you must have gone out with some really dense guys because your ass is perfect," he said softly. "In fact, just looking at it makes want to do all kinds of naughty things."

Kate's pulse quickened as she remembered the spanking he'd given her the other night. Surely she deserved another one for making him chase her around the hotel room. "Such as?"

He put his mouth close to her ear. "Such as sliding my very hard cock right in there."

She turned in his arms to look at him in wide-eyed surprise, but when she opened her mouth to speak, nothing would come out.

He reached up to gently tuck her hair behind her ear. "Have you ever been fucked in the ass before?"

She blushed and shook her head.

He considered that for a moment. "Would you like me to slide my cock in your ass?"

Kate didn't answer right away. She'd always been curious about anal sex, but had never trusted any of the other men she went out with enough to try it. But despite just meeting Dawson a few days ago, she trusted him more than any man she'd ever been with. And after all the other things they had done in bed, she instinctively knew it would be good with him.

She wet her lips and nodded.

He cupped her face in his hand, then bent his head and kissed her tenderly on the mouth. "I'll be gentle with you, baby. I promise."

She reached up to cover his hand with hers. "I know you will be."

He kissed her again. "Get on your hands and knees on the bed."

Pulse racing, Kate did as he told her. Behind her, she heard Dawson open the drawer to the bedside table and she glanced over her shoulder to see him taking out a condom and a tube of lubricant. She expected him to put on the condom, lube up, and slide in her ass, but instead he coated his finger with the clear jelly.

Even though she knew Dawson would be gentle, she couldn't keep from tensing a little as he came up behind her. He must have sensed she was nervous because he soothingly ran his hand down her back and over the curve of her bottom. She immediately felt herself relax at his touch. It was like he knew exactly which buttons to push.

"I'm just going to tease you with my finger, sweetheart," he said softly.

Kate let out a little moan as he slipped his lubed-up finger between her cheeks and lightly massaged the opening of her ass. She'd never thought of that area as being particularly erogenous, but what he was doing felt good and she found herself arching her back to lift her ass higher in the air.

Dawson slowly pushed his finger in her hole a little bit at a time. Even though it was pleasurable, Kate still stiffened and clenched her muscles around his finger. He stopped moving immediately.

"Relax," Dawson coaxed softly.

She exhaled as she slowly unclenched her muscles. As she did so, he slid his finger in deeper, opening her wider. She automatically tightened her muscles again, but then quickly relaxed. Dawson kept his finger where it was for a moment, to let her get used to having something in her ass, she supposed, but then he gently began to move in and out of her.

Kate moaned.

"Does that feel good?" he asked.

"Very good," she breathed.

He slid his finger a little deeper. "My cock's going to feel even better."

She wasn't sure how that could be possible. His finger felt pretty damn good. If he was right, though, and his cock did feel even better, then she might just pass out from the pleasure of it.

Since Dawson had brought up the subject, she thought he would slide his finger out and replace it with his cock, but he must have decided she needed more foreplay because he continued to slowly work his finger in and out of her ass for several long delicious moments. Kate was just starting to wonder if she might actually orgasm when he slipped his finger out completely.

Kate looked over her shoulder, watching as Dawson rolled on a condom, then coated his erection with a serious amount of lube. It occurred to her then that his cock was a lot bigger than his finger, which had seemed like a very snug fit when it was in her ass.

She eyed him skeptically as he stepped up behind her. "Are you sure that's going to fit?"

He chuckled. "I'm sure. Just relax for me."

Kate wasn't convinced he'd fit regardless of how relaxed she was, but she didn't say anything. She trusted him to take things slowly, and she had to admit her pulse was racing at just the thought of what they were about to do.

Dawson cupped her ass and tenderly spread her cheeks. A moment later, Kate felt the head of his cock pressing against the tight ring of muscle back there. She instinctively held her breath, then remembered that would only make her body tighten up and forced herself to let it out. Dawson must have been waiting for her to relax because the moment she did, he slowly began to slide in.

As he entered her, her asshole stretched to accommodate him, and Kate let out a moan. While his cock definitely filled her a whole lot more than his finger had, it wasn't really uncomfortable. In fact, the feeling was more pleasurable than she'd imagined it could be. Better even than his finger. Like her whole ass was tingling from the inside out. Of course, that probably had a lot to do with how careful Dawson was being with her. Even after the head of his shaft was inside, he didn't force himself in the rest of the way, but continued to inch in deeper ever so slowly, matching his movements to her breathing. Then before she knew it, he was completely and snugly inside. Even then, he didn't thrust right away, but instead stayed nestled there.

"Does that feel okay?" he asked softly.

She let out a sigh. Okay was an understatement. She felt like she was floating. Why the heck hadn't she ever done this before? Maybe because she'd never been with a guy like Dawson. "It feels wonderful."

He pumped his hips gently. "How about if I thrust a little?"

She moaned as his shaft slowly slid in and out. "Mm-hmm."

He grasped her hips more firmly and let out a groan. "You're so tight."

She glanced at him over her shoulder. "That's a good thing, right?"

He groaned again, deeper this time. "It's a very good thing. Is this okay for you? I'm not thrusting too hard, am I?"

"It's perfect."

As Dawson continued to thrust in and out, Kate found herself automatically rocking back against his hips. The motion drove him deeper each time, sending huge shivers of pleasure rippling through her, and she clutched at the bed sheets. Though the sensations felt different than they did when he was in her pussy, they were no less intense, and as he moved a little faster inside her, she felt an increasing tingle in her ass that she knew must be the beginnings of an orgasm. Eager to see if that's what it really was, she arched her back and pushed against him as forcefully as his hands on her hips would allow. The pleasure that came with it almost took her breath away.

"You going to come for me, baby?" he asked.

"Yes," she breathed, the words caught somewhere between a sigh and a moan.

He tightened his hold on her hips and began to thrust a little harder. That was enough to send her into orbit and she threw back her head and cried out as the tingling in her ass intensified even more and she was coming over and over in an orgasm that was completely unlike anything she'd ever experienced. Behind her, Dawson pulled her back hard against him, surging his cock into her as he found his own release.

It was a long time before he slowly pulled out and when he did, all Kate could do was lie there in blissful amazement. She'd had no idea having anal sex could be so pleasurable and all she could think about was doing it with him again.

Dawson ran his hand down her back. "You okay?"

She pushed herself up to sit on her hip. "Perfect," she said, leaning forward to give him a kiss on the mouth. "That was incredible."

He reached up to gently brush her hair back from her face. "You're the one who's incredible. I'm just honored you let me initiate you in the pleasures of anal sex."

Kate didn't say anything as he climbed into bed beside her and pulled her into his arms. She couldn't imagine any other man being as careful and considerate as Dawson was. He'd been as sweet and gentle as any woman could ever desire. Just one more thing about him that was perfect.

As she snuggled close to him, Kate couldn't imagine sex with another man was ever going to be as good as it was with Dawson.

Chapter Five

❧

Dawson watched from beneath half-closed eyes as Kate got dressed the next morning. "Sure I can't persuade you to stay in bed?"

"I wish," she groaned, slipping her feet into her shoes. "But we've already skipped out on almost all the other organized events. As maid of honor, I really need to go spend some quality girl time with the bride."

He sighed. "I suppose I see your point. What are you girls doing anyway?"

Kate sat down on the edge of the bed and gave him a smile. "Going to the hotel spa so we can get beautiful for the wedding."

He reached out to curl the end of her long, silky hair around his finger. "Waste of money. You're already beautiful."

Her cheeks colored at the compliment. "You always say the sweetest things."

"It's easy when they're true."

She blushed even deeper at that. "So, what are you going to do today?"

He shrugged. "I don't know. Maybe go down to the gym and get in a run. But more likely, I'll lie in bed and watch ESPN all day." He grinned. "You're welcome to come back and join me after you're done getting pampered, if you want."

"Tempting as that is, I'd better not. If I did, we'd end up having mad, passionate sex instead of watching television and I'd show up at the wedding looking like I just rolled out of bed."

He chuckled and pulled her down for a kiss. "I think you look sexy like that."

She laughed. "Yeah, well, I don't think Rachel would agree. But once my maid of honor duties are done, I'm all yours."

"All mine." He reached up to brush her hair back from her face. "Mmm, I like the sound of that."

Something flickered in Kate's eyes and for a moment, Dawson thought she looked almost sad, but it was gone before he could be sure.

"Me too," she said softly, then leaned close to touch her lips to his. "I'll see you at the wedding."

As Kate moved to go, Dawson had to resist the urge to pull her into his arms and keep her there. It was silly and stupid and completely out of character for him, but it was the only thing he could think to do. He was falling for Kate in a big way and he didn't want to lose her.

He flopped back on the pillow and stared up at the ceiling. It was almost laughable, really. He'd gone out with plenty of women who were willing to get married, but he hadn't been able to see himself settling down with any of them. Now he'd finally met someone he could envision spending the rest of his life with and she wasn't interested in a long-term relationship. At least not with him.

Dawson groaned. Shit, he sounded like a chick.

Kate was the one who made the rules that first night about them going their separate ways after the weekend was over and she hadn't done anything to make him think she felt differently now. She wasn't interested in him for anything other than sex. He should just be satisfied they had a wonderful weekend together and leave it at that. Thanks for the memories, and all that.

Swearing under his breath, he grabbed the remote from the nightstand and switched on the television. He and Kate still had one more night together. He'd be damned if he let anything spoil it.

* * * * *

"Earth to Kate."

Kate shook herself from her musings to look at Rachel. She and the other girl were getting a French manicure in one room of the hotel's luxurious spa while the bridesmaids were in another getting their hair styled in a fancy updo. They would flip-flop after everyone was finished, then all get their makeup done together. If Kate weren't so preoccupied, it would have been the perfect way to while away the hours before her best friend's wedding. But getting all pampered for the big event only reminded her she only had one more night with Dawson. The thought made her want to curl up in a ball and cry. Kate didn't want Rachel to know how miserable she was, though, so she forced herself to give the other girl a smile.

"Sorry. I must have zoned out."

"Zoned out? Honey, you were on another planet." Rachel regarded her thoughtfully. "Is everything okay? Did something happen with Dawson? Did you two have a fight or something?"

Kate shook her head. "No, no. Everything with Dawson is fine."

"Then why do you look like you're about to cry?"

Kate swallowed hard. She never was very good at hiding her emotions, especially from her best friend. This was Rachel's big day and Kate knew it wasn't right to burden the other girl with her problems, but she really needed to talk to someone. She glanced at the red-haired girl doing her nails, wondering if she should ask her to leave so she and Rachel could have some privacy, but then realized whatever they said, it probably wouldn't be anything the manicurist hadn't heard before.

Kate looked at her friend. "I never should have slept with Dawson."

Rachel frowned. "What? Why not? You said the sex was amazing."

"It is amazing. It's better than amazing. It's just that..."

"It's just what?" her friend prompted when her voice trailed off.

Kate caught her lower lip between her teeth and chewed on it for a moment before finally answering. "I think I'm falling in love with him."

She braced herself for the lecture she knew was coming, but instead Rachel's eyes lit up. "Oh my God, that's wonderful!"

"No it isn't."

"What are you talking about? Why wouldn't it be wonderful?"

Kate groaned. "Because I made it clear to Dawson the first night that I wanted this to be a weekend fling, no strings attached."

Rachel shrugged. "So, tell him you changed your mind. It's a woman's prerogative, after all."

Kate stared at her friend incredulously. "Wait a minute. You were the one who told me I shouldn't think of Dawson as anything more than a walking, talking sex toy."

Throughout their conversation, the manicurist had been doing her best to look like she wasn't listening, but at that, the redhead lifted her head to look at Rachel in astonishment. Kate was surprised to see her friend blush.

"Okay, that was totally out of context," Rachel explained to the girl before turning her attention to Kate again. "And it was before you fell in love with him anyway, so what I said then doesn't apply now."

Kate shook her head at the other girl's logic. "It doesn't change anything. I can't tell Dawson how I feel, not after I told him I wasn't interested in anything more than sex."

He would just think she was changing the rules and she knew from experience that men hated when a woman changed the rules.

"Sure you can," Rachel insisted. "It's a well-known fact that men are very open to the idea of turning a hookup into a relationship."

Kate gave her a skeptical look. "It is?"

"Yes. I read about it in *Cosmo*."

The manicurist nodded. "I read that, too. It makes complete sense to me."

God, they both made it sound so easy. "Rachel, I don't even know if he feels the same way."

The other girl smiled. "I've seen the way Dawson looks at you, honey. He's definitely into you. Trust me."

Kate wanted to point out that just because Dawson had been "into her" several different ways already this weekend, it didn't mean he wanted to take their relationship to the next level. He might not be interested in her for anything other than sex. If she said something, she'd end up looking like a desperate fool when just a few days ago she'd been a modern liberated woman. On the other hand, if Rachel was right and she walked away from Dawson, she knew she would end up regretting it for the rest of her life.

She looked at her friend. "Do you really think I should tell him?"

"Yes!" both Rachel and the manicurist said in unison.

Kate couldn't help but smile as she looked from one girl to the other. "Okay, I'm outnumbered, I guess."

"So, that means you'll tell him?" Rachel asked.

She nodded. "I'll tell him. I don't know how, but I'll tell him."

Kate wanted to run up to Dawson's room right then and tell him how she felt, but she knew if she did, they'd never make it to the wedding. So she forced herself to stay where she was and let the spa staff pamper her along with the other girls, something that was much more enjoyable now that she was no longer depressed. As a result, the rest of the day seemed to fly by and before Kate knew it, they were all making their way outside to the bluff where the ceremony was being held.

Since she was standing behind the other bridesmaids, Kate couldn't see Dawson from where her vantage point and she ran her hand down the front of her peach colored gown nervously.

"You look beautiful," Rachel said in her ear.

Kate turned to give her friend a smile. "Shouldn't I be the one telling you that?"

"You told me upstairs, remember?" Rachel wrapped her arms around her in a warm hug, then pulled back to give her a grin. "Dawson won't be able to take his eyes off you."

Kate hoped so. She smoothed her gown again, then realizing the hand holding the bouquet was trembling, she steadied it with the other. Sheesh, she was so nervous, she felt like she was the one getting married. Her pulse skipped a beat at the thought.

As Kate followed the other bridesmaids up the aisle a few minutes later, her gaze automatically went to Dawson, who was standing with the other men up front near the beautifully decorated gazebo where Rachel and Bob would say their vows. She caught her breath at the sight of him. Good heavens, she'd never seen a man look more handsome in a tuxedo in her life. But Dawson was so gorgeous she almost stopped right where she was just so she could gaze at him. Then he gave her that devastating grin of his and she practically melted on the spot.

Abruptly realizing she actually had stopped, Kate blushed and forced herself to continue up the aisle and take her place with the rest of the bridesmaids at the front. As she turned to watch Rachel's father escort her up the aisle, Kate couldn't help but notice that Dawson hadn't taken his eyes off her. Kate barely registered when Rachel held out the bouquet for her to hold. Hoping none of the guests had seen, Kate blushed and quickly took the flowers before turning to watch her friend step into the gazebo with her soon-to-be husband.

Kate tried her best to focus on the ceremony, but her gaze kept straying to Dawson. Each time it did, she found him looking her way, so it wasn't surprising when the priest had to ask him twice for the rings. As he hastily dug in his pocket for them, Kate saw Rachel give her a knowing smile from the steps of the gazebo.

Fortunately, she and Dawson didn't have to do anything else but stand there for the rest of the ceremony. When Rachel and Bob descended the steps of the gazebo after it was over, Kate surprised herself by actually remembering to give the other girl her bouquet of flowers. As soon as the couple started down the aisle, Dawson offered Kate his arm and they followed.

Thankfully, Rachel and Bob had to stand in the receiving line when they got to the back of the bluff, which gave Kate a few moments alone with Dawson before they had to pose for pictures.

He reached up to gently finger a tendril of hair that had been artfully left loose from the updo to frame her face. "You're enough to take my breath away."

The compliment warmed her all the way to the tips of her French-manicured toes. "Thank you," she said softly. "You look pretty breathtaking yourself in that tux."

His mouth quirked. "It's uncomfortable as hell to wear, but I'm glad you like it."

She laughed. "I most definitely like it."

Dawson glanced around, then lowered his voice. "You have no idea how much I want to kiss you right now."

"So, what's stopping you?" she teased.

Chuckling, Dawson bent his head to kiss her, but just as his lips were about to touch hers, the wedding photographer loudly announced he needed the bridal party to gather together so he could take pictures. Dawson groaned and lifted his head.

"Think they'd notice if we slipped upstairs for a quickie?" he asked.

"I think they might," Kate laughed. "Since it would probably take me an hour to get out of this dress."

He sighed. "I don't know why you'd have to take the dress off for a quickie, but I suppose you're right. Okay, pictures it is then. But I'm going to thoroughly ravish you after the reception."

Kate smiled up at him. "I can't wait."

While Kate wouldn't have minded going up to his room for that quickie Dawson suggested, posing for pictures along with the rest of the wedding party was rather fun, especially since she and Dawson were together in almost all of them. When they were done with the photos, they all went into the ballroom, where the bride and groom made their big entrance to a round of applause from their guests.

Although the chicken cordon bleu Rachel and Bob had decided on for dinner looked delicious, Kate was too busy having a good time with Dawson to pay much attention to what they were eating. She hadn't even realized it was possible to fall for a guy as quickly as she'd fallen for Dawson, but as she listened to him give the toast, she realized he was the man she'd been searching for her whole life and this time, she hadn't even been looking. Maybe that was why she'd found him.

Kate was still marveling at that as she and Dawson walked out to join the rest of the bridal party in the traditional first dance a little while later. As he took her in his arms and pulled her close, she discovered he was as talented on the dance floor as he was in the bedroom. But then she'd always thought dancing was a little like making love. All those rhythmic motions were quite erotic. And feeling his body move against hers as they danced was one very erotic experience.

She would have been content to stay on the dance floor for the rest of the night, or at least until they went up to Dawson's room, but a little while later, the DJ announced it was time for the bride and groom to cut the cake. As they sat down along with everyone else, Kate eagerly reached for her water glass and took a sip.

"I'm glad we decided to hook up for the weekend," Dawson said as he reached for his own glass and took a long swallow of water. "It was a good idea."

Something about the offhand way he said the words made Kate's heart suddenly squeeze in her chest. Was this his subtle way of reminding her that he was only in this for some casual sex? Had he somehow figured out she'd started having feelings for him and wanted more than a simple weekend fling? Her hand began to tremble and she quickly set the glass down on the table.

She forced herself to smile. "Yeah. Me, too."

Kate supposed she should have said more, but right then, she couldn't trust herself to speak. She wasn't even sure she could breathe. Tonight was it. This thing with him was really going to end. But how could she spend the night making love to Dawson now when all she wanted to do was go up to her room and cry her eyes out? At the same time, how could she not? It was her last chance to be with him. There would be time enough for tears on the ferry ride home tomorrow. Tonight at least, she was going to enjoy herself.

But that was easier said than done. Fortunately, Dawson didn't seem to pick up on how quiet she'd gotten and Rachel was too busy being the blushing bride to notice. Or so Kate thought. Unfortunately, the other girl was still observant enough to realize Kate hadn't gathered around with the rest of the single women when it was time to catch the bouquet.

"Kate!" she called. "Where are you, girl? Get over here!"

Kate groaned inwardly. Damn. She'd forgotten all about catching the bouquet. Considering the man she was in love with wanted nothing to do with her after their little weekend fling was over, she wasn't really in the mood to take part in the silly tradition. But now that Rachel had singled her out, there was no way she could get out of it. Not that it mattered, she supposed. She never caught the stupid thing anyway.

She got to her feet. "I'm coming, I'm coming!"

As Kate made her way to the center of the dance floor to join the other single women, the other bridesmaids clapped and cheered, as did the rest of the guests.

At all her other friends' weddings, Kate always made sure she was front and center for the bouquet toss, desperate to get her hands on the darn thing, but this time, she purposely positioned herself at the back of the group, figuring there was less chance of catching it there. However, when Rachel threw the bouquet over her shoulder, it sailed over all the other women to land right in her hands like it was guided by GPS. How was that for ironic?

Around her, everyone clapped and cheered again, more loudly this time. Though her heart really wasn't in it, she picked up her gown and gave the room a small smile and a curtsy all the same. As she straightened up, Rachel hurried over to wrap her in a big hug.

"Congratulations, future Mrs. McKenna," her friend whispered in her ear.

Tears stung Kate's eyes and she quickly blinked them back, not wanting the other girl to see. She even managed to give Rachel a smile when her friend pulled back to look at her. This was Rachel's wedding day and she wasn't going to do anything to bring her down. Luckily, Bob swooped in and whisked his wife away before Kate could reply.

"I think someone's impatient to get his bride up to the honeymoon suite," Dawson whispered in her ear.

Kate shivered as his warm breath tickled her cheek. She'd been so caught up in her own thoughts she hadn't heard Dawson come up behind her. She took a deep breath, then turned to smile at him. "I think you're right."

"You know what that means."

"What?"

He flashed her a sexy grin. "That you and I can finally be alone."

Kate's pulse fluttered at the promise in his eyes and she went up on tiptoe to give him a kiss. "And you can ravish me just like you promised."

As it turned out, it was another hour before Rachel and Bob left the reception, but once the bride and groom were gone, Kate and Dawson said good night to the rest of the wedding party and hurried upstairs. In his room, he took her in his arms and covered her mouth with his. She closed her eyes and melted against him, shutting out everything else as she kissed him back. If this was going to be her last night with Dawson, she wanted it to be perfect.

Letting out a groan, Dawson tore his mouth away to kiss his way down her neck to the curve of her shoulder as he reached around to undo the zipper on her dress. With his help, the straps slipped over her shoulders and the gown landed in a puddle of peach satin at her feet to leave her standing in nothing but a lacy bra and matching panties of the same color. He took a step back to slowly look her up and down before he bent his head to kiss her again.

His mouth was hot and demanding on hers and Kate parted her lips with a moan as his fingers found the pins holding up her long hair and began removing them one by one. When he'd gotten all of them out and the tresses tumbled down her back, he slid his hand in her hair and tilted her head back, plunging his tongue into her mouth to take sweet possession of hers.

Still kissing her, Dawson ran his hands down her back to find the clasp of her bra. Opening it deftly, he slid the straps off her shoulders and down her arms, releasing her breasts from their confines. Kate waited breathlessly for him to cup them in his hands, but instead he hooked his fingers inside her panties and slowly pushed them down, then slipped off her high-heeled sandals. As he straightened, he ran his hands up her bare legs and over her hips to bury his hands in her hair and close his mouth over hers once again.

Kate grabbed onto the lapels of his tux, pulling him closer. Her nipples tingled where they brushed against his jacket, and she slid her hands inside to push it off his shoulders. She reached for his bowtie next, giving it a little tug before undoing the buttons on his shirt. She eagerly yanked it out of his waistband and would have reached for the zipper on his pants when he swung her up in his arms and gently set her down on the bed.

He stood gazing down at her, his gaze caressing her naked body with an intensity that made Kate catch her breath. No matter how many other men she took her clothes off for, she would never forget the way Dawson McKenna looked at her.

That thought brought a pang with it and tears suddenly clogged her throat. She swallowed hard, wondering how she was going to keep from losing it. Dammit. She didn't want to spend their remaining night together crying. But Dawson didn't seem to notice and she was relieved when he finally stripped off his shirt and pants so she could focus on his magnificent body instead of how much she was hurting inside.

Tossing the last of his clothes on the floor, Dawson climbed onto the bed and settled himself between her legs. He braced himself on his forearms and teasingly rubbed the head of his cock up and down the lips of her pussy for one long delicious moment before slowly sliding inside.

Kate gasped, her arms and legs going around him to pull him in even deeper. Dawson mumbled something she couldn't make out and before she could ask what it was, he bent his head to claim her lips in a searing kiss. She moaned against his mouth and tightened her arms around him, instinctively lifting her hips to meet his when he gently began to thrust.

Unlike the other times they'd made love, she didn't beg him to go faster or take her harder. This time, she wanted to make it last all night if she could.

Dawson seemed to want the same thing, because he kept his thrusts slow and steady, sliding out until just the tip of his cock was inside her before sliding back in to completely bury his length in her pussy again. Then he would hold himself there, pressing so firmly she swore she was going to come just from the fullness of it.

But as much as she wanted it to, there was no way they could last all night. It just felt too good. When neither of them could hold off coming any longer and Dawson buried his face in the curve of her neck and exploded inside her, the orgasm that coursed through Kate was so powerful and so beautiful that it brought tears to her eyes. This time she didn't try to stop them, but let them roll silently down her cheeks, hoping Dawson wouldn't see them in the semi-darkness of the room.

Kate lost count of how many times she and Dawson made love after that first time. All she knew was that whenever they came down from their passionate high, they would reach for each other and do it all over again until they finally both fell into an exhausted sleep.

Chapter Six

ജ

Leaving Dawson the next morning was the hardest thing Kate ever did in her life. Which was why she took the coward's way out and decided to leave before he woke up. No matter how much she hated herself for doing it, she simply couldn't trust herself to say goodbye to him without bursting into tears. She was on the verge even now. And that would completely ruin everything.

Swallowing hard, she tore her gaze away from the handsome man sleeping soundly beside her and carefully slipped out of bed. Tiptoeing across the room, she picked up her bra and panties from where they lay on top of her dress and put them on, then stepped into the satin gown and zipped it up as quietly as she could. She bent down to pick up her shoes next, but then hesitated as a twinge of guilt assailed her. While this thing she had with Dawson might just be a weekend fling, it wasn't right to just leave without a word. She should at least leave him a note.

Forgetting about her shoes for the moment, she padded over to the desk. Behind her, Dawson stirred in bed and she threw a nervous glance over her shoulder. Getting caught sneaking out of his room would require more explanation than she could give without crying. But to her relief, he was still asleep.

Breathing a soft sigh, Kate took out a piece of hotel stationery and picked up a pen, but then hesitated again. What did a girl say to a guy like Dawson? Words didn't seem enough, so in the end, she kept it simple.

Dawson,

Thank you for the most wonderful weekend of my life.
Kate

She stared at the paper for a moment, then let out a sigh. Putting it in an envelope, she wrote Dawson's name on the front, then walked over to the bed and placed it on the pillow beside his, careful not to disturb him. Fighting the urge to bend over and give him one last kiss, she picked up her shoes and the bridal bouquet she'd caught from Rachel the night before and quietly slipped out of the room.

Kate hurried down the hall to her room, tears blurring her vision. Her chest hurt so much she could barely breathe and once inside, she had to lean against the door to steady herself. Dear God, it felt like her heart was actually breaking.

Choking back a sob, she took off her gown and carelessly stuffed it into her suitcase along with the rest of her clothes, then changed into fresh underwear before putting on jeans and a T-shirt. After that, she grabbed her stuff from the bathroom and shoved everything haphazardly into her toiletry bag. Later, she would probably regret packing so hastily, but right now, all she wanted to do was get out of there. She didn't even take the time to redo her makeup or brush her hair, but just ran her fingers through its long length on her way to the door.

Hand on the knob, Kate turned back and gave the room a quick look to see if she'd forgotten anything when her gaze settled on the bridal bouquet she'd tossed on the bed. Her first instinct was to leave the damn thing, but for some reason, she found herself snatching it off the bed to take it home.

Fortunately, the rest of the hotel was still asleep at that time of morning, so Kate didn't encounter anyone on her way down to the lobby. The desk clerk seemed a little surprised she was checking out so early, but made no comment other than to tell her to have a nice day. As she pulled out of the parking lot a little while later, she berated herself for not checking the ferry schedule before she left, but to her relief, it was still at the dock when she got to the marina. Parking her car on board, she got out and went up to take a seat in the enclosed deck.

Since the ferry wasn't due to leave for Anacortes for almost half an hour, Kate had a lot of time to wonder if she'd done the right thing by leaving. What if she'd been wrong about Dawson? What if he was the kind of guy who was open to a long-term relationship? She was thinking maybe she should go back when the ferry pulled away from the dock.

Her heart sank. Well, it was too late now. It was probably for the best anyway.

Letting out a sigh, Kate walked outside to stand at the railing. No one else was out there, so she could be alone with her thoughts and as she watched San Juan Island retreat in the distance, she blinked back fresh tears. She wondered if Dawson had read her note yet. Did he regret their parting as much as she did? The idea that he might just shrug and toss her letter in the trash hurt almost as much as leaving him and she swallowed hard.

Kate was so lost in her own misery she didn't even know someone had come out on deck until they were standing right beside her. Confused and a little annoyed that another passenger had to invade her space when there was a whole deck to make use of, she turned her head to see who it was, only to gasp in surprise when she realized it was Dawson.

At first, she thought she was imagining him, that her mind had somehow conjured up his jean-clad form to torture her even more, but when his beautiful brown eyes met hers, she knew for a certainty he was really there. His hair was tousled as if he'd just run his hand through it, and he was breathing hard, too, like he'd been running.

"Dawson," she breathed. "What are you doing here? I-I mean, I thought you'd be taking a later ferry."

"I was, but then I woke up and found your note and..." He shook his head as if searching for the right words. "God, this is really awkward. I don't even know if I should have followed you. But I just knew I'd be kicking myself for the rest of my life if I let you go without telling you how I feel. So, when I discovered you'd checked out of the hotel, I decided to come after you."

Kate's heart seemed to stop in her chest. Was he saying what she thought he was saying?

"Look Kate, if my chasing after you like this makes you uncomfortable, then I'm sorry. I know we both agreed to hook up for the weekend and that it was just supposed to be about the sex, but it ended up being more than that for me. I didn't plan on falling for you, but somewhere between making love to you that first night, having dinner on the balcony off my room, and dancing with you at the wedding reception last night, I did fall for you. Hard." He reached out to gently cup her face in his hand. "What I'm trying to say is that I'd really like to keep seeing you when we get back to Seattle. I want to see where this thing between us can go. I hope you feel the same."

She gazed up at him, too stunned to do anything but stand there.

The corner of his mouth edged up. "When I practiced this whole speech in my head as I was hauling ass to catch the ferry, I imagined you saying something encouraging at about this point in the conversation."

Kate blushed. She opened her mouth to tell him she did feel the same way, but nothing would come out. Deciding to just show him how she felt instead, she threw her arms around his neck and kissed him. That must have been good enough for Dawson because he kissed her back with a passion that left her breathless.

"I take it that means you're okay with us continuing to see each other," he teased when he lifted his head.

She laughed. "Okay with it? Dawson, it's what I wanted since the first night we slept together."

His brow furrowed. "Then why did you leave?"

She gave him a sheepish look. "Because I wasn't sure you'd feel the same. And because I wasn't as brave as you are. If you'd been the one who left, I would never have had the courage to come after you."

He reached up to gently brush her hair back from her face, his mouth quirking. "I didn't stop to think about being brave when I decided to come after you. I just knew if I didn't, I'd be making the biggest mistake of my life."

She kissed him again. "Well, I'm glad you did. It's just good you were able to make the ferry before it left. You must have checked out of the hotel in record time."

"Speaking of that, I'm going to have to turn around and go back to San Juan Island when we get to Anacortes."

It was her turn to frown. "Why?"

"Because I was in such a hurry to catch you before you left I didn't check out of my room. Actually, I didn't even bother to take any of my stuff."

She shook her head in amusement. "No problem. I'll go back with you."

His eyes darkened with a look she was coming to recognize. "You know, I don't have to be out of the room until noon. If we get back in time, we might be able to slip in a quickie."

Her pussy tingled at the suggestion and she let out a little moan as she went up on tiptoe to kiss him again. "And what if I can't wait until we get back to your room?"

He chuckled. "Well, then I suppose we'll just have to find someplace on the ferry to make do until we get back."

She shivered with anticipation. That added a whole new meaning to the phrase *love boat*. "What do you suggest?"

He took both her hands in his and started backing toward the door that led inside. "Ever make love in a storage room on a ferry?"

She laughed. "I'm pretty sure I haven't."

Dawson gave her a wolfish grin. "Me, either. Let's go find one and try it out."

Kate couldn't follow fast enough.

GOOD COP, BAD GIRL

Dedication

ℰ℘

With special thanks to my extremely patient and understanding husband, without whose help and support I couldn't have pursued my dream job of becoming a writer. You're my sounding board, my idea man, my critique partner, and the absolute best research assistant any girl could ask for! Thank you for talking me into finally taking the plunge and submitting to Ellora's Cave.

Trademarks Acknowledgement

ℰ℘

The author acknowledges the trademarked status and trademark owners of the following wordmarks mentioned in this work of fiction:

Abercrombie & Fitch: Abercrombie & Fitch Company Corporation

Chippendales: Chippendales, USA, LLC.

Cosmo: Hearst Communications, Inc.

iPod: Apple, Inc.

Chapter One

ဢ

Julie Hanson couldn't believe her friends had forgotten her birthday. She'd waited all day for one of them to call her at the ad agency where she worked and tell her they were going to take her out for a big night on the town in honor of the big event—it wasn't every year a girl hit the big 3-0, after all—but no one so much as sent her an e-card. It hurt they hadn't remembered, especially since she never forgot any of their birthdays.

Resigned to spending her night alone curled up on the couch with a movie and a pint of ice cream, she dropped the mail on the small table inside the entryway, then went into the kitchen to stick a frozen dinner in the microwave so it could heat up while she changed clothes. Maybe she would treat herself to a bubble bath later, too, she thought as she opened the freezer. And after that, she'd climb into bed with her vibrator. She let out a groan. Talk about a pathetic way to spend her birthday.

Shaking her head, she took out two frozen dinners and looked from one to the other. Neither one was very thrilling. She was still trying to decide between the Chicken Mediterranean and the Roasted Chicken Chardonnay when the doorbell rang. With a sigh, she threw both boxes back in the freezer and went to answer the door. Unlocking it, she yanked it open without bothering to look through the peephole.

"Surprise!"

Julie blinked in astonishment. Half a dozen of her friends stood there, their arms filled with gifts and huge grins on their faces.

"You didn't think we'd forgotten your birthday, did you?" Becca asked, walking past her into the apartment.

Julie felt her face flush as the rest of her girlfriends filed in. "N-no, of course not," she stammered as she closed the door. "I figured you guys would give me a call later and wish me happy birthday."

Megan whirled around to give her a wide-eyed look of disbelief. "Call and wish you a happy birthday? Girl, you only turn thirty once. That calls for a celebration, complete with chocolate cake and loads of presents!"

"And my famous margaritas!" Valerie added, holding up a bottle of strawberry margarita mix.

Julie laughed, ashamed now she'd even thought they had forgotten her birthday. "You guys are the best."

"We are," Becca agreed with a grin. "So, let's get this party started already!"

Deciding to leave the margaritas in Valerie's capable hands, Julie grabbed a stack of plates from the kitchen cabinet while Becca stuck her iPod in the speaker dock. A moment later, the sexy sounds of Nelly Furtado's *Promiscuous* filled the apartment.

"So," Valerie said, handing Julie a margarita, "What's it going to be, Jules? Do you want to cut the cake or open your presents first?"

Julie's gaze went from the beautifully decorated cake sitting on the kitchen counter to the stack of colorfully wrapped gifts on the coffee table in the living room as she considered her friend's question. While the chocolate cake was definitely calling to her, the presents were too enticing to resist.

She grinned. "You guys know I'm not very patient when it comes to opening presents. The cake's going to have to wait."

Taking a seat on the couch, Julie waited impatiently for her friends to crowd around her before reaching for the first box on the stack. Eager to see what they had gotten her, Julie tore into the wrapping paper and yanked off the lid to find a gift card for her favorite day spa tucked in a bundle of pastel-colored tissue paper.

She smiled at Valerie. "I love this place."

"I know. You talk about it all the time. But then again, you talk about going to Quickie Lube to get your oil changed in your car, too, so it was a real tossup." Valerie winked at her. "I figured you'd rather pamper yourself than your car. Besides, Quickie Lube didn't have gift cards."

Laughing, Julie gave the other girl a hug, then grabbed the next box from the table and excitedly ripped off the wrapping paper. Inside was a jar of decadent chocolate body paint designed to make foreplay even more of a "hands-on experience", or so the package claimed.

"Now if I just had a hot guy to lick the stuff off," she teased. "I don't suppose you brought one to go with this, did you, Melanie?"

"I would have, but the store was all out." The other girl gave her a grin. "They told me they'd have the shelves restocked by the weekend, though, if you want to go pick one out for yourself."

Julie laughed. If only finding a guy were as simple as selecting one off a shelf. It'd be a lot easier than trying to meet one at the supermarket or the health club. She hadn't had much luck at either of those places.

"Open mine next," Becca said, holding out a small box with huge bow on top.

Julie happily did as instructed, bursting into laughter when she saw Becca's gift was a waterproof vibrator shaped like a rubber ducky.

"Hey, don't laugh!" Becca protested. "That little guy works like a charm."

Valerie grinned. "Are you speaking from personal experience?"

"Damn right I am! Don't knock it until you try it."

Everyone laughed at that as Julie reached for the next gift. The rest of her presents were just as frivolous as the first few, including a gift card to her favorite lingerie store and a skimpy pair of shortie pajamas. As much as she liked the gift card and the pjs, however, Julie had to admit she was most intrigued by the heart-shaped leather paddle Megan gave her. She picked it up, admiring its highly polished surface.

"Like it?" Megan asked.

Julie could only nod, her imagination started to run wild.

Megan must have seen the naughty gleam in her eye, though, because the other girl gave her a knowing grin. "I thought you'd like it. I always figured you were a little kinky."

Julie looked at her friend dubiously. "You did, huh?"

Her friend shrugged. "Sure. I could tell just by looking at you."

"I don't know how kinky I am. I mean, I've tried a lot of off-the-wall things in bed, but spanking isn't one of them." She grinned, then added, "Yet."

"Yet?" Becca squealed. "Does that mean you want to?"

Julie smacked the paddle lightly against her palm, both surprised and a little excited by how much it stung. "If the right guy came along, I'd be only too willing to drape myself over his lap."

"Maybe we should head out to the club later and find you the right guy then," Megan suggested.

The other girls all agreed, but Julie wasn't so sure. She couldn't imagine how she could possibly ask a guy she just met to spank her.

Between Justin Timberlake's *Sexy Back* blaring from the speakers and her friends' merciless teasing about getting spanked with the paddle, Julie was still laughing so hard ten minutes later she didn't even realize the doorbell had been ringing until whoever was outside in the hallway finally banged loudly on the door with their fist.

Setting her margarita down on the coffee table, Julie got to her feet and hurried over to the door.

"Hang on a minute!" she said, shouting to be heard over the music. "I'm coming."

"Not yet you aren't," Becca called from behind her. "But you will be once you take a bath with Mr. Ducky!"

Laughing, Julie yanked open the door and found herself face to face with the most gorgeous guy she'd ever seen. Tall, with short-cropped brown hair and a perfectly chiseled jaw, he had a wide, sensuous mouth and soulful dark eyes. More gold than brown, they were the kind of eyes a girl could end up getting lost in.

She forced her gaze to move lower, taking in his broad shoulders and muscular biceps before coming to rest on the shiny badge on the front of his dark blue uniform. Directly across from it was a nametag that read Chandler. This hot hunk was a cop?

Abruptly realizing she was just standing there staring at him, she reached up to tuck her long, ash blonde hair behind an ear. "Can I help you, Officer?"

He glanced at the other girls still sitting in the living room before those incredible eyes settled on her again. "Is this your apartment, ma'am?"

She stifled a groan. Even his voice was sexy as sin. "Yes."

"We got a complaint about the noise you and your friends were making."

Julie automatically opened her mouth to apologize, only to close it again as the obvious suddenly struck her. God, she was slow sometimes. This mouthwatering specimen of a man wasn't a real cop; he must be a male stripper her friends had hired for her birthday. And if he looked even half as good naked as he did in that uniform, then she was in for a real show. Her friends were the best!

She glanced at the other girls over her shoulder and gave them a wink before turning back to him. Her lips curved into a sexy smile. "And you're here to arrest me, right?" she teased. "Or maybe you'd rather give me a birthday spanking instead?"

He lifted a brow, clearly caught off guard by the suggestion.

Julie was a little surprised by it herself. So much for not being able to ask a guy she'd just met for a spanking. She wasn't usually quite so bold. Then again, she was already on her second margarita. Not that she was tipsy or anything. She was just feeling a little naughty. And if she couldn't be naughty on her birthday, when could she be naughty?

When he didn't answer, she gave him a pout. "No? And one of my friends just gave me the cutest heart-shaped paddle, too." She shrugged. "Maybe later then. I'd much rather see you strip anyway."

His brows drew together. "Strip?"

Damn, he was really good at staying in character. She nodded. "Yeah, you know, take off your clothes. Though I wouldn't do it out in the hallway if I were you. Not unless you want my neighbors to really call the cops."

When he didn't move, she reached out and grabbed the front of his belt to give it a tug. He didn't resist, but let her pull him into the entryway. As much as she would have liked to keep her hand right where it was, maybe even move it a little lower, she forced herself to release him. She should probably let him start dancing before she got too familiar. She waited, expecting him to make suggestive little moves with his hips and unbutton his shirt, but he only continued to regard her with that same authoritative expression on his face. Sheesh, this guy was seriously into his role.

Julie took a step closer to him. He was taller than she was by almost a foot and she had to tilt her chin to look up at him.

Up close like this, she could see light flecks of green in his golden eyes.

"You're really good, you know that? If I didn't know better, I'd think you were a real cop." She circled him slowly, running her hand up his arm and over his shoulder, then across his back. "The uniform looks real, that's for sure." She let her fingers trail over his opposite shoulder and down his other arm, her gaze going to the gun in the holster at his hip as she walked around to stand in front of him again. "So does the gun. And the handcuffs." She ran a finger over the badge on his chest. "And that badge is the best I've ever seen."

As she studied the radio clipped to his left shoulder, she realized it looked real, too. She didn't know male strippers wore such authentic getups. She was about to say as much to him when the radio suddenly hissed.

"All units in the vicinity of Bayview, we have a 2-11 in progress..."

She frowned. Bayview was a neighborhood in the southern part of the city, across town from where she lived in the Lower Pacific Heights section of San Francisco. *Oh...crap.* This guy wasn't a stripper. He was a real cop! She jerked her head up to look at him, her eyes wide.

A slow smile curved his mouth as he folded his arms across his broad chest. "That's right, ma'am. The uniform is real. The gun is real. The handcuffs are real. The badge is real. And you," he added meaningfully, "are in real trouble."

Julie took a step back, her face crimson. "I-I'm really sorry," she stammered. "I just naturally thought you were a male stripper my friends had hired for my birthday party. It was an honest mistake." She looked up at him from beneath her long bangs and chewed nervously on her lower lip. "Are you going to arrest me?"

He lifted a brow. "For what? Disturbing the peace? Or thinking I was a stripper?"

She cringed with embarrassment. "Both."

His mouth twitched. "I'm pretty sure mistaking a police officer for a stripper isn't a crime. As for disturbing the peace, that's a misdemeanor, so I'm just going to write you a citation and ask you keep the noise to a minimum for the rest of the party. If you'll step out into the hallway with me, we can do the paperwork while your friends," he gave the other girls a pointed look, "turn the music down." He held out his hand toward the door. "After you."

Julie stepped out into the hallway, then turned to face him, feeling completely mortified. How could she have been so foolish?

Leaving the door slightly ajar, he pulled out his citation pad and a ballpoint pen. "Name?" he asked, glancing at her as he flipped to a fresh page.

"Julie Hanson."

She might have been embarrassed, but that didn't keep her from letting her gaze run over his broad shoulders and well-muscled arms as he wrote her name down. She probably should cut herself a break. Who would think a guy this hot would be a cop? With a body like his, he should be working at Chippendales or modeling for Abercrombie & Fitch or something.

He tore off the top sheet from the pad and handed it to her. She scanned the page until she came to the section at the bottom. Beside the words "Issuing Officer" was the name Kirk Chandler. Damn, that had a sexy ring to it. Like he belonged in a romance book. Or had stepped off the pages of one.

"Try to keep the noise down." His gold eyes narrowed warningly as he put his pen and notepad away. "If I have to come back tonight, you will be in serious trouble."

She lifted her head to look at him. It might be worth getting in a little trouble just for the chance to see him twice in one night. The thought had her wondering just how loud her iPod speakers could go.

"We will," she promised.

"Have a good night, then."

Giving her a nod, he turned to head down the hallway. After a few steps, he stopped and turned back to flash her a sexy grin. "By the way, happy birthday."

His voice, softer and less authoritative than it had been before, was almost like a caress on her skin, and her pulse fluttered. "Thanks."

Julie watched him walk down the hallway, her eyes automatically going to his backside. Damn, he had a great ass. Too bad she didn't get to see him naked.

She waited until he had completely disappeared around the corner before pushing open the door and going back into her apartment. Closing it behind her, she fixed her friends with an accusing look.

"Why the heck didn't any of you stop me?" she demanded.

The other girls shared a look, then dissolved into fits of laughter.

"Because we were having way too much fun watching you come on to him," Becca finally admitted.

"Totally," Valerie agreed. "It was like watching an X-rated episode of *Cops*."

Melanie nodded. "I was waiting for him to pin you up against the wall and frisk you."

"Frisk her?" Megan said. "I was waiting for *her* to start frisking *him*! Or ask to see his nightstick."

The rest of the girls burst into another round of giggles at that. Though Julie wanted to stay mad at her friends for letting her make a fool of herself, she couldn't help but laugh with them. Frisking the hunky Officer Chandler to see if he was carrying any concealed weapons sounded like some seriously sexy fun to her.

"He was hot, wasn't he?" she said, letting out a dreamy sigh as she threw herself down on the couch beside Megan.

Across from them, Melanie took a sip of her margarita. "He thought you were pretty hot, too."

Julie looked at the other girl in surprise. "He did?"

Her friend grinned. "Oh yeah. He was definitely checking you out."

Julie sighed again, this time in frustration. "Just my luck. I meet a hot guy on my birthday and all he does is give me a stupid citation for disturbing the peace."

"At least he didn't arrest you," Megan pointed out. "Then again, it might be kind of fun to be led away in handcuffs by a smokin'-hot cop like him."

Becca winked. "Especially if he's leading you into the bedroom."

"I wish," Julie groaned. "A girl can dream, though, right?"

"Sure," Valerie said. "But can you do it while we have cake? I fantasize better with chocolate."

Julie laughed, but as she took a bite of birthday cake a few minutes later, she had to admit it did make her fantasies even more delicious. Of course, that was probably because Officer Chandler and his well-muscled biceps were the main topic of conversation for the rest of the night.

By the time her friends left a few hours later, she was so turned-on she was seriously considering taking a bath with Mr. Ducky. She only hoped the cute, little vibrator worked as well as Becca said it did because she was definitely in need of an orgasm.

She had just grabbed the sex toy from the coffee table and was about to head for the bedroom when the doorbell rang. Wondering which of her friends had forgotten something, she tossed the vibrator on the table and went to answer the door. When she opened it, however, she was surprised to see the gorgeous Officer Chandler standing there.

Chapter Two

ഔ

Her pulse quickened. Damn, he looked hot in that uniform. But then she remembered what he said about her being in serious trouble if he had to come back.

"Oh no! Did my neighbors call to complain about the noise again?"

He lifted a brow. "Did you and your friends give them a reason to call and complain again?"

She shook her head. "No. We turned the music down just like you told us."

He chuckled. "Good. Because I'd hate to have to arrest you."

A sexy image of him pushing her up against the wall so he could frisk her popped into her head unbidden, and she blushed.

"I'm not actually here on police business this time," he continued. "I picked up a little something for you after I got off duty. I thought I'd take a chance and see if you were still up."

As he spoke, he held up a small box. It was wrapped in shiny silver paper and topped with a blue bow.

She looked at him in surprise. "You got me a birthday present?"

The corner of his mouth edged up. "To make up for the citation I issued you."

Her lips curved. "You didn't have to do that. But it was sweet of you." She reached out to take the box, her fingers lightly brushing his. The contact sent a little spark running through her that had nothing to do with static electricity and she caught her breath. "Do you want to come in while I open it?"

"Sure." He glanced around her small, one-bedroom apartment. "Did your friends go home already?"

"They just left."

Keenly aware of his gaze on her, she plucked off the bow with suddenly nervous fingers and set it on the table in the entryway. Tearing off the paper, she opened the lid and smiled. Inside, there was a cherry-flavored ring pop.

"Oh my gosh! I haven't had one of these things since I was a kid."

"I saw it and thought of you," he said, then sheepishly added, "Plus, it was really the only thing I could find at the all-night convenience store where I stopped."

She laughed. "It's perfect. Thank you."

"You're welcome." He looked around the apartment again, then back at her, a teasing glint in his golden brown eyes. "So, did you ever get that birthday spanking you were looking for?"

She blinked. "Wh-what?"

"Your birthday spanking. Did you ever get one?"

"Oh!" Julie felt her face color. Dang it, why did she have to blush so easily? "No, I didn't."

Actually, she'd completely forgotten about it. But now the mere mention of one made her think of the heart-shaped paddle she'd gotten for a present, as well as her promise to put it to good use if she ever found the right guy. And Officer Kirk Chandler definitely looked like the right guy.

He gave her a slow, sexy smile as he took a step closer. "Do you still want one? If you do, I'd be happy to do the honors."

The thought of draping herself over his knee for a spanking made her pussy spasm and she bit her lip to stifle a moan. She looked up at him from beneath lowered lashes. "It's after midnight, so technically it isn't really my birthday anymore. Do you think it would still count?"

He let out a soft chuckle. "I don't think there are any rules when it comes to birthday spankings."

She nodded. "Probably not."

"Is that a yes, then?"

Her lips curved into a smile. Go for it, she told herself. "It's most definitely a yes."

He grinned. "I was hoping you'd say that."

Now that she had given him the okay, Julie expected Kirk to take her hand and lead her over to the couch so he could administer her spanking, but he surprised her by sliding his hand in her long hair and bending his head to kiss her first. His mouth was gentle on hers, his tongue teasing as it persuaded hers to come out and play. She melted against him, her hands gliding up the front of his shirt to settle on his shoulders. She'd been all set for a spanking, but kissing was fine, too. The muscles of his shoulders flexed and bunched beneath her fingers as she gave them a firm squeeze. She'd been right. He was extremely well built under his uniform.

The urge to see what he looked like beneath that crisp, navy blue shirt was almost too powerful to resist and she was just about to say to heck with the spanking and go for the buttons on the garment when he lifted his head with a groan.

"Time for that spanking," he said softly.

Julie's pulse skipped a beat as he took her hand and led her over to the couch. After all that talk about spanking with her friends earlier, she was even more eager to experience one, and the knowledge that she was about to have her bottom reddened by a guy as hot as Kirk Chandler made her pussy tingle with anticipation. Still holding onto her hand, he sat down and slowly guided her over his lap so she was lying stretched out on the couch. When he expertly rested one hand on the small of her back to hold her in place, she found herself wondering if he had done this before. She opened her mouth to ask him, but at the feel of his other hand lightly cupping her ass through her short skirt, she forgot all about his qualifications for the job and told herself to just be glad he knew what he was doing.

"Since it wouldn't be very gentlemanly of me to ask how old you are, I'll just spank you until I think you've had enough," he said. "How does that sound?"

"Mmm," she purred. "Sounds good to me."

She wondered if she should mention this would be her first spanking, but then decided against it. She didn't want to come off as inexperienced. Especially since she was the one who had suggested he give her one. Besides, she was a *Cosmo* girl. Fun and fearless, that was her. And more than a little eager for him to warm her bottom.

She held her breath as she waited for Kirk to begin, but he didn't start spanking her right away. Instead, he gently caressed her ass cheeks through her silky skirt. That part of her body had always been one of her favorite erogenous zones, so she wasn't surprised to feel her pussy immediately start to get wet. Of course, that probably had something to do with the position she was in. Not only did it give Kirk a delicious view of her long legs, but it also made her feel very submissive. That was a new experience for her, but she discovered it was a huge turn-on.

Julie was so caught up in her newfound submissive side she didn't realize Kirk had stopped massaging her bottom until she felt a light smack on her right cheek. Even though it didn't sting, she still let out a startled little gasp.

"Too hard?" he asked.

She lifted her head to look at him over her shoulder. "No, it just surprised me. You can spank me a little harder, if you want."

Giving him a provocative little smile, Julie turned back around to rest her head on her arms again. Kirk chuckled and lifted his hand to smack her on the other ass cheek, this time a little harder. It stung more than the first spank, but in the best possible way, and she lifted her bottom up a little higher for the next one. When it came, she almost let out a little moan. She had no idea getting a spanking could be this erotic, but as Kirk went back and forth from one cheek to the other, she felt herself get more and more aroused. It was as if there was a direct connection between her ass and her pussy, because both were tingling. She got even more turned-on when he stopped the spanking to rub her bottom again. Her skirt had ridden up a little to expose the edges of her skimpy panties and she caught her breath as his fingers brushed the parts of her derrière left exposed. She could only imagine how much more exquisite his hand would feel on her bare skin.

She held her breath, wondering if he might pull down her panties. Her pussy was practically gushing. When Kirk stopped in mid-rub, she thought he was actually going to yank down her panties, but he only started spanking her again. Not that she was complaining. She definitely liked this spanking thing, bare bottom or not. He delivered a series of firm smacks to both cheeks that made her bottom feel hot all over. Even though she didn't want him to stop, Julie couldn't help but squirm around on his lap all the same. That earned her an extra-hard smack and she squealed in surprise. The sound was quickly followed by a moan, however, when Kirk abruptly stopped spanking to give her ass a firm squeeze.

"I think it's time to try out that paddle you got for your birthday, don't you?"

Her pulse skipped a beat at the mention of the heart-shaped paddle. As impatient as she was to try it out, she couldn't ignore the little tremor of nervousness that ran through her as he reached for the implement. Then again, she thought as he rested the paddle against her right cheek, it could just be excitement. She tensed as she waited for him to use it on her. But to her surprise, he instead caressed her ass with it. Unable to help herself, she let out a little moan.

"Does that feel good?" he asked softly.

She sighed. "Mmm."

Getting spanked with it was going to feel even better, though. She just knew it. When he brought the paddle down on her upturned ass with a resounding smack a moment later, she discovered she was right. The paddle stung more than his hand and she could feel heat spread over her bottom almost immediately. She wasn't sure how having her ass spanked could feel so good, but it did, and as Kirk paddled first one cheek, then the other over and over, she began to rotate her hips so she was grinding against his leg. God, how she wanted to slide her hand between their bodies to finger her clit. But she was afraid if she did, he might stop spanking her and she didn't want him to stop. She wanted him to keep spanking her until she orgasmed from it. Since she'd never been spanked before, she wasn't sure such a thing was even possible, but she was definitely getting hotter and hotter by the second. If she didn't come soon, she thought she might just explode. She let out a groan, torn between demanding he paddle her bottom some more and begging him to slide his hand between her legs and touch her clit.

She lifted her head to give him a pleading look over her shoulder. "Touch me. Please."

The corner of his mouth curved. "My pleasure."

Julie waited for him to pull down her panties, but he surprised her by slipping his hand between her legs and fingering her through the thin material. She opened her mouth to tell him to pull them down, but all that came out was a moan. The material was thin enough not to get in the way of her pleasure and she ground against his hand as he made slow, lazy circles on her clit. If anything, the tiny bikini panties made what he was doing even hotter. Like he wanted her so much he didn't want to take the time to pull off her clothes. God, it was so sexy!

"Oh yeah," she breathed, undulating her hips. "Faster. Move your fingers faster."

He obeyed, immediately moving his fingers more quickly. Julie sighed. Usually it took guys a while to figure out how she liked to be touched, but Kirk seemed to know exactly what she needed, exactly what would get her off, and he gave it to her.

"Just like that. Don't stop. Please don't stop."

"I won't. I'm going to make you come like this, baby."

The words, combined with the magic his fingers were working on her clit, had her doing just that. Her orgasm started right beneath his fingers, then spread to the rest of her body, sending shock waves of pleasure rippling through her until she was letting out one long, continuous moan.

When the tremors finally subsided a few moments later, Julie could do nothing but lie there draped over his lap. She'd had some great orgasms before, but that was off the charts. She should thank him for it.

She pushed herself up to sit back on her heels, then, sliding her hand in his dark hair, leaned forward to give him a kiss. This time, she was the aggressor, her tongue tangling with his in an erotic game of Twister that left them both breathless. He cupped her breast, his thumb finding her nipple through the thin material of her cami-top and making tiny circles around the peak. As exquisite as what he was doing felt, though, she had other things in mind. Breaking the kiss, she climbed off the couch, then stepped between his legs to kneel down in front of him.

"It might be my birthday," she said, "but that doesn't mean I can't give you a present, too. Especially after such a wonderful spanking."

Giving him a sultry smile, she reached out and tugged at his belt. Never having gone out with a cop, she hadn't realized how much stuff they wore attached to their belts, and she was glad when Kirk gave her a hand. When his cock finally sprang free of its confines a moment later, all she could do was stare. He was big, thick and hard. Just the way she liked it. And on the tip was a glistening droplet of pre-cum.

Reaching out, she wrapped her hand around the base of his shaft, then leaned forward and ran her tongue over the head. He tasted sweet and just the slight bit musky, and she let out a soft murmur of appreciation. Rather than close her lips around him right away, however, she slowly ran her tongue up and down his shaft a few times before finally taking him completely in her mouth.

Kirk let out a throaty groan and slid his hand in her long hair, gently guiding her when she started to move her mouth up and down. Julie kept her movements slow and deliberate, sliding all the way up to the tip of his cock and swirling her tongue over the head before taking him deep again. She repeated the motion over and over, constantly changing her technique to keep things interesting. Sometimes she would follow along with her hand, squeezing his shaft as she went. Most of the time, though, she only used her mouth on him, cupping his heavy balls in her other hand and lightly caressing them with her fingers.

"God, you're good at that," he said hoarsely.

Julie felt a little surge of pride at his words. She took him deeper and deeper in her mouth with every bob of her head until he was as deep down her throat as he could go. She kept him there for a long moment before she slowly slid her mouth up his length and started the whole process over again. Kirk only let her do that a few times, however, before he tightened his hand in her hair. She lifted her head to give him a curious look.

"I need to be inside you now," he said, his voice husky with lust.

She couldn't get to her feet fast enough. The thought of having his big cock inside her already had her pussy throbbing with anticipation. Grabbing the hem of her top, she lifted it over her head and tossed it on the coffee table. On the couch, Kirk was hurriedly unbuttoning his shirt, but he stopped halfway down to gaze at her bare breasts. And from the hunger in his eyes, he definitely liked what he saw. Pulse quickening, she unzipped her skirt and let it fall to the floor at her feet, then pushed down her panties, wiggling her hips a little so they could slide down to the floor, too. By the time she stepped out of the tiny scrap of material, Kirk had stripped off his shirt, gotten to his feet, and was pushing down his pants.

Julie stared at him, taking in his broad shoulders, washboard stomach and long, well-muscled legs. She didn't think she'd ever seen a more perfect guy.

Noticing the tiny foil packet he was holding, she plucked it out of his hand then pushed him back onto the couch with a little shove of her hand. If Kirk minded her taking command, he didn't say so. Instead, he wrapped a hand around the base his cock and waited. Tearing open the packet, Julie took out the condom and slowly rolled it onto his rock-hard shaft. Straightening up, she put her hands on his shoulders and climbed on the couch so she was straddling his lap. She didn't take him inside her right away, but stayed poised above him, gazing down into his eyes. The desire she saw there made her catch her breath. Tightening her hold on his shoulders, she slowly lowered herself onto his shaft.

Julie gasped. He was hot and hard inside her. She had never been with a man who filled her so completely, but it was like the gorgeous Officer Chandler's cock had been made expressly for her. He felt so good in her pussy she almost didn't want to move, but she knew if she did, it would feel even better. When she began to undulate her hips a moment later, she discovered she was right.

As she slowly rode up and down on him, she slid her hands in his hair, tilting his head back so she could kiss him again. He reached out to cup her freshly spanked ass, giving it a firm squeeze as he guided her movements. Her bottom still tingled a little from the paddling he'd given her, and she murmured her approval against his mouth. While getting a spanking from a gorgeous guy might be hot as hell, having sex with him right afterward was too incredible for words.

Kirk dragged his mouth away from hers to trail kisses along the curve of her jaw and down her neck. "Keep riding me."

Julie let out a moan as he pressed his mouth to the curve of her shoulder. She couldn't have stopped riding him if she wanted to. He felt too damn good inside her. Even so, she did get a little distracted when he slid his hands over her hips and up her tummy to gently cup her breasts. She moaned again, this time more loudly, only to gasp a moment later when he bent forward to take one of her nipples in his mouth. She arched against him as he suckled first on one sensitive peak, then lavished the same exquisite attention on the other. By the time he lifted his head, she was practically dizzy from the pleasure of it.

"You stopped moving," he pointed out, sliding his hands back down to cup her ass again.

She glanced down to realize he was right. She smiled. "I got distracted, I guess."

His mouth quirked. "Really?"

"Uh-huh." She ran her hands over his smooth, muscular chest then back up to his shoulders again. "You're very distracting."

He chuckled. "Maybe I should do something to help you focus, then."

Julie wondered exactly how he intended to do that. She found out a moment later when he gave her a sharp smack on the ass. Startled, she let out a little gasp. But as warmth spread over her bare bottom, she gave him a slow, sexy smile.

"*Oooh.* Do that again."

Kirk's mouth twitched with amusement. Lifting his hand, he spanked her on the ass again, this time a little harder. "Ride me," he said, his hand coming down on her other cheek with a loud smack.

Julie let out a little yelp but did as he commanded, riding up and down on his cock in perfect rhythm with the spanks.

Kirk smacked one cheek then the other until her bottom was stinging. And still she wanted more.

"Harder," she breathed. "Spank me harder!"

He obeyed, the spanks echoing in the small living room. Julie bounced up and down on him wildly, her pussy clenching around his cock each time his hand connected with her ass. With a groan, Kirk grabbed her ass cheeks in both hands and began to thrust up into her.

She clutched at his shoulders. "Harder!" she cried. "Fuck me harder!"

At her words, he tightened his hold on her ass and pumped into her so forcefully his thrusts sent her right over the edge and into another orgasm that was better than any she'd ever had in her life. She threw back her head and screamed out her pleasure loud enough for the whole apartment building to hear. If they'd called the cops for disturbing the peace before, then they were really going to do it now.

The last tremors of her climax were just leaving her body when Kirk grabbed her hips and stopped her from moving. Startled, she opened her eyes to look down at him and found him clenching his jaw, a strained expression on his handsome face. He was right on the edge of coming, but was holding back for some reason.

She leaned forward to kiss him on the mouth. "Why don't you let yourself go ahead and come, too?"

"Because I'm not ready to come yet," he said hoarsely. "The night is far from over and I have lots of things I want to do with this hot little body of yours."

She wrapped her arms around his neck. "Mmm, I like the sound of that."

His lips quirked. "Good. That means you won't mind if I take charge for a little while."

It seemed to her that he was in charge before, regardless of the fact she'd been the one on top, but she didn't point that out to him. "Not at all."

"Then slide off my cock and bend over the coffee table."

Although Julie was reluctant to get off his lap, she was eager to see what he had in mind, so she obediently got up, then turned around and leaned over to place her hands on the table. She glanced over her shoulder to see Kirk sitting back on the couch with his hand wrapped around the base of his rigid cock while he admired the view. Giving him a seductive look, she slowly wiggled her bottom back and forth in front of him.

Kirk sucked in a breath. "Damn, you've got a gorgeous ass. Just made for spanking."

His compliment made her go warm all over, but before she could thank him for it, he leaned forward and cupped her cheeks in his strong hands, making her completely forget what she'd been going to say. She arched her back and pushed her derriere up higher in the air in anticipation of another spanking, but to her surprise, Kirk bent and pressed his lips to her right ass cheek. She caught her breath as the stubble on his jaw scraped lightly against the tender skin, unable to contain the shiver that went through her when she felt him do the same to the opposite cheek. She never had a guy do that before, but she'd definitely been missing out.

Then he did something that made her think she might melt into a puddle right there on the living room floor. He spread her cheeks and slowly ran his tongue along the folds of her pussy.

Julie moaned and parted her legs even more, silently begging him to continue. Kirk obliged her, grasping her hips in a firm hold and plunging his tongue inside her pussy from behind. He certainly didn't learn that little maneuver at the police academy, that was for sure.

After a few moments of pleasuring her with his tongue, Kirk let out a groan and got to his feet. Julie opened her mouth to protest, but could only gasp as he thrust his cock inside her in one smooth motion. She closed her eyes, savoring in the feel of him as he slowly pumped in and out of her pussy. Not only could he go deeper in this position than when she'd been on his lap, but his cock seemed to be touching her in new and exciting places that had her moaning over and over.

Julie was barely even aware Kirk had taken his hand off her hip until she felt a sharp smack on her bottom. She let out a startled gasp, but it was quickly followed by a moan as he began spanking her in time with his thrusts. The combination was more erotic than she would have imagined and she eagerly pushed her ass back to meet his hand.

"Do you like that?" he asked.

"God, yes!" she breathed. "Do it harder!"

"Spank you harder or fuck you harder?"

"Both!"

He didn't need any further encouragement, but delivered a series of firm spanks to her ass as he pumped into her more and more forcefully. Julie grabbed the edge of the coffee table and held on tight, throwing back her head and crying out in ecstasy as she had her third orgasm of the night. She was so caught up in its riptide of pleasure she didn't even realize Kirk had stopped spanking her until he grasped her hips in both hands and buried himself deep inside her as he found his own release. Though not nearly as vocal as she was, his own hoarse groans had a sexy, almost primal sound to them that made her shiver in delight.

As Kirk slid out of her, Julie straightened up to lean back against his chest, completely spent. She'd never had orgasms that strong in her life. She wondered absently if the spanking had something to do with it and decided while it almost certainly had, Officer Chandler played a bigger part. He definitely knew how to pleasure a woman, that was for sure.

Letting out a little sigh, she turned in his arms and looped hers around his neck. "That was a whole new level of mm-mm good."

His mouth curved. "For me, too. Though I'm pretty sure we can top it if we try."

Her pussy quivered anew at the mere thought of surpassing that performance. She lifted her head to give him a teasing look. "You think so, huh?"

He pulled her close for a long, hot kiss. "I know so."

The quiver in her pussy turned into an insistent throb at the promise in his words. "In that case, what do you say we go into the bedroom?"

"Lead the way."

Julie took his hand and turned to head for her bedroom when a naughty idea came to her. Stopping, she whirled around to face him.

"Hold that thought," she said.

Ignoring the curious look Kirk gave her, she hurried back to the couch and picked up the plastic container of chocolate body paint, then grabbed the handcuffs from his belt.

"I thought we might need these," she said, giving him a sexy smile as she took his hand and started to lead him toward the bedroom again.

To her surprise, Kirk didn't follow. Instead, he spun her around and pulled her into his arms for another kiss. Julie parted her lips beneath his with a moan, ready to give him an all-access pass to her tongue again, when she felt him take the handcuffs away from her.

"Hey!" she protested. "I had plans for those."

He grinned. "So do I. And since I'm trained in the use of them, I'll be the one in charge of them."

While the thought of being completely in his control made Julie practically breathless with anticipation, she couldn't resist giving him a little pout. "Whatever you say,

Officer. But next time, I'm going to be the one putting you under arrest."

The words were out of her mouth before she could stop them. If Kirk picked up on the hint she was hoping this would be more than a one-night stand, he gave no indication of it. He only chuckled in reply as she led him toward the bedroom. Halfway there, though, he stopped her again, this time to press her back against the wall. His erection was hot and hard against her tummy despite the fact he'd just orgasmed a few minutes ago. She'd never been with a guy who could get it up again so fast.

"That beautiful ass of yours drives me crazy, do you know that?"

He didn't give her a chance to answer, but instead covered her mouth with his in a searing kiss. As his tongue took possession of hers, Julie thought she heard something fall to the floor, but it wasn't until Kirk cupped her breasts in both hands that she realized he'd dropped his handcuffs. She moaned as he took her nipples in his fingers and twirled them back and forth. She went ahead and let the jar of body paint join the cuffs on the floor. She had the feeling she and Kirk weren't going to get to the bedroom anytime soon.

Dragging his mouth away from hers, Kirk lifted his head to gaze down at her, his eyes molten with desire. Without a word, he grasped her ass in both hands, then he lifted her up and buried himself deep inside her in one forceful motion. She glanced down and noticed he'd already put another condom on. When the heck had he done that? Damn, he was good.

Moaning, she wrapped both legs around him, clinging to him as he fucked her fast and hard against the wall. Each thrust shoved her back against it so hard she could barely catch her breath in between, but she absolutely loved it. She'd never experienced anything so erotic or primal in her life.

He tightened his grip on her ass, sending little tingles of pleasure dancing over her tender skin. The feel of his hands reminded her of the spanking he'd just given her, making her breath quicken and her pussy clench down on his cock. As unbelievable as it seemed, she experienced yet another orgasm, this one just as mind-blowing as the others.

Kirk buried his face in the curve of her neck as he came, muffling the sounds of his groans, but Julie knew by the way he drove his cock into her and held himself there that his climax was just as earth shattering as hers.

He didn't release her until both their orgasms had subsided. She slid slowly down his body to stand on trembling legs. She wanted to tell him how amazing that had been, but she couldn't seem to speak. All she could do was lean against his chest and try to catch her breath.

As if somehow sensing that, Kirk tilted her face up to his and tenderly kissed her on the mouth. Bending to pick up the handcuffs in one hand and the chocolate body paint in the other, he handed the latter to her, then swung her up in his strong arms and carried her into the bedroom.

Once there, he gently set her down on the floor. Wrapping her arms around his neck, she pulled him down for another kiss. Finding his tongue with hers, she drew it into her mouth and sucked on it gently. He slid his free hand up her rib cage to palm one of her breasts. His fingers found her nipple, giving it a little squeeze, and she gasped against his mouth. God, his touch was magic.

Lifting his head, Kirk released her nipple and urged her onto the big bed. Julie set the container of body paint down on the bedside table, then lay back on the pillows, her breath quickening as he bent over her, the handcuffs dangling from one hand. She'd had a guy tie her up before, but that had been with a scarf. While being bound with the scarf had been sexy, there was something even more exciting about the idea of being in handcuffs. On second thought, she decided as Kirk gently took her wrist and expertly snapped the cuff around it, maybe it had more to do with the fact that the guy she was with was so damn hot. From the way her pussy purred, she concluded that was definitely the reason.

Looping the cuffs through the wrought iron headboard, Kirk secured her other wrist, effectively making her his prisoner. Julie caught her lower lip between her teeth and gave the handcuffs an experimental tug. While she could still move her hands around, she couldn't get them more than a few inches away from the headboard.

"Too tight?" he asked.

She shook her head, her lips curving into a slow, sexy smile. "They're perfect."

His eyes smoldered as he gazed down at her. "You're the one who's perfect."

Lowering his head, Kirk pressed his mouth to the inside of her wrist and slowly kissed his way down the curve of her arm. Although his lips felt warm and delicious on her skin, they also tickled like crazy, and Julie couldn't keep from squirming. Of course, she couldn't get very far handcuffed to the bed like she was, and the reminder that she was completely under his control was hot as hell.

He paused to run his tongue over the sensitive skin on the inside of her elbow before continuing down her arm. When he got to her shoulder, she turned her head on the pillow, giving him access to her neck, and she let out a sigh of pleasure as he nibbled her there. Mmm, he definitely knew his way around the female body.

Kirk kissed his way up to her ear, swirling his tongue inside and making her shiver, before retracing his path back along her neck and down to her breasts. She held her breath as she waited for him to play with them, but instead he reached for the container of chocolate body paint. Her pulse quickened as he took off the protective seal and unscrewed the lid. Putting the top down on the bed, he dipped his fingers into the chocolate.

She smiled. "I'm pretty sure that came with a brush."

"I prefer the hands-on approach." He gave her a sidelong glance at her as he placed the jar back on the nightstand. "Besides, I always loved finger painting."

Giving her a wicked grin, he let the chocolate body paint drip off his fingers onto one nipple, then the other, before rubbing it all over her breasts. When he was done, he held his finger to her lips. She drew it into her mouth, licking it the same way she had his cock earlier.

Kirk slid his finger out with a groan. "You have no idea how sexy that is."

Cupping her breasts tenderly in his hands, he took one chocolate-covered nipple in his mouth and suckled on it gently. Julie moaned and arched against him as he swirled his tongue 'round and 'round the sensitive tip. He alternated soft, gentle flicks of his tongue with naughty little love bites that made her wiggle like crazy. He was going to drive her wild. Just when she was sure she would go insane from what he was doing, he lifted his head to inflict the same exquisite torment on the other nipple. Then he started licking the chocolate off the rest of her breasts. God, she could have him do that all night!

Kirk, however, clearly had other things in mind because after one more flick of his tongue, he lifted his head from her breast. Julie's moan of protest quickly turned into one of pleasure when he slowly began to kiss his way down her stomach a moment later. She definitely liked where this was going.

She waited in breathless anticipation for him to make his way down to her pussy, but to her surprise, he stopped at her bellybutton for a moment to swirl his tongue around the tiny indentation. She'd never had anyone make love to her bellybutton before, and decided she definitely liked it. She was practically panting with excitement when he began to slowly kiss his way farther south. The closer he got to her clit, the more she ached there. If he didn't put his mouth on her soon, she was going to go insane!

He seemed determined to tease her, though. Cupping her ass cheeks, he pressed a kiss to the inside of one thigh, then the other, before lightly running his tongue up the slick folds of her pussy. If she could have moved her hands, she would have threaded them into his hair and forced him to pay attention to her clit. Instead, she was completely at his mercy.

"*Mmm*," he breathed "You taste good."

He swiped his tongue along her pussy lips a second time, once again stopping before he reached her clit. She yanked at the handcuffs holding her prisoner, but they held her fast. She wanted to reach down, grab his head and put his mouth where she so desperately needed it. And yet, the fact that she couldn't aroused her even more.

Even so, that didn't stop her from begging him. "Kirk, please."

He pressed another kiss to the inside of her thigh before lifting his head to look at her. His golden brown eyes glinted with amusement. "Please what?"

"Please lick my clit," she demanded. "I need to feel your mouth on me!"

When Kirk bent his head to lick along the folds of her pussy again, Julie was half afraid he was going to tease her some more, but then she felt his tongue on her clit. He flicked at the plump little nub before making lazy circles around it.

Julie arched off the bed, clutching at the wrought iron bedframe she was handcuffed to.

"Just like that," she moaned. "Don't stop!"

He tightened his grip on her ass and moved his tongue more firmly and deliberately on her clit. Julie writhed beneath him, moaning and moving her head from side to side on the pillow as she felt her orgasm build. He took his time, pushing her higher and higher until she swore it couldn't get any better. But it did. And when she finally reached her peak, her entire body was trembling as if she had been running a marathon. The climax that hit her was so powerful she had no choice but to throw back her head and scream again. Kirk kept lapping at her clit until the sensations became so intense she thought she might actually pass out. She strained at the handcuffs, trying to free herself so she could wrap her fingers in his hair and pull his mouth away. The steel around her wrists refused to give, though, and she could do nothing but writhe on the bed and moan in pleasure as the orgasm went on and on.

He only stopped licking her clit after he had coaxed every last bit of pleasure from her, and all Julie could do was lie back against the pillows and gasp for air. She'd never been with a guy who was so damn good at licking pussy, but that had to be the best oral sex she'd had in her life.

Kirk pressed a tender kiss to the inside of her thigh, then sat back on his heels to open the foil packet he'd brought with him from the living room. Rolling it down on his rock-hard cock, he crawled up her body to settle between her thighs. Bracing himself on his forearms, he pressed against the opening of her pussy but didn't slide in. Instead, he bent his head and closed his mouth over hers.

He tasted of chocolate and her own pussy juices, and she murmured her approval as she parted her lips and suckled on his tongue. As he kissed her, he rubbed the head of his cock up and down along her wet slit. She moaned in frustration.

"Stop teasing me," she begged him hoarsely. "I need you inside me. Now!"

At her entreaty, Kirk immediately stopped tormenting her and slid into her wetness inch by incredible inch. Julie gasped against his mouth as she felt her pussy expand to accommodate his large cock. She locked her legs around him, taking him as deep as he would go. She would have wrapped her arms around him, too, if she hadn't been handcuffed to the bed. She wasn't completely submissive, though, and when he started to pump into her, she lifted her hips to meet his.

Kirk made love to her slowly and deliberately, sliding his cock all the way out of her pussy before plunging back in again. He buried himself deep with every thrust, touching parts of her she was sure no man had ever touched. But while she loved the slow and steady rhythm of his lovemaking, right then her body screamed out for something more forceful, more primal.

She dragged her mouth away from his, her breathing ragged. "Harder," she demanded. "Fuck me harder!"

His eyes blazed at her words and he immediately began to obey, pumping into her harder and harder until the bed was shaking beneath them and the headboard was slamming against the wall. If her neighbors had complained about the noise before, they definitely weren't going to like what they were hearing now. Who the hell cared? She'd move out and get a new place tomorrow if she had to. Right now, she didn't want him to ever stop fucking her.

"Oh God, I'm coming!" she cried as his pounding sent her into an orgasm that made all the previous ones seem like foreplay. "Don't stop. Please don't ever stop!"

He didn't. Instead, he began to fuck her even harder, thrusting into her until she was crying out in ecstasy. Kirk buried his face in her neck then, letting out a hoarse groan as he reached his own climax.

It was a long time before he finally lifted his head, and when he did it was to cover her mouth with his in a long, intoxicating kiss.

"I guess I should get those cuffs off, huh?" he said, giving her a grin.

She let out a little laugh. She had almost forgotten about them in all that orgasmic bliss. "I don't know. I'm thinking I could fall asleep just like this."

He chuckled as he climbed off the bed. "You say that now, but wait until your arms start going numb. Then it's not so fun."

She wondered how he knew that little piece of information, but didn't ask. As Kirk walked out of the bedroom, Julie's gaze went to his backside, and she let out an appreciative sigh. He really did have a great ass.

When Kirk came back into the room a moment later, he unlocked the cuffs, then tossed them on the bedside table along with the keys. Lying back on the pillow beside her, he pulled her into his arms. Julie snuggled up close to him and put her head on his shoulder. Talk about a wonderful birthday present. She only hoped it was the kind of gift that kept on giving.

"You know," she said, running her fingers up and down his muscular chest. "Maybe I should plan on disturbing the peace every night, if you're going to be the responding officer."

He chuckled and tightened his arm around her. "You don't have to go to all that trouble. All you have to do is ask me to come by."

Her breath hitched and she lifted her head to look at him. "Well, in that case, what's your schedule look like for tomorrow night?"

Kirk's mouth twitched. "I think it just opened up." He captured the ends of her long hair in his fingers and curled it around the tip of one. "Any chance I can get you to demonstrate the proper usage of that cute, little yellow duck out there in the living room when I come over?"

Julie shivered at the thought of luxuriating in a hot bath and using that vibrator on herself while he watched. "I think I can do that," she said, leaning close to give him a kiss. "Just remember to bring your handcuffs."

Also by Paige Tyler

ဢ

eBooks:
Erotic Exposure
Good Cop, Bad Girl
Just Right
Mr. Right-Now

About the Author

ଚ୍ଚ

Paige Tyler is a full-time, multi-published, award-winning writer of erotic romance. She and her research assistant (otherwise known as her husband!) live on the beautiful Florida coast with their easygoing dog and their lazy, I-refuse-to-get-off-the-couch-for-anything-but-food cat. When not working on her latest book, Paige enjoys reading, jogging, doing Pilates, going to the beach, watching Pro football and vacationing with her husband at Disney. She loves writing about strong, sexy alpha males and the feisty, independent women who fall for them. From verbal foreplay to sexual heat, her wickedly hot stories of romance, adventure, passion and true love will bring a blush to your cheeks and leave you breathlessly panting for more!

Paige Tyler welcomes comments from readers. You can find her website and email address on her author bio page at www.ellorascave.com.

Tell Us What You Think

We appreciate hearing reader opinions about our books. You can email us at Comments@EllorasCave.com.

Why an electronic book?

We live in the Information Age — an exciting time in the history of human civilization, in which technology rules supreme and continues to progress in leaps and bounds every minute of every day. For a multitude of reasons, more and more avid literary fans are opting to purchase e-books instead of paper books. The question from those not yet initiated into the world of electronic reading is simply: *Why?*

1. *Price.* An electronic title at Ellora's Cave Publishing and Cerridwen Press runs anywhere from 40% to 75% less than the cover price of the exact same title in paperback format. Why? Basic mathematics and cost. It is less expensive to publish an e-book (no paper and printing, no warehousing and shipping) than it is to publish a paperback, so the savings are passed along to the consumer.

2. *Space.* Running out of room in your house for your books? That is one worry you will never have with electronic books. For a low one-time cost, you can purchase a handheld device specifically designed for e-reading. Many e-readers have large, convenient screens for viewing. Better yet, hundreds of titles can be stored within your new library — on a single microchip. There are a variety of e-readers from different manufacturers. You can also read e-books on your PC or laptop computer. (Please note that Ellora's Cave does not endorse any specific brands.

You can check our websites at www.ellorascave.com or www.cerridwenpress.com for information we make available to new consumers.)

3. *Mobility.* Because your new e-library consists of only a microchip within a small, easily transportable e-reader, your entire cache of books can be taken with you wherever you go.

4. *Personal Viewing Preferences.* Are the words you are currently reading too small? Too large? Too... ANNOYING? Paperback books cannot be modified according to personal preferences, but e-books can.

5. *Instant Gratification.* Is it the middle of the night and all the bookstores near you are closed? Are you tired of waiting days, sometimes weeks, for bookstores to ship the novels you bought? Ellora's Cave Publishing sells instantaneous downloads twenty-four hours a day, seven days a week, every day of the year. Our webstore is never closed. Our e-book delivery system is 100% automated, meaning your order is filled as soon as you pay for it.

Those are a few of the top reasons why electronic books are replacing paperbacks for many avid readers.

As always, Ellora's Cave and Cerridwen Press welcome your questions and comments. We invite you to email us at Comments@ellorascave.com or write to us directly at Ellora's Cave Publishing Inc., 1056 Home Avenue, Akron, OH 44310-3502.

COMING TO A BOOKSTORE NEAR YOU!

ELLORA'S CAVE

Bestselling Authors Tour

UPDATES AVAILABLE AT
WWW.EllorasCave.com

ELLORA'S CAVE
Romanticon

Annual convention
for women who
refuse to behave

COLUMBUS DAY WEEKEND

www.JasmineJade.com/Romanticon
For additional info contact: conventions@ellorascave.com

*Discover for yourself why readers can't get enough
of the multiple award-winning publisher*
Ellora's Cave.
Whether you prefer e-books or paperbacks,
be sure to visit EC on the web at
www.ellorascave.com
*for an erotic reading experience that will leave you
breathless.*